I0573597

BAD TASTE IN MEN

KYLIE GILMORE

Copyright © 2014 by Kylie Gilmore

All rights reserved. No part of this publication may be reproduced, distributed, or transmitted in any form or by any means, including photocopying, recording, or other electronic or mechanical methods, without the prior written permission of the writer, except in the case of brief quotations embodied in critical reviews and certain other noncommercial uses permitted by copyright law.

This is a work of fiction. Names, characters, places, brands, media, and incidents are the product of the author's imagination or are used fictitiously. The author acknowledges the trademarked status and trademark owners of various products referenced in this work of fiction, which have been used without permission. The publication/use of these trademarks are not authorized, associated with, or sponsored by the trademark owners. Any resemblance to actual events, locales, or persons, living or dead, is purely coincidental.

Bad Taste in Men: © 2014 by Kylie Gilmore

Cover design by Sweet 'N Spicy Designs

Published by: Extra Fancy Books

ISBN-13: 978-0-9912665-5-5

Something's brewing between friends…

1

Rachel Miller loved weddings as much as the next thirty-one-year-old single woman with a closet full of wretched bridesmaid dresses.

Yeah. That much.

At least she wasn't a bridesmaid this time. She'd come here as Shane O'Hare's plus one, a favor to her friend. And it was nice that the wedding was on the beach. It was the first time she'd made it to the beach all summer. She stepped away from the wedding pavilion, where Shane's older brother Travis and his new bride, Daisy, were still celebrating with family and friends. Shane was one of Trav's three best men and was slow dancing with his assigned bridesmaid. Rather than sit around watching everyone couple off for the slow dance, Rachel decided to take a walk on the beach.

The sun was dipping low in the sky. She kicked off her tan pumps, glad she'd skipped the pantyhose, and wiggled her toes in the warm sand of the Long Island Sound. She headed for the gently lapping waves, wanting to feel the water run over her feet, and stepped in. *Ahhh*. She stayed like that for a few minutes, enjoying the quiet and the gentle splash of water.

Shane appeared at her side, and she startled. For a six-foot guy, he moved as quietly as a cat.

"Are you having a good time?" he asked.

Fabulous! I love watching everyone else get married while my ovaries shrivel and I hurtle toward forty more likely to get struck by lightning than get married. How else could I prepare for my future as a spinster with ten cats?

But it *was* his brother's wedding, so she mustered a smile. "Sure."

It wasn't his fault she was becoming bitter and jaded. She was cursed, really.

Cursed with bad taste in men.

There was Brandon. Took her a year to realize he was gay. Jake, who thought his bipolar meds were bogus. Mark, a guy who picked her up in a club, never once mentioning he was married. The blind date who thought he was Superman and insisted she dress up as Lois Lane. Justin, the nice Jewish boy from JDate with the unfortunately high-pitched voice. (She knew she shouldn't judge, but in the dark, Justin sounded like a woman whispering sweet nothings in her ear.) And the worst, Drew, who stalked her for two months after she broke up with him.

"How's the water?" Shane asked.

"A little cool, but good. Come on in."

Her cute teal dress with spaghetti straps ended just above the knee, so she could move in a little deeper without getting it wet. She tiptoed over the slippery rocks and some broken shells.

"I don't have a towel, and these shoes are leather," Shane said.

Shane was so vanilla. Ha! That was probably a compliment for him, a gourmet ice-cream maker. She turned to face him where he stood on shore in his tux. The wind picked up, messing up the side part in his red hair. He smoothed it back down.

"Live a little," she teased.

He crossed his arms. "I'll live it up on the sand."

She rolled her eyes and bent to run her fingers through the cool water. Her glasses slipped down, and she pushed them back up. She only wore her contacts when she was trying to pick up men. But today she was with Shane so no need. She never bothered with makeup or contacts or taking her hair out of its usual braid when they hung out. She was just herself—comfortable, snarky, relaxed. Though she'd put her hair up in a twist today. The braid didn't seem right for a wedding.

She eyed him playing it safe on the sand, arms crossed against fun. "Don't be such a—"

"Rach, look out!"

She looked behind her as a powerful-looking wave approached, moving fast and high. She only managed one step to shore before it hit the back of her legs. Her ankle twisted on the slippery rocks, but she managed to stay upright. The wave receded, and the undercurrent pulled at her. Pain shot up her right ankle. *Shit.*

She limped back to shore, wincing with every step. "I twisted my ankle."

Shane offered his arm. "Hang on. I'll help you back to a chair. We'll get some ice."

Rachel was no damsel-in-distress. "I got it. I'm fine."

She took another step, and the sand shifted under her, twisting the ankle worse. "Ah!" she cried as her leg gave out from under her. She hit the sand. "Oof."

She held her poor ankle. It looked so normal, yet hurt like a mother.

"I'll carry you," Shane said, bending down to her, already sliding one arm under her legs, the other wrapped around her shoulders.

"That's not..." Her words died in her throat as he lifted her and carried her over the sand. For once she had no snappy reply. She'd never been carried in a man's arms before. She'd read about it in novels, saw it in plenty of chick flicks, and always thought, *What's the big deal?* But now that she was cradled in Shane's strong arms, she had to admit to feeling almost...petite. A little cherished.

A little...turned-on.

Cool it. This is Shane we're talking about. Your friend.

As he carried her back to the pavilion, she took the time to appreciate all the work he'd put in at the gym lifting weights these past few months. She casually rested her hand on his hard bicep. She felt her face flush and quickly dropped her hand. She'd teased him plenty about his new muscular physique. She'd called him gym rat, Arnold, and Popeye, but she hadn't actually touched the muscles until now. At least she didn't have to worry he'd drop her.

Her best friend Liz Garner rushed over to them when they reached the pavilion. "What happened?"

Liz wore a pale blue matron-of-honor dress. Her sister Daisy was the bride. Ryan, Liz's husband of one month and Shane's oldest brother, stood at her side, assessing the situation in that cool cop way of his. (Could this family be more incestuous? Two brothers marrying two sisters. Geez.)

"Do we need an ambulance?" Ryan asked, already pulling his cell from his tux pocket.

"No!" Rachel exclaimed.

Shane set her down gently in a chair. "Yes."

"It's just a twisted ankle!" Rachel protested. "I just need ice. Please. I hate hospitals."

"I'll get ice," Liz said, rushing off.

Shane brought over a second chair and lifted her leg to rest it there. She bit back a cry of pain, and sweat broke out on her upper lip.

"Don't touch my leg again," Rachel ground out. She shooed everyone out of her personal-space bubble. "Everybody stay away."

Shane and Ryan exchanged a look.

"Rach, you should get it checked out," Shane said. "You can't even put weight on it."

"I can," Rachel said, though even now she could see it was swelling. "I just need to rest a little with ice."

"You're going," Shane said. He turned to Ryan. "I'll drive her to the emergency room."

Ryan gave a curt nod and stepped away.

"I'm not going to the emergency room," Rachel said. They always poked you with needles at the hospital. She hated needles. And she didn't want to embarrass herself by passing out in front of Shane.

"I'll stay with you the whole time," Shane said in a soothing tone.

"It's not necessary!" she hollered. "I'm fine!"

Liz reappeared with a bag of ice and gently placed it on Rachel's ankle. Rachel sucked in a breath.

"Sorry!" Liz said. She glanced at Shane. "Do you think it's broken?"

"Either broken or a really bad sprain," Shane replied. "A wave hit her, and she slipped on some rocks."

Rachel gritted her teeth. "Stop talking about me like I'm not here."

"Do you want me to come with you?" Liz asked.

"I'm not going anywhere," Rachel insisted. "Besides, it's your sister's wedding." She turned to Shane. "And your brother's. I'll rest up, then head home. Go! Enjoy yourselves. I feel fine as long as I'm just sitting here."

Just let me suffer and pass out without any witnesses.

Liz took her hand and squeezed. "Are you sure?"

"Positive."

"I'll check on you in a bit." Liz rejoined her husband, who immediately tucked her close against his side.

Shane hadn't moved. He just stood there, studying her.

"You don't have to babysit me," she said. "Go dance with someone."

"Don't fight me, or you'll end up hurting yourself," Shane said, handing her the bag of ice.

"Why would I—Shane!" He was carrying her again, out of the pavilion, through the parking lot, over to his Chevy Tahoe SUV. He opened the door and slid her into the passenger seat.

"Keep the ice on your ankle," he said in an authoritative tone that she'd never heard from him in the past seven months of hanging out. She actually got goose bumps. Shane was a little shy, but once he'd warmed up to her, he normally had a very gentle demeanor.

He reappeared a moment later in the driver's seat. "I'll

take you to the hospital in Eastman so you're closer to home, unless you want me to look one up near here?"

She seethed over the non-choice. Her ankle throbbed. "Eastman is fine," she said through her teeth.

"You got it." He put the car into gear and peeled out of the parking lot.

They drove in silence. Rachel knew this was a complete waste of time. And if anyone came at her with a needle, she was outta there. She'd hop out the door if she had to.

Four hours later, Rachel sported an ankle brace and Shane was pushing her out of the hospital in a wheelchair. She had a severe ankle sprain and crutches with instructions to stay off it for forty-eight hours. She also had to do physical therapy daily at home for the next four to six weeks. Just perfect. Not only did she have a business to run, the struggling independent bookstore Book It, she was also helping with the Clover Park summer street fair, the biggest sales day for all the local stores next to the holiday season. And she couldn't drive with her right ankle in this condition.

She complained to Shane about her lack of time for all this sprained-ankle business on the drive back from the hospital.

"The doctor said six weeks and you'll be good as new," Shane said.

"In the meantime my business will go bankrupt and the street fair will never get off the ground."

He glanced over. "I'll help you with work. And Barry's running the street fair this year. Don't worry."

Shane was so sweet. Rachel was not.

"Barry's only been in the chamber of commerce for a few months," she said. "He's going to need help. And you have your own business to run." She stared out the window at the passing scenery. "I'll figure something out."

Shane ran Shane's Scoops, an ice cream/coffee/candy shop across the street from hers. It was one of the things they had in common, both owning their own shop in town. The other thing they had in common, what had moved them from passing acquaintances to friends, was the Liz-Ryan connection. Rachel and Shane were thrown together often because of them—parties, family barbecues, town celebrations. Liz included Rachel in her new social life revolving around the O'Hares, and Ryan, her husband, always included his brothers, Trav and Shane. She knew Shane from as far back as middle school, but had paid him little attention then. He'd been a tall, quiet boy and not nearly as interesting as the books she loved to lose herself in.

"You don't have to figure anything out because I'm helping you," Shane said. "That's just how it's gonna be."

She scowled, not liking this new bossy side of Shane. Still, she did need help, and no one would understand better how to make both the business run smoothly and get the street fair going than him.

"I'll pay you," she said.

He snorted. "You don't have to pay me. I'm helping out a friend."

She didn't know why she said that. Pride, maybe. She barely had enough money to pay the part-time cashier she had. That was why her plan to add a café in the space next door just had to work. She needed to make Book It more of a destination to draw people not just from Clover Park, but all the neighboring towns. When she'd brought up the idea of a café to Shane, he'd agreed to be her food and drink supplier. He'd wanted to expand his offerings, but didn't have the room in his ice-cream shop, so the café was a good idea for both of them.

"Okay," she finally said. "Thank you."

Shane stopped at a light and gave her a smile. Two adorable dimples appeared. "You're welcome."

Rachel faced front. Why was she noticing his dimples all of a sudden? He always had a dimpled smile. She was getting punchy. It was late, and she was exhausted from a long and painful day.

A short while later, they pulled into the small parking lot behind her store. Her apartment was on the second floor. Shane fetched her crutches from the back seat and walked around to open her car door. She tucked the crutches under her arms and made her way awkwardly to the rear entrance.

"Thanks again," she told him. "I got it from here."

He exhaled sharply. "Gimme the keys. I'm not leaving you."

She pulled her keys from her purse. "I'm fine. You've done your part. Thank you. Good night."

He snatched the keys from her, unlocked the door, and slipped a crutch out from under her arm, replacing it with his body. His voice rumbled low in her ear. "Relax."

She suppressed a shiver. That would've happened with anyone speaking so close to her. Sound waves and physics and neurological stuff. She glanced at him, so close. His eyes were blue with flecks of gold. She'd never noticed the gold flecks before. Her eyes widened as he leaned the other crutch against the building and scooped her up in his arms.

"Careful of my ankle!" she screeched.

He grunted, pushed open the door, and carried her upstairs to her apartment. If her pulse was racing, it was only because of the risk of falling down an entire flight of stairs. He carried her in and set her down gently on the bed.

"Really, Shane, there are easier ways to get me into bed."

His voice went low and husky. "When I want to get you into bed, you'll know it."

Her face flushed. She opened her mouth for a snappy retort, but nothing came out. Was he coming on to her or insulting her?

He chuckled. "I'll bring your crutches."

He left, and she propped up the pillows behind her so she could sit up in bed. He returned and placed the crutches next to her bed.

"I'll take the sofa," Shane said, "so I can carry you downstairs again in the morning."

"That's ridiculous. I've got crutches. I can do it."

"If you don't want me to stay, then call me when you wake up and I'll come over. I'm not letting you tumble down those stairs."

"You're not sleeping on my sofa."

"Then call me."

"Sure," she said just to get rid of him.

His eyes narrowed. "I'll be on the sofa."

"No!" She thought fast. *How to get him out of her hair?* "Sleep in my bed instead," she offered, lifting the covers.

His eyes lit up. "I thought you'd never ask."

And to her absolute shock, he scooted in next to her.

2

Shane stifled a laugh at Rachel's shocked expression. He'd wanted to be more than friends for months now, but Rachel was prickly, and he'd been biding his time. She had a laundry list of flaws that kicked a guy out of her good graces—too high a voice, too pushy if they paid for her meal, too cheap if they didn't offer, too much hair gel, too much lip-smacking when they chewed. Of course, some guys she was better off without—that stalker guy for one. As her friend, he spent a lot of time with her and got the inside scoop. So far he hadn't fallen onto her list of unforgivable flaws.

Here they were.

In bed.

She may have been joking with the invitation, but he sure as hell wasn't.

He kicked off his shoes, propped up some pillows behind his head, and grabbed the remote. He'd take it slow. Give her time to get used to him being so close. "What do you feel like watching?"

"Excuse me?" Rachel's voice hit a jarring high note. "I was joking." She shoved him with both hands, but he didn't budge. "Get out!"

He turned on his side and propped up on one elbow. "Rach?"

She blinked rapidly. He was making her nervous. Good, that made two of them. If there was ever a time to cross the line of friendship, it was when they were in bed.

"What?" she asked in a voice much softer than her usual tone.

He took a deep breath. "Do you ever think about being more than friends?"

She studied the comforter, appearing to consider the question. His heart thundered in his chest. It was out there. He couldn't take that whopper back. He'd taken a risk, and he hoped like hell it paid off.

Her chocolate brown eyes met his. "I can't lose you, Shane. Let's not mess up a good thing. Okay?"

His ears and cheeks burned. Damn Irish genes. He wished he wasn't a blusher. He could never play it cool when he wanted to. "Whatever, your loss," he mumbled.

He turned on the TV and settled in to watch the History channel, something they had in common. They both also loved running their own business, good coffee, and British comedy. They were a match in so many ways, but if she didn't feel *that* way about him, he wasn't going to force the issue. *Dammit.* He couldn't believe he'd misread her so badly. He'd thought there was something there.

"You don't have to stay," Rachel said.

"Yeah, I do." He couldn't look at her, so he kept his eyes fixed on the small TV. "Just for a while. I'll come back in the morning."

"All right. Thanks."

"Yup." He tried to focus on the show, something about Lewis and Clark. Having her so close, her flowery scent wrapped around him, it was very, very hard not to touch her. Why was he torturing himself like this? He should just go. She was fine. Yet something kept him pinned in place.

He really should move on. It was just...he'd connected with Rachel. Something that didn't happen for him that often. Ever since that New Year's party at Garner's when they'd spent most of the party talking in a quiet corner. Rachel had been alone since Liz spent the entire party wrapped up with

Ryan. Shane didn't much like parties, but he'd gone since his brothers and Gran would be there, and he hated being alone even more than he hated parties. He was very glad he'd gone. Sure he'd known Rachel as a kid, but he'd never talked to her back then. She always had her nose in a book, and he'd been tongue-tied around most girls anyway.

Maybe his timing was bad. She wasn't feeling well.

Half an hour later, he finally risked a glance over at Rachel. She was sleeping. He removed her black-rimmed glasses and set them on the nightstand. He took a moment just to gaze down at her; something he could never do when she was awake. Locks of dark brown hair fell around her face out of the twist she'd put it in for the wedding. He'd love to let her hair loose and run his fingers through it. Her lips were parted. A small bow in the upper lip drew him in. If he kissed her good night, would she wake?

He leaned down slowly, his heart kicking up. So close. He eased in. Almost there.

She sighed and threw an arm over her head, smacking him in the face.

Ow! That's what you get for trying to steal a kiss.

He leaned back and tucked her in. Then he quietly got out of bed and left, feeling like an absolute fool.

Rachel woke the next morning, grabbed her glasses from the nightstand, and tried to get up, momentarily forgetting about her ankle. *Ow-ow-ow.* Her leg was so stiff. Shoot. What had the doctor said to do? They gave her instructions. She grabbed the paper from her purse on the nightstand. She was supposed to elevate it above her heart to reduce swelling and ice it twice a day. She sighed. All she really wanted was a hot shower and coffee. Should she call Shane for help like he'd told her to?

Nah, she could do this.

She grabbed the crutches and swung herself to the kitchen, getting the coffee going and grabbing a granola bar.

Her ankle throbbed, reminding her she needed ice. She tossed the granola bar to the kitchen table, grabbed an ice pack from the freezer and tossed that on the table too.

Coffee first. She hobbled over to fetch the coffee and returned to the table. Lifting her foot up on a nearby chair, she undid the brace and placed the ice pack on her poor ankle. Still swollen. She stayed like that for a while, sipping coffee and icing her ankle, and pulled her book from the large, flat basket that served as both fruit bowl and book holder. *The Nitwit's Guide to Running a Coffee Bar* was surprisingly thorough. She'd created a business plan from it.

She'd already talked to the landlord about expanding into the abandoned deli next door to Book It, and he'd even agreed to ninety days rent-free while she got the café up and running. Now she was just waiting to hear from the bank on her loan application. She really needed this. Book It was in the red, and she was nearly at the point of either giving up her apartment and moving back in with her parents (Please, no. Her parents were nice people, but they radiated a tense civility of a marriage long gone south.) or letting her cashier go.

The doorbell rang. Shoot. It was probably Shane. How did he expect to help her down the stairs if she had to go down the stairs to let him in?

She heard the door rattle, then turn, and open. "It's just me," Shane called.

Her eyes widened. He had a key?

"Uh...come in?"

He walked into her kitchen and smiled at her sheepishly. "I grabbed your keys on the way out yesterday."

She was torn between furious and grateful. She held out her palm for the keys. He dropped them in her hand.

"Don't do that again," she said.

"It was an emergency." He pulled up a chair. "How's the ankle?"

"It hurts like hell," she admitted.

"The doc said you should take ibuprofen. Did you take it?"

"I barely got the coffee. No, I didn't get the medicine."

He stood. "Where do you keep it?"

It was in the bathroom medicine cabinet along with tampons, bikini wax, a box of condoms—more a measure of hope than of any practical use—and who knew what else she'd left in there. Not fit for Shane's eyes, that was for sure.

"I'll get it," she said, grabbing the ankle brace and leaning forward to put it back on.

"Just rest," he said. "I can get it."

"I can do it!"

He put his palms up. "Okay, okay." He pushed her hands out of the way and quickly redid the brace.

"Thank you," she said through a clenched jaw, annoyed with all his fussing over her. She didn't like needing help. She grabbed the crutches and made her way to the bathroom. Her mouth dropped as she caught sight of herself in the mirror. Her mascara made black smudges under her eyes. Her hair was half out of the twist in a tangled knot. Her dress was wrinkled. Geez, Shane was kind to act like he didn't notice anything odd.

She opened the cabinet. It was worse than she remembered—she also had press-on nails (she never could bother with polish) and cherry massage oil from Maggie's bachelorette party. Maggie, Shane's grandmother, was a hoot, and Shane...he was apple pie. Warm, comforting, sweet. At least the other wildly inappropriate party favors—edible underwear and a vibrator—weren't here. She'd thrown out the underwear, and the vibrator was hidden in her nightstand drawer for easy access.

She tossed back some ibuprofen, washed off the mascara, and brushed her hair into its usual neat braid before making her way back to the kitchen.

Shane was poking through her refrigerator. He straightened. "You want me to make you something?"

He was a trained chef, but she didn't want him cooking for her and making a big deal out of this ankle thing.

"I have a granola bar." She headed back to the table and

plopped down. Coffee. She'd be much more pleasant with more coffee in her.

"Those granola bars taste like cardboard," he said, turning his nose up at it.

"It's the perfect balance of fiber and protein," she said, reading the label. "Besides, I'm not a big breakfast person. What I really need is a shower."

"Need help?"

She leveled a suspicious gaze at him.

His lips twitched. "I won't peek."

Yeah, right.

"I can do it. Why don't you come back in half an hour to help me downstairs?"

"I'll wait here in case you need help." He sat at the table and picked up her book. "Seriously, Rach? *The Nitwit's Guide*?"

"It's a good book," she said defensively. "I made a business plan from it."

"I can help you plan the café. I know the food business."

"Sounds good. We'll talk more once I hear from the bank on my loan." She finished her coffee and granola bar while he flipped through the book. She grabbed the crutches and stood. Then she remembered the zipper on the back of her dress. "Could you just unzip me?"

He stood, one corner of his mouth tilting up. "I'd love to."

She gave him her back. "Cool it, Don Juan."

He chuckled, and his warm hand brushed over the back of her neck as he moved her hair out of the way. She focused on the pain in her ankle so she wouldn't think about what he was doing. She'd ask her sister to do it if she were here. Same thing practically.

His warm fingers grazed her spine as he inched the zipper down. A shiver ran through her. Ankle throbbing. Terrible pain. Omigod, could he go any slower?

She heard him suck in a breath. She looked over her shoulder. "What?"

His eyes met hers in a heated gaze. "You're not wearing a bra."

She looked away. "So?"

She wore pasties because of the spaghetti straps. Not that she was going to explain that to him. She didn't wait for a response; instead she headed for the bathroom. "I'll be back in a bit."

To her relief, she heard him settle back at the table. She really didn't want him following her into the bathroom. She made her way to the bedroom, slipped off the dress, pasties, and undies, took off the brace, and hobbled over to the shower. Fifteen minutes later, she was clean and exhausted. She wrapped a towel around her body and headed to the bed, needing to sit down for a bit.

Shane was already sitting there.

"Shane! Get out of here!"

"Think of me as your nurse, here to help. I see naked bodies all day long. Ho-hum." He faked a yawn.

She sat on the bed next to him. Sweat broke out and ran down her back purely from the exertion of getting ready.

"Go get me a towel for my hair." She shoved him toward the bathroom. "Please."

He went to fetch it.

She used the break from him to make her way over to the dresser and caught her reflection in the large mirror above it. Her hair was a tangled lump, and she wore no makeup. *Oh, who cares! It's just Shane.* The towel drooped, and she tucked it tighter. She grabbed a bra and pulled it on. One crutch slipped out from under her arm and hit the floor. *Dammit.* She readjusted the towel around her waist and slipped her favorite rhinestone-studded "Reader" T-shirt over her head. It was one of a series of reading-themed T-shirts she'd made herself. She got her panties and shorts. Okay. She'd have to sit down for this next part.

She considered the floor and realized she'd have to drop pretty far with her bad leg out in front of her to get down. Better not.

She considered how to get to the bed with one crutch. She could hop. Yes. With one hand clutching her panties and shorts, the other holding the crutch, she hopped in a little half-circle and made her way to the bed.

Shane threw the extra towel on the bed and headed toward her. "Wait. Let me get your crutch."

"Stay right there," she warned, continuing her hop journey. "I got this." He kept walking toward her. "Back up!"

Hop, hop, whoosh. Omigod.

The towel had given up its precarious hold and dropped to the floor.

Rachel closed her eyes. Shane saw. She knew he saw. She could just die of embarrassment. Right here, right now.

She felt the towel wrap securely around her waist again. His warm hands tucked it in.

"You are one stubborn woman," Shane said.

She opened her eyes, expecting to see him holding back a laugh at her expense, but he looked damn serious. His eyes burned into hers, and a frisson of awareness ran through her body. The air felt suddenly charged between them. Her mouth went dry over the sarcastic reply her brain couldn't seem to formulate.

She quickly averted her eyes and hopped the rest of the way to the bed. "Turn around," she told him. "No more peep show."

He turned, giving her his back. His voice came out hoarse. "I wasn't peeping. The towel just—"

"Never speak of this again." She yanked on the panties and shorts, leaning back on the bed to wiggle them up over her hips. "I mean it."

"Never," he agreed. "I'll be in the kitchen. Call me if you need me."

He left quickly, and Rachel collapsed on the bed, unsure how she'd ever look her friend in the eye again.

3

_____

Shane poured a glass of ice water and held it against his forehead. The image of Rachel's lush curves burned into his brain. How could he go on pretending he just wanted to be friends when all he wanted was to strip her naked and lick every inch of that delicious body?

He stuck his head in the freezer.

By the time Rachel returned to the kitchen, fully dressed, hair back in a neat braid, he'd managed to cool off.

"Ready to go?" he asked, looking at a spot just over her ear. She always worked the Sunday shift at her store.

"I'm ready," she said softly.

He tried not to read into that soft tone. She'd already turned him down flat last night. "I'll take the crutches down first. Sit."

She made her way to a kitchen chair and handed him the crutches without a word. Their eyes met and held, and he felt it, like an electric current in the air. There _was_ something there. This attraction wasn't just one-sided. Hope surged through him. He took the crutches downstairs and pondered what his next move should be.

He returned to her side. "Come on, princess."

She blushed, something she never did, but had done twice

today already. Maybe he could make her blush just one more time. He bit back a smile.

She stood. "The doctor said I can put weight on it again after forty-eight hours."

"Yup." He scooped her up and briefly considered carrying her straight to the bedroom. She felt wonderful in his arms, warm and soft. Instead, he carried her downstairs as promised, setting her down by the crutches.

"Thank you," she murmured, putting the crutches under her arms.

"I'll be back tomorrow morning," he said.

She met his eyes, and he saw a flash of regret, like she was about to shut him down again. "Shane—"

He moved swiftly before he could lose his nerve. His lips met hers in a soft kiss. He pulled back to gauge her reaction.

Her eyes were wide, clearly surprised. Then her expression darkened, brows furrowed. "That never happened. It can't. I value our friendship too much to muck it up with a fling."

"Who says it would be a fling?" He stroked her cheek. "I care about you."

He was, in fact, stupidly, helplessly, deeply in love with her. But he knew better than to tell her that. She'd run screaming for the hills.

She looked away. "I just don't feel that way about you, okay?"

His heart squeezed painfully at the slam. She set off for her store.

"I'll see you," she called over her shoulder.

"See ya," Shane mumbled.

He headed across the street back to his apartment, dragging his feet. His own shop didn't open until noon on Sundays, so he had plenty of time to contemplate Rachel's rejection. Two painful rejections in two days. *Strike three and you're out.*

He couldn't face his empty apartment, briefly considered cooking something in the commercial kitchen in the back of his shop, but quickly nixed the idea. He knew Sam would be there making the ice-cream base as he did every morning, and he didn't feel up to small talk. He started walking down Catoonah Street, where rows of houses, some beautiful old Victorians, lined both sides of the tree-lined street. Where to? He passed Gran's house. She was all wrapped up in Jorge now, newly married as of last September. He passed his older brother Trav's house across the street from Gran. Newly married as of yesterday. His other older brother Ryan's house was a few blocks away. Newly married as of last month. Everyone around him was getting married.

He was starting to feel like the black sheep of the family. Funny because, of the three brothers, Shane was the only one who'd ever had a long-term relationship. Two, in fact. When he connected with someone, which wasn't that often, he went all-in. He'd had a three-year relationship in high school, until Kerri left for college, and a five-year relationship with Laura from culinary school. A few several-months-long relationships after Laura. Nothing in a couple of years, though, not since Rachel moved back to town.

He'd waited patiently as Rachel went through loser after loser, finally settling in as her friend. Well, now he knew the score. For whatever reason, despite what felt like A-grade chemistry percolating between them, she didn't want to cross that line.

He jammed a hand through his hair. Dammit, he wanted to cross that line. Enough with this patient waiting shit. He wanted her, and it was past time he did something about it. He knew her well, very well. She told him everything—every detail of her day, every bad date, every dream for the future— and he listened, soaking it all in, wanting to know all of her. That knowledge should help him navigate those defenses she was so good at putting up, keeping every guy at a distance. He just had to figure out how.

It wouldn't be easy, that was for sure. Rachel was not an easy woman. She was strong, tough, and sarcastic, but he actually liked that about her. His other girlfriends had been sweet and gentle, and he'd spent a lot of time trying to protect their feelings and keep them happy. With Rachel, he didn't have to do all that. He could relax.

Whatever it took. He was all-in.

He kept walking, wishing he was the kind of guy who could do casual hookups. It had been embarrassingly long since he'd gotten any. It was part of the reason he'd started lifting weights at the gym. Looking good for Rachel, hoping she'd see him as more than a friend. Not that it did him any good. The other part of the reason he'd started working out was his brother Ry's relentless teasing about his ice-cream paunch. Ry had been right about that. He did feel better now that he'd lost the gut. As if conjured from his thoughts, Ry called from behind him.

"Hey, bud."

Shane turned to see his brother out for a jog. Ry was four years older and had been more like a father to Shane than a brother. Their father was an unpredictable alcoholic, and their mother had been severely depressed. Their mom had always seemed fragile, like anything could set her to crying. She'd committed suicide when Shane was thirteen. Ry had been solid as a rock, helping him and Trav through that hellish time.

"Run with me," Ry said, jogging in place. He grinned. "I'll go slow so you don't get winded."

Shane hated running, but he rarely got to see Ry without Liz glued to his side, so he set off at a slow pace next to him. Not that he didn't like Liz. It was just that he didn't always want to feel like the guy on the outside of Loveland.

"How's Rachel?" Ry asked, picking up the pace.

"It was just a sprain," Shane said. "After a couple of days she can move to an Ace bandage and hiking boots. Then she has to do exercises at home."

Ry nodded. They ran in silence for a few minutes.

"How far you going?" Shane asked. He hoped Ry was on his way home.

"Just another couple miles. I'm circling around, going up to the high school and back."

Shane inwardly groaned. The high school was on top of a

hill. But what else did he have to do? He didn't want to go home and wallow in the bitterness of rejection. Rachel was so damn stubborn too. He'd have to balance working around her stubbornness and pushing through it. Why couldn't she just see how right they were for each other? It was so damn obvious to him.

"You okay?" Ry asked.

"Yeah."

Ry said nothing more. That was his way. He was just there for you: solid, strong, silent.

Thoughts of Rachel tumbled through his head. Her surprised expression when he'd kissed her, when that towel dropped and he'd glimpsed paradise, her stinging rejection. *I value our friendship...friendship...friendship.* Shane couldn't take the thoughts on repeat anymore.

"Did you hear the new fro-yo place opened?" Shane asked just to say something, *anything* to distract him from Rachel.

"Yeah, The Dancing Cow opened in April."

Shane grunted. It *was* July. But his irritation with Barry Furnukle was a good distraction.

"I heard Barry's giving away wacky glasses now," Shane bit out. "Bastard."

Ry glanced over. "So?"

"So he's stealing business from me. Kids are excited about stupid wacky glasses and ask for frozen yogurt instead of ice cream. It's not the same! Those probiotics are dead by the time it gets into their bowls. It's not even healthy! I bet he doesn't even make it fresh!"

Ry's brows shot up. Shane never raised his voice. But Rachel had gotten under his skin, and now that he thought about it, Barry was a real pain in his ass too.

"Pick up the pace," Ry said. "You need to get some endorphins kicking in to counteract all that bitchiness."

Shane picked up the pace. His feet were going numb, sweat poured down his face, and he couldn't suck in enough air to talk. Finally they made it to the hill. He bent at the waist, panting. "I'll wait here."

Ry pulled at his arm. "Come on, pokey. It's just one hill. If you get to the top, I won't even make you spit out what's really bugging you." He coughed out, "Rachel."

How did Ry know?

"Race ya," Ry said, taking off.

Shane watched his brother go. Geez, running was for the birds. He never got anything but tired from it. He must be missing whatever triggered those feel-good endorphins. Ry made it to the top and carefully worked his way back down.

"Come on, keep up," Ry said, elbowing him.

Shane reluctantly started running again back toward Ry's place.

"Let me guess," Ry said, not even out of breath. "She just wants to be friends."

Shane stumbled, and Ry's arm shot out to steady him. "How did you know?"

Ry raised a brow. "Because if she wanted more than that, you wouldn't be bitching about wacky glasses."

"So what's my next move?" Shane asked.

Ry shook his head. "Friends is your only move unless she starts giving out a different signal."

"That's what's so frustrating. I swear it's not one-sided, but she's pushing me away."

"She'll let you know when she wants more." A ghost of a smile crossed his brother's face. Probably thinking of Liz again.

Shane sucked in air. Where were those damn endorphins?

"You know what would make you feel better?" Ry asked.

Shane panted. "What?"

"A daily run. It'll give you something to focus on, and it'll help your mood too."

"Fuck that," Shane managed to wheeze out.

Ry laughed. "Language, my dear."

Shane bent over as a cramp hit his side. They were almost to Main Street, where he lived in the apartment over his shop. "Augh..." *Pant. Pant.* "I'm gonna..." *Pant.* "...walk home." He waved him away. "You go."

"See you tomorrow at seven a.m. sharp for our run," Ry said with a devious smile before hightailing it home. Shane knew his brother would carry through too, pounding on his door until he got up and joined him.

Shane groaned. Fucking older brothers with their fucking advice. Ry told him to cool it, but Trav probably would've told him to do the opposite. He'd pursued Daisy for a good six months before he caught her. Now they were on a honeymoon in Bermuda.

He walked slowly, trying to breathe through the pain in his side. He got to Rachel's shop and saw her sitting at the front register, head bent over her papers.

He broke into a run. At least if she looked up, she could see him running, not staggering like an old man. He made it across the street, up the stairs, and into his apartment.

He collapsed on the floor, where he planned to stay for the foreseeable future.

4

Rachel moved off crutches just in time for her loan meeting at the bank. Shane had been, um, helpful with all that carrying her up and down the stairs gallantry, but she was an independent businesswoman who needed to face this next step alone. Her mind flashed to Damon or, as she liked to call him, Demon. Her old boss at the accounting firm. She'd worked her ass off her first two years in no small part due to his demands on her time, his harsh tirades against even the smallest error, his constant micromanaging over her shoulder. Until one night in the late hours of a long day she'd finally snapped and told him off good.

Instead of firing her or yelling at her, he got up, walked around his massive desk, and stood very close to where she was standing clutching a client's folder. He stroked a finger down her cheek. "I wondered when I'd break you." He flashed a predatory smile. "You lasted longer than most. Come home with me. I'll show you what you need."

"I'm not going home with you." She backed toward his office door.

"I want you. And when I don't get what I want, it shows." He put a hand on the door above her head, blocking her exit. "You think I was tough on you before?" He shook his head, an evil smile playing there. "Make the easy choice and you will be richly rewarded."

"Okay." She kneed him in the groin, and he dropped like a rock. She made her escape and filed a sexual harassment suit the next day. Demon lost his job.

Work was no picnic after that. The mostly male management gave her a wide berth, and no matter how hard she worked, she was passed over again and again for the higher level jobs. She couldn't wait to own her own business and work only for herself. She took another job at a competing accounting firm out of necessity and spent the next several years squirreling money away for her dream of owning her own bookstore. Finally, she'd broken free. Book It was all hers, and she answered to no one.

She took in a deep breath of still-cool early morning air, feeling optimistic as she made the short walk down the street to the bank. She'd dressed up a bit with a black pencil skirt and white button-down short-sleeve shirt with a purple floral scarf. The ensemble was unfortunately less than stellar because she had to wear hiking boots for the ankle support.

Her small-business contact, Zach Cukor, already knew her well from when she'd applied to start Book It two years ago. He'd been so friendly and helpful the last time she'd applied for a loan. Most independent bookstores were struggling with the ease of online shopping, but he'd agreed with her that Clover Park needed a bookstore. Plus, there was no competition within thirty miles of her shop.

She stepped into the air-conditioned lobby and crossed slowly to Zach's office in the back, still limping a bit. "Hi, Zach, how are you?"

He stood in a sharp navy suit and shook her hand. "Good. But what happened to you?"

She maneuvered herself into a chair and blew out a breath. "Sprained my ankle when a wave hit me on the beach. I'll be okay in six weeks."

He sat across from her. "Sorry to hear that."

"Thanks."

Zach shuffled some papers on his desk, then folded his

hands across the top of them. "Rachel, I'm afraid I have bad news."

Her heart started pounding. "Was there a problem with my paperwork? I thought I had everything in there you asked for. The business plan, the store's financials, my old tax returns—"

"The paperwork was fine." His mouth set in a flat line. "I'm sorry, the bank turned down your loan. Book It's financials are not good. You haven't turned a profit in two months. Banks don't like risk."

Her mind reeled. She needed this. Book It needed that extra something to draw customers. Something they couldn't get from browsing online. She knew good coffee, snacks, and tables to hang out would make people linger. She used to love to do that at the Borders in Eastman before they closed down.

"What about that line of credit you told me about when I opened Book It?" she asked. "Could I get one of those?"

Zach brightened. "You could still do that. But I'm afraid that would be capped at twenty-five thousand due to your current financial situation."

She needed more than that to open the café. She'd applied for a hundred-thousand-dollar loan. She'd need equipment, décor, inventory, employees. What was she going to do?

"That's not nearly enough money," she said. "Any suggestions?"

"You could find some investors."

Investors. Ha! She didn't know anyone with that kind of money. Well, there was her dad, but she already knew his answer would be no. He thought her bookstore was a bad financial move from day one, and he never let her forget it. Her head throbbed. All of her plans, her dream for Book It, all crushed. She pushed up unsteadily from the chair. "I guess that's it, then."

Zach held up his palms. "I'm sorry we couldn't do more."

Rachel waved that away and made her stiff-legged, hobbling way out the door. Fricking fuckity-fuck-fuck. She was screwed. Book It was screwed. She'd end up living with her parents. Her store would go out of business and be turned into a nail salon or a sub shop or something equally more horrible than picking out the perfect book.

Tears stung her eyes. She quickly blinked them away as she walked back to her shop. She was *not* a crier. She pushed open the door, and the bell overhead jingled cheerfully.

Her only employee, Janelle Wilcox, looked up from the book she was reading at the register, where no one was buying books. "How'd it go?"

"Not good," Rachel replied. "I didn't get the loan."

"I'm so sorry, Rach."

"Yeah. I'll be in my office."

"Don't worry," Janelle called over her shoulder. "I heard a new book club is forming with some of the seniors in town. I'm sure they'll order from us every month."

"Great," Rachel managed. She went into her small office and sat at her desk. She took a few calming breaths before opening the laptop and pulling up the accounting system. She looked at the next three months. It was bad. She'd have to break the lease on her apartment. She'd rather sleep in the storage room of her shop than go back to her parents' cold war of pleasantness.

Or she'd have to let Janelle go. Her friend. Her loyal employee, who'd been with her from the very beginning.

She dropped her head in her hands and moaned. Why had she opened a bookstore? She'd left a perfectly respectable soul-sucking job doing recordkeeping for retirement plans. Her older sister, Sarah, had gotten her the job at her old firm. Luckily for Sarah, she hadn't had Damon for a boss. Who was she kidding? Her accounting career was laughable in light of her degree in literature. She hadn't wanted to be a teacher, and she couldn't do much else without an advanced degree. All she'd ever wanted was to live and breathe books.

Somehow Rachel made it through the rest of the day, greeting each of the five customers with the enthusiasm of a long-lost family member, trying not to sound desperate. *Please buy a stack of books. Just one, really?*

She let Janelle go early and closed up the shop herself. She had some hard thinking to do. Hard decisions to make. And for that she needed chocolate. She headed across the street to Shane's Scoops for a fudge brownie sundae.

Shane's shop was hopping. People came from all over for his homemade gourmet ice cream. And this was the season for it. She waited in a long line and checked the whiteboard for today's flavors—cherry vanilla, chocolate, vanilla, salted caramel, cookies and cream, blueberry sorbet, and lemon sorbet. Her mouth watered. She knew Shane used fresh, in-season ingredients, each flavor an intense burst on the tongue. Everything was made in-house, the ice cream, the cones, the whipped cream, even the cookies and cream had fresh-made chocolate cookies that were mixed in. Today was a chocolate day, so those other flavors would have to wait.

"Hey, Rach, the usual?" Shane asked when she got to the counter. She normally went for the cookies and cream.

"Nope. Fudge brownie sundae with chocolate ice cream."

His brows drew together in a look of concern before he snapped into action. "You got it."

That was how well he knew her—fudge brownie sundae meant a really shitty day.

A few minutes later, she sat on a cushioned stool at a counter lining one wall of the shop, with an orgy of chocolate in a large cup. Chocolate ice cream over a homemade brownie, all of it covered in hot fudge, whipped cream, and chocolate sprinkles. Shane had given her extra hot fudge at no charge. She closed her eyes and let it roll over her tongue. Heavenly. The rich chocolate transported her for a moment from the darkness weighing her down.

When she opened her eyes, Shane was sitting on the stool next to her. She startled. The man was forever sneaking up on her.

"What happened?" he asked.

The pure caring she heard in his voice made her throat tight. If she spilled, she'd likely break down right in the middle of his busy shop with all these innocent children.

"Don't you have to work?" she asked. "Your shop is crazy busy."

She felt a stab of jealousy that her shop was empty while

his was so busy. Obviously she was in the wrong business. She jabbed her spoon in the ice cream.

"I can take a fifteen-minute break," Shane said. "Let's go upstairs."

It was a measure of how low she felt that she picked up her sundae and followed him out the door without a second thought. The last time she'd seen him he'd carried her down the stairs of her apartment while they'd awkwardly tried to pretend the kiss from the day before had never happened. But it couldn't happen. She'd meant it when she said she couldn't lose him. His friendship was everything to her. He was the only guy she'd ever known that was really there for her, day in, day out. She could tell him anything, absolutely anything, and he never judged. He was her rock.

When they got to the back staircase leading to his apartment, he took the sundae from her and set it on the step. He bent down, offering his back. "Climb aboard."

She stared as his T-shirt stretched across broad shoulders and bulging biceps, and felt herself flush. Also, she was wearing a skirt. She didn't want to dry hump his back. Friends don't let friends hump each other.

"Don't be silly," she said. "I can do the stairs. I've been doing them at my place."

"Not on my watch. Climb up." He peered over his shoulder at her. "Or should I carry you?"

Did she want to feel like a princess carried in his arms again? No way. They. Were. Friends.

She wrapped her arms around his neck, hiked up her skirt, and boosted herself on. He stood, reached under her bare legs, and boosted her up a little more. Omigod, this was a huge mistake. His large warm hands on her bare thighs, the heat of his back burning through the thin fabric of her panties. Was she really going to ride his back to orgasm up a flight of stairs? She was just about to pound his back and demand he put her down when he snagged her sundae and began to climb the stairs.

She hung on and bit back a moan as the friction of rocking up and down his back made her go damp. She needed to spend more time with her vibrator if she could get off on a piggy-back ride. Dear Lord, she'd never even hugged him before she sprained her ankle. She prayed he didn't notice. At least he only touched her with one hand on the back of her upper thigh—the other hand held her sundae—though that one hand did seem to be spread wide for maximum skin contact.

He carried her into his apartment and set her down at the kitchen island next to a bright red cushioned stool that matched the stools in his shop.

She yanked her skirt down, hoping he wouldn't notice what felt like a full-body blush. "Thanks," she mumbled.

"My pleasure."

Her gaze jerked to his, and he gave her a slow smile. Had he put special emphasis on pleasure? The way he said it ran through her like warm chocolate. Flustered, she took a seat and focused on her sundae.

He walked to the other side of the island and poured them both a glass of ice water. She drank greedily, desperate to cool off.

"So tell me what brought on the fudge brownie sundae," he said in that sweet, thoughtful tone that always made her want to talk his ear off. She'd spent many hours telling him about all of her horrible dates and getting the guy perspective on them. She took a deep breath. She had to tell someone about the demise of her career, the crushing of her dream, and her imminent failure as a businesswoman.

She set her spoon down. "The bank turned down my loan for the café. I mean, I know my financials don't look great, but they'd seemed so understanding about the struggles of an independent bookstore." She exhaled sharply and studied the large wooden spoon mounted over the sink. "I really thought the café would save Book It."

"Are you going to have to close your store?"

"I hope not. We're a little in the red, but not too bad. I'll either have to let Janelle go, or let my apartment go and live rent-free with my parents. Thirty-one and moving back home." She dropped her head in her hands, all appetite gone.

"Tell me more about your plan for the café."

She looked up. "What does it matter now? It's not happening."

His jaw tightened. "Just tell me."

She rubbed her forehead. "I was going to open up the wall between the café and bookstore to make it all one. Then I'd have your awesome coffee and fresh-baked stuff. That way, when you're browsing for books, you've got all these delicious aromas wafting over, then you have a snack, go back to browsing and, hopefully, buying books. I wanted it to be a place to hang out. Someplace where people not just from here but from nearby towns would stop by too." She played with the end of her braid. "I can't let Janelle go. She's been with me from the beginning."

Shane nodded, all concern and sympathy.

Rachel leaned forward and rested her forehead on the island. "Mommy, get my old room ready."

Her life officially sucked. If she were in a Jane Austen novel, this would be the perfect time for an anonymous benefactor to show up.

"The bank suggested I find investors," she told the counter.

A warm hand rubbed her back. She straightened. She swore the man was half cat, she hadn't even heard him move.

The back rub felt amazing. *Back rubs between friends are fine. The back is neutral territory.*

She closed her eyes as warmth stole through her. "Who'd want to invest in the café knowing how Book It is failing?"

"Me."

She turned. "You?"

"Yes."

She shook her head. "You're just feeling sorry for me. Besides, you don't have that kind of money."

His hand stopped moving, resting on the small of her back. "How much?"

"The loan was for a hundred thousand."

He whistled. "Wow."

"Yeah."

Should she tell him to move his hand? Now it kinda felt like he had his arm around her.

"I'd need to see the business plan before I committed to it," he said.

Her jaw dropped, and she completely forgot about his hand. "Are you serious?"

He smiled. "Yup."

She stood and paced his living room. She couldn't help her disbelief. Was this some weird sacrificial gesture on his part to convince her to be more than friends? Going into business with Shane? Would it ruin their friendship? Would he expect more from her than friends? Why would he do this?

She stopped pacing and returned to sit on the stool across from him. "Why?"

"I like the idea of a café. I even like the name. Something's Brewing Café." He nodded in approval. "Investing in the café would help me diversify. I'm feeling the crunch from the new fro-yo shop."

"Barry's a competitive threat?"

"He's giving out wacky glasses. The kids love 'em. I never thought to give out cheap party favors. I thought quality ice cream would bring people back for more."

"Barry with his pro-bee-otics?" She giggled. Barry couldn't even pronounce probiotics right, yet he said it all the time. She and Shane had a running joke to see how many times they could get him to say the word.

Shane snorted and did his Barry impression. "Fro-yo is much healthier than ice cream thanks to the—" he lifted his nose in the air "—pro-bee-otics."

She laughed. Shane was spot-on. Then she started thinking about his offer. "How would this work? You'd take out a loan and invest in the café?"

"We'd be partners, fifty-fifty. I'll loan you your half, and you can pay me back when the café starts turning a profit."

"You seriously have a hundred grand?"

He raised one shoulder up and down. "I can get it."

His shop *was* doing well. Plus he supplied a network of restaurants with ice cream and had his own delivery truck and a crew of employees. Maybe he could afford it. Just because he chose to live in an apartment above the shop didn't mean he had no money. Maybe he just socked the money away.

It was so generous. Too much. But what if it worked? What if the café was a success and Book It was saved *and* she paid him back? It could be her dream come true.

She played with the end of her braid. "I don't know."

He inclined his head. "Think about it. I hate to make you eat and run, but I do have to get back."

She looked down at her half-melted sundae. Her spirits were lifted more by Shane than the chocolate anyway. She tossed the rest in the trash.

He bent in front of her. "Up you go."

She stared at his back. No way in hell was she taking that ride again. Not when they might go into business together. "I can walk."

He stood and turned, a small smile playing over his lips. Did he know what that ride did to her? She felt herself flush.

"What's the big deal?" he asked. "You seemed happy with the ride up."

Dammit! He did know!

"I was *not* happy."

"No?"

"Absolutely not." She raised her chin. "I was actually uncomfortable." She nodded to emphasize the point. "And bored," she added. "In fact, this whole conversation is boring."

"Uh-huh."

She bit back a curse, not willing to let him see that he'd hit on a sore spot, and headed for the door.

"Rach, come on, you just got off crutches yesterday."

"I'm fine," she called over her shoulder. She opened the door and went flying backwards as his arms went around her waist and lifted her. "Shane!"

She wiggled to get away.

"Stop fighting me. You're gonna end up hurting yourself worse."

She went still because either way—riding his back or carried in his arms—she enjoyed it way too much. This *might* be a problem. If only she hadn't sprained her ankle, they wouldn't be in this ridiculous, confusing mess.

He set her back on the ground, and they had a stare down.

Shane blinked first and took a step closer. "Okay?"

"Okay, fine! But this whole carrying me around routine has gotten very—"

He scooped her up and cradled her in his arms. She got the crazy feeling that he might just carry her off to bed. Her breathing hitched, and she ran hot all over.

"Very what?" he prompted.

"Old," she breathed.

He chuckled and carried her out the door. "I agree. I can't wait until you start carrying me around instead."

She giggled.

I'm taking an elevator downstairs. That's all. A warm, muscled elevator.

He set her down inside his shop and grinned. "Want another sundae?"

"I'm good, thanks."

He nodded once and went back to work.

She worked her way through the crowd of people in his shop, thinking again of the future for Book It, her baby, her passion project. She'd have to set firm boundaries with Shane. That was all. Business would be business, friendship after hours, and nothing more than that. It could work. It really could. It *had* to work.

She smiled to herself and stepped back out into the sunshine.

Shane drove to his dad's house in Fieldridge after work. Usually he stopped by on Sundays, but he didn't think his dad would mind the midweek visit. Shane was the only one of his brothers willing to spend time with their dad. It had been a year since Jack O'Hare had first contacted Shane about getting to know each other again. Before that, the last time Shane had seen his dad was when he was thirteen. Jack had walked out on him and his brothers shortly after their mom died. Jack had explained how his alcoholism combined with grief over the loss of his wife had proved too much for him to handle back then. He'd asked Shane for forgiveness and let him know he'd been sober for three and a half years.

Shane wasn't one to turn his back on family. He'd already lost his mom, so if his dad wanted back in his life, he'd been willing to give him that chance.

They'd started spending time together every Sunday, working on a '67 Shelby Mustang GT 500 his dad had inherited from his dad. Shane knew cars and tools, thanks to his dad, so working on the car was a natural fit. Before his mom had died, his dad had kept his drinking to nights so the boys knew if they caught him in the afternoon on a weekend, he'd play catch with them. But, unlike his brothers, Shane had been terrible at sports and had stayed away. He never got much attention from his dad until he was nine and asked for an E-Z Bake Oven for Christmas.

He got a toolbox instead with real tools. Jack dedicated himself to making sure Shane knew tools, cars, and how to fix stuff around the house. Everything Jack thought a man should know. Somehow working with his hands came easier to Shane than catching a ball. Maybe because he wasn't afraid of something hurtling through the air at him.

Shane had ended up at culinary school despite his dad's efforts. Still, it was good to know how to fix stuff too.

He rang the bell of the modest ranch home his dad rented. The door swung open, and Shane was struck once again at how much Ryan looked like their dad. His dad smiled, and wrinkles formed around his eyes with the gesture. "Shane! What a nice surprise. Come in."

Shane stepped inside. The place was neat and sparsely decorated with old furniture his dad had picked up at Goodwill. "You feel like going for a ride?"

"Absolutely. Let me grab the keys." His dad went to the kitchen to fetch the Shelby's keys from their hiding spot behind the spice rack. Now that the Shelby was running, they'd been going for rides for the past couple of months.

They walked to the detached garage, and his dad punched in the code. The Shelby was valuable and highly collectible, since there weren't many around like this beauty from '67 signed on the dash by Carroll Shelby himself. Once they'd gotten the car running, his dad had given him the car as a thank you for spending time with him. Shane had never told his brothers about the gift. He hadn't wanted to further any hurt between his brothers and his dad. Ryan and Trav were polite to their dad at the few family events Gran had invited him to, but that was as far as it went. Shane kept the car hidden at his dad's place and never drove it in Clover Park.

His dad opened the garage, and they both took a moment to admire the car's beauty.

"That wax really brought out the red, didn't it?" his dad asked.

The original candy apple red. Shane resisted touching it so as not to leave a smudge. "She's beautiful."

Shane slid onto the smooth black vinyl of the driver's seat and gripped the original wood steering wheel. He admired the brushed aluminum accents and the old-fashioned speedometer. No computers working in this car. Just pure gears, metal, and raw horsepower. His dad got in and shut the door.

Shane turned the ignition, and the engine roared to life. He glanced at his dad, and they exchanged a grin.

He pulled out and headed for the open roads just outside of town, where horse farms dotted the landscape. The roads were curvy, mostly deserted, and lined with trees and stone walls. He hit the accelerator, enjoying the guttural sound of raw power that he felt as much as heard. The steering was tight, the brakes tight, beautiful shifting. They'd done a great job pulling this car back to its top form.

They rolled the windows down and let the warm breeze carry through. Shane soaked it all in for several miles before he finally told his dad what was on his mind.

"Dad, you know how much this car means to me, right?"

"That's why I gave it to you. I knew you'd take good care of her."

"You know what means even more to me?" He glanced over. "Just hanging out with you."

His dad's voice came out hoarse. "Me too, son."

Shane's chest ached. They drove in silence for a few minutes. He really didn't want to hurt his dad's feelings. The car had brought them together. It had given them something to focus on when conversation was still difficult in those early visits. It had given them something to look forward to and, ultimately, to connect with. But the important thing now was that they did have a bond. A good one.

"Dad, I want to sell the car."

"What! I thought you loved this car! I love this car. When I gave it to you, I pictured you giving it to your son one day."

Shane's chest tightened like his heart was in a vise. Geez, this was hard. But if he wanted to have a son of his own, he first had to sweep Rachel off her feet. Investing in the café, becoming her business partner, and ultimately much more, all depended on selling this car, his only real asset. He hoped to get at least a hundred grand for it. He couldn't take out another business loan, he was still paying off the one he'd taken to open his own shop. And he'd invested most of his profits right back into the business when he expanded with the equipment, staff, and delivery truck needed to supply ice cream to restaurants.

Whatever it took.

Shane slowed the car a bit to make conversation easier with less wind whipping through the windows. "You know I love the Shelby, but something's come up. An investment opportunity. I need the money to get in on the ground floor."

He congratulated himself on sounding reasonable and very business-savvy.

At his dad's silence, he glanced over. His lips were pressed into a line. His dad finally spoke. "This is about a woman, isn't it? That Rachel you're always talking about."

Shane didn't want to sound like a total lovesick fool, even if he was. "No, it's business."

He hit the accelerator, and the engine's roar combined with the wind made further conversation difficult. Finally, a couple miles down the road, he had to stop at a stop sign.

"Rachel's business?" his dad asked.

Shane sighed. "Yes."

His dad shook his head. "You're just gonna blow thousands of dollars to impress a woman."

"I told you this is business." Shane's cheeks burned. "You up for a drive to the beach?"

"Hell yeah."

"One last drive."

"One last drive, son."

Shane made his way east. The beach was about forty minutes away. The same beach where he'd held Rachel in his arms for the first time. She'd felt so right there. Ever since they started spending time together, Rachel was all he could think about. He'd seen glimpses of a tender heart under that prickly exterior. He was determined to win her heart. It was only fair. She already had his.

"Dad, I hope you're not mad. I know the Shelby has kinda been our thing."

His dad exhaled sharply and patted the dash. "I'll be sorry to see her go, but we'll get a new thing. Besides, I was in love once. Tell you the truth, I still love your mom. Not even death can take that away."

Shane swallowed hard over the lump in his throat. "I still love her too."

"She, uh, would've been so proud of you."

"Thanks," Shane choked out.

"All right, enough of that. Let her rip."

Shane punched the accelerator, and they raced around curves, the summer breeze running through their hair on their last glorious drive in perfection. God, he'd miss this car.

But he wanted Rachel more.

5

Rachel rang the bell at Liz and Ryan's house the next morning and nearly jumped out of her skin to hear a ferocious barking on the other side of that door. What the hell?

Liz answered, holding the collar of a lunging, barking, huge black and white puppy. "Hold on, let me just get him back."

Her friend's usually perfect straight blond hair was in a drooping ponytail with frazzled pieces that kept dropping in front of her face. "Sit, Hagar. Sit." Hagar jumped up on Liz and licked her. Liz giggled. "Thank you for kisses. Now sit. Sit, sit, sit."

Hagar did not sit. Instead he started jumping all over Rachel. "My ankle. Watch my ankle!"

Liz dragged Hagar with her into the living room. "Have a seat. He'll calm down in a minute."

Rachel made her way to the living room. Liz sat on the sofa, and Hagar immediately put his front legs on her lap, half sitting on her.

"Did you walk here?" Liz asked around the huge lapdog.

Rachel sat a respectable distance away from the beast. "Yeah, I can't drive yet."

"Rach! You should've called. I'm driving you home."

Rachel knew better than to argue. "Sure, thanks." She

stared at the slobbering creature with his tongue hanging out. "So you finally got the dog."

Liz smiled and shook her head. "You know I've been wanting a nonshedding dog for a long time, and I just mentioned to Ryan that we should start thinking about a puppy. You know, see how we do taking care of that as sort of a practice run before kids."

Rachel rolled her eyes. Like a puppy was the same deal. Her sister had four kids, the oldest only seven. You couldn't just stick a kid in a crate and leave the house. "You remember Bryce as a newborn, right?"

Bryce was Daisy's son. Liz had been helping her sister raise the baby before Liz had moved in and later married Ryan. Her friend had been a wreck with that colicky up-all-night baby.

Liz wiped dog drool off her cheek. "Of course I remember Bryce. That's why I wanted practice."

"You know that's not a nonshedding dog. It looks part lab."

Liz scooted Hagar over and held out her button-down pink shirt already covered in black and white fur. "I know! I wanted a cute little bichon frise or a miniature poodle, but Ryan found Hagar abandoned by the Little League field and brought him home. Hagar's so happy to be here I couldn't turn him away."

Hagar, hearing his name, took the opportunity to lick Liz all over her face again. Liz closed her eyes, smiling with her lips closed.

Eww. Did Liz know where that dog's tongue had been?

"The vet says he's eight months old," Liz said. "He probably has some Great Dane in him." She lifted a giant paw. "See these paws?"

"He's going to destroy your house."

Liz hugged him. Hagar nibbled at the ponytail band in her hair, pulling more hair out of its ponytail. "Hagar!" She put him on the floor, and he rolled over, showing his stomach. She gave him a belly rub. "He's already chewed through Ryan's phone charger and ate a remote. That's why Ryan changed his name to Hagar the Horrible. Hagar for short. I had named him Dumpling."

Rachel snorted. Dumpling? This huge guy?

"So what's up?" Liz asked. "Tell me everything that's new with you."

"Well, you know how I wanted to open a café next to Book It?"

Liz's eyes lit up. "Did you get the loan?"

"No."

"Oh, I'm so sorry. Maybe try another bank?"

"I don't think I'll get a different answer from a bank that doesn't know me from Adam. My financials aren't great. Anyway, Shane offered to invest in it. He said we'd be partners. He'd loan me the money for my half."

Liz's brows shot up. "Really?"

"Yeah. It's a generous offer."

"Egg?"

The old nickname referred to the fact that Liz thought Rachel was an egghead, always in her head and not noticing life going on around her. Rachel called Liz "chicken" because she never seemed to go for what she really wanted, but look at Liz now—married to the guy she'd crushed on as a teen, living in a house with a yard, and the dog to boot. Everything Liz had always dreamed of. The two kids to go along with it would likely be happening soon.

Rachel sighed. She couldn't call Liz chicken anymore. "What?"

"About Shane. I think he might have feelings for you, and maybe those feelings led him to offer to help you out financially."

Rachel knew that. But that didn't mean they couldn't still go into business together. "I told him we should just be friends." She lifted a finger triumphantly. "Actually I told him that before he made the business offer, so he definitely knew."

Liz looked at her sympathetically. "People don't just turn their feelings off and on that quickly."

Rachel felt a stab of guilt. She really needed this to work. She couldn't lose Book It.

"Is there any way I can do this without being a total jerk?" Rachel asked.

Liz considered, pulling her ponytail smoothly back into place. "You'd have to be very clear. Spell it out. This is a business deal, and you don't want to mix business with pleasure."

"Strictly business. Firm boundaries. That's what I've been thinking."

"Absolutely. You're a professional. Pretend it's some fancy-pants rich investor that came along. You'd have papers drawn up, get a lawyer to look it over, and never once take your clothes off."

"Well, if he's rich…"

They cracked up.

"You can do this," Liz said. "Just…be careful with Shane. He's special to me too. I don't want to see him get hurt."

Shane was Liz's brother-in-law now. Geez, Rachel was surrounded with O'Hares. And now it felt like Liz was with them instead of her.

"I thought you'd be on my side," Rachel said.

Hagar leaped up and barked at something by the front window. Liz joined him. "Bird," she said over her shoulder. She coaxed Hagar back with a huge bone. "Of course I'm on your side. I love you both. Now be the professional business-woman you are and make your café the most exciting thing to hit Clover Park since the O'Hares." Liz grinned.

"You are definitely drinking the Kool-Aid now. I remember when you couldn't bear to even look at Ryan. All you could think about was The Humiliation."

The Humiliation was what they called an embarrassing incident at Grand Lake one summer when Liz was only thirteen with a monster crush on Ryan, the seventeen-year-old lifeguard.

Liz smiled mysteriously. "You never know when love will sneak up on you."

Please. Spoken like only a newlywed could get away with. Rachel stood. "I'd better get back."

Liz jumped up. "Let me just put Hagar in his crate, and I'll drive you."

Hagar leaped up at his name, tail wagging hard. Liz took him back toward the kitchen. A few minutes later, Rachel and Liz headed out the front door.

"Stop by on Sunday for a barbeque," Liz said as she unlocked her car. "One o'clock."

An O'Hare family barbeque. Rachel had been to many. They were a fun crowd, but Liz was right, she had to be careful to keep firm boundaries with Shane, personally and socially, if this business partnership was going to work.

"Can I bring Janelle?" Rachel asked.

Liz started the car. "Absolutely. We'd love to have her."

Rachel marveled over the changes in Liz as they made the short drive to Book It. The Liz she used to know would never have let a giant, slobbery, shedding dog into her meticulously neat home. Yet here she was, a happy mess. What happened to her cool, calm, and collected friend? Liz had changed so much since getting together with Ryan last year. She fell in love and got married. Was that what love did to you? Turned you into a different person?

Rachel had never been in love, and for that she was glad. She liked her life just as it was, surrounded by books, being her own boss, coming and going as she pleased. Only cleaning up after herself.

"You need any help with the street fair?" Liz asked. "I've got time this summer. I just have a few kids for tutoring." Her friend taught third grade at Clover Park Elementary.

"That would be great!" Rachel enthused. Why hadn't she thought to ask her best friend since sixth grade? Liz had always been there for her. She realized with a start that as Liz had spent more time with Ryan, Shane had filled the space left behind by her best friend. Shane had become her closest, best friend.

Just one more reason to keep things strictly business. She couldn't afford to lose another best friend.

~

I am a professional businesswoman, Rachel reminded herself as she waited for Shane to arrive at her apartment the next night for their planned business meeting. She'd called him yesterday after her talk with Liz and then gone straight to her lawyer. She had a business plan copied and bound for Shane, as well as the paperwork for a partnership and a loan contract that spelled out the terms of the loan. She set the interest rate to the same as the bank would have offered (if she'd actually gotten the loan) to keep everything at a fair market value.

She hadn't dressed for a business occasion, thought that might be taking it a little too far; instead she wore the *Readers Rock* T-shirt she'd designed, with shorts. She sat at the kitchen table with the papers all laid out. She'd left the door unlocked so they wouldn't have to go through that awkward *Officer and a Gentleman* routine again. She was so over that petite feeling with those strong, muscular…*professional* arms. No, not professional arms. Geez. Who ever heard of professional arms?

If they were going to go into business together, she couldn't have any weirdness between them. The success of Book It was everything to her. After being in business for only two years, she wasn't ready to see it shut down. Clover Park needed a bookstore. Otherwise it was just food and antiques, doctors and dentists, nothing soul-satisfying the way a good book like *Pride and Prejudice* could be.

The doorbell rang.

"It's open!" Rachel hollered.

She heard Shane's footsteps on the stairs, and then he stood in her kitchen, smiling his dimpled smile at her. "I got the money."

She did a double take. "How did you get it so fast? My business loan application took two weeks."

Shane grinned. "I had something stashed away for a rainy day, and it came through in a big way."

"You're not gonna tell me?"

"What's all this?" he asked, pulling up a chair and gesturing to all the papers.

She pushed the laminated business plan toward him. "It's

everything you need to know to be a partner in Something's Brewing Café. Business plan, partnership papers, loan contract."

He picked up the business plan and flipped through it. "Not much on the type of coffee or food you're going to offer."

"I was still figuring that part out."

He closed the business plan. "I've got plenty of ideas for that. I'll come up with a menu."

"Aren't you going to read it?"

"I'll read it later."

"O-kay." She gave him a pen and pushed the partnership papers toward him.

He looked it over. The lawyer had spelled out a fifty-fifty split with Shane supplying the food and coffee as well as training the baristas while Rachel ran the shop.

"Do I need to get Gabe to look at this?" Shane asked, referring to his lawyer friend. Gabe Reynolds had been in their grade and recently moved back to town.

"Gabe's the one that handled it for me."

Shane's brows shot up. "What'd he say about it?"

Rachel played with her braid. "Just that he thought it was interesting that we would be business partners."

"Interesting how?"

Gabe had given her a knowing look and his exact words were: "So you and Shane, huh? 'Bout time." But Rachel wasn't about to share that with Shane. That would be unprofessional.

"I don't know," Rachel said casually. "I figured he meant interesting as in something different since we were never partners before." She pushed the loan papers toward him. "I set up a loan repayment schedule too." She pointed out the interest rate. "Same as the bank's rate."

Shane rubbed his temple. "You don't have to pay me interest."

"Yes, I do."

He blew out a breath and looked over the numbers. "You really think we need all this? Can't we just shake on it?"

"This is business. We have to do it right."

"Ten-year loan? We could do twenty if you want."

"Ten," she said firmly.

He studied her. She wasn't budging on this. She didn't want any special treatment just because they were friends. Part of keeping things strictly business was having all the paperwork in place. She didn't want any hard feelings and definitely no misunderstandings about exactly what they were getting into here.

Shane grabbed the pen and signed everything with a flourish. "Done." He flashed a smile. "Partners." He held out his hand.

She shook it. His hand was surprisingly warm in hers. Their eyes met, and the moment hung between them as they just stared at each other.

"Rach, I…"

She yanked her hand back. "Janelle wants to go out with you," she blurted.

It wasn't true. Janelle had never mentioned any interest in Shane, but Rachel needed a buffer and fast.

Shane's brows crinkled in confusion. "Janelle from your store?"

Rachel nodded. "She's into you. She asked me to ask you if you'd ask her out."

Shane narrowed his eyes. "Why does this sound like something out of junior high?"

"She's shy."

Janelle had never been shy. Rachel grabbed a napkin from the fruit bowl and scribbled Janelle's number on it. "Call her, okay?"

Shane stared at the napkin. "Rach—"

"Just do it!" She shoved the napkin in his hand. "You have to. I already told her you'd call."

"What'd you do that for?"

"I knew you'd take forever to ask her out, and I was sick of hearing her moon over you."

"I wouldn't take forever if I actually…" He stood abruptly, shoving the napkin in his pocket. "I'll look over the business plan tonight. We can hammer out the details tomorrow. My place."

"Actually I have my family Shabbat dinner Friday night. I can't miss." The Sabbath dinner was the only time her parents were in perfect accord, which made it her preferred time to visit. Plus she'd get to see her sister and her nieces and nephews. She loved the little guys to pieces.

"Oh, yeah, I forgot about that," Shane said. "Saturday night, then."

She couldn't be alone in Shane's apartment. He'd probably cook dinner for her, and it would be all intimate with more of that weird, crackling tension between them. Things were much more serious now that they had a business to launch. It simply wasn't a smart decision. Not until he was safely coupled up with someone else. All of their meetings from here on out would be in public places.

"How about we meet at my shop after closing?" Rachel asked.

Her shop had huge windows overlooking Main Street. Definitely not private.

He stared at her. "What's wrong with my place?"

"Nothing. I'm just more comfortable at the shop."

"All right," he said slowly. "I'll bring pizza."

She beamed. "Sounds like a plan."

He stared at the ground and blew out a breath. "See ya."

He sounded deflated. Definitely not how she wanted to begin their business partnership.

"Smile, Shane. With your good food and my retail skill, we'll turn a profit within a few months." She attempted a British accent, a nod to their favorite comedies. "This will be a smashing success!"

He merely raised a hand in acknowledgment and headed downstairs. She felt a little bad for pawning him off on Janelle, but the more she thought about it, the more she thought they'd make a nice couple. She'd planned on bringing her friend to the barbecue as a buffer, but having her as Shane's date was even better. She was doing them both a favor, in fact. They were both nice, good-looking, single adults. They should be thanking her. Maybe they'd name their firstborn after the woman who made it all happen.

On that note, she called Janelle. "Shane wants to go out with you. Please go, just for one date. I told him you'd love to."

To Rachel's surprise, Janelle was delighted. "Ooh, first a family barbecue, then a date. I'd love to go out with him. I've been drooling over his new sleek, muscular bod. Like a panther, mrow! Thanks, Rach, for making it happen. I never wanted to say anything because I thought maybe you had a thing for him, but this is *perfect*! I'll get him to break out of that shy routine with my patented Janelle seduction spell."

Rachel suddenly felt uneasy. "Seduction spell?"

"Top secret, honey. I'll call him right now. Thanks so much!"

"Wait! You have his number?"

"Sure. I've seen it on the shop's caller ID enough times. Bye!"

"Oh. Bye." Rachel hung up and poured herself a tall glass of chardonnay. "I'm such a good friend," she muttered.

6

Shane woke before dawn, unable to sleep without thoughts of Rachel and his spectacular, dumbass blunder running through his head. He'd never understand women. So much for sweeping Rachel off her feet with his white-knight routine, dashing in to save her business. Instead of falling into his arms, she'd set him up with another woman. He still didn't know how that had happened so fast.

He made his way downstairs to the kitchen in his shop. Sam wasn't even here yet to start the ice-cream base. He felt like baking. He'd take some of those fresh blueberries and make muffins. He already knew he wanted muffins for the café's menu. He could change the mix-in with the season—cherry, lemon, cranberry, pumpkin spice, cinnamon. But first blueberry because it was blueberry season.

He turned on a speaker dock he kept in the kitchen and pulled up his favorite playlist. Beyonce's "Drunk in Love" was up first. Like it or not, he could relate. He sang along as he gathered the ingredients. He washed the blueberries and tasted one. The berry burst in his mouth, tart and sweet. Perfect. Nothing like fresh-picked local blueberries.

He gathered the dry ingredients, then pulled out the butter, eggs, and milk. He eyed the basket he kept with lemons and limes and decided to grate some lemon zest in along with the juice to enhance the flavor of the blueberry. He got in the zone, working from memory the right proportions of flour, sugar, and baking powder. He prepared a teaspoon of fresh ground cinnamon, taking a moment to breathe deep and savor its aroma. Whisking the dry ingredients together, his mind flashed to working in the kitchen with Gran when he'd first come to Clover Park.

He'd been shell-shocked over the collapse of his family and the loss of his mother. He went mute at his new school, unable to handle jumping into the deep end as a seventh grader with the boys who were way into sports and the girls who asked him strange questions (Do you like four-leaf clovers? How tall are you? Do you have a girlfriend?) and then giggled at his answers (Yes, five foot ten, no), even though nothing was funny. Gran's kitchen was a cheerful oasis. She played top 40 music every night as she cooked delicious dinners, so unlike the food he'd grown up on—burnt fish sticks, hot dogs, and pizza. Suddenly there was lasagna, spicy stir-fry, and roast chicken. And the vegetables, always fresh, like roasted peppers, tangy Swiss chard, and perfectly steamed broccoli.

At first, he'd just sat at the kitchen table and watched, used to sorta fading into the background. A week passed like that until Gran suddenly turned to him.

"Boy, you've blended into the wallpaper long enough. Now I need you to be my sous chef."

"Me?" he asked, his voice cracking in excitement. No one had ever *needed* him for anything before. And what the heck was a sue chef?

"You see anyone else hanging around here?"

Ryan was always at some sports practice or game and usually got home late. Trav was out doing who-knew-what, getting into trouble. It was just him. He stood and crossed to her just as she slid open a drawer and pulled out a blue and white striped apron. She put it on him.

"Fits perfectly," Gran said. "Turn around."

He turned, and she tied it in back. "Used to be your

grandpa's. I don't know if you remember, but he was a whiz at the barbecue."

"Cool." His grandpa had died when he was ten, and Shane had only ever eaten hamburgers when he'd visited, but he believed her. "What's a sue chef? Is that a girl thing?"

"It's a French term. Sous like s-o-u-s. It's the assistant chef. You'll do all the washing and chopping while I do the cooking. When I think you're ready, I'll let you do the whole shebang. First things first, every chef washes their hands before preparing food."

He headed for the sink and scrubbed up.

"You'll start with washing these carrots and potatoes; then I'll show you how to peel and chop for the roast chicken I'm making."

He'd quickly moved up to full chef. His hands were strong and sure from working with tools for years. Once Gran showed him the right technique, he peeled and chopped efficiently. He loved handling the fresh herbs and vegetables, many he picked that same day from her garden. The fresh scents and flavors were an awakening from what felt like a black-and-white existence into a full-color life.

Gran let him make whatever he wanted after school all by himself, reserving the dinner hour for the two of them to work together. He dove in with appetizers and desserts, saving entrées for them to work on together. Leaving the daily grind of school, where he felt like the odd man out, to the absolute freedom of total control in the kitchen had been nothing short of amazing. His family loved his cooking, and he knew he'd found his purpose in life.

Now he wiped the flour off his hands on the blue and white striped apron he kept for sentimental reasons. He'd had new aprons made just like it with Shane's Scoops embroidered on the front for his staff, but this one was special, the original, the one that had started it all. He smiled at the memory and whisked the wet and dry ingredients together. He had just enough time to bake the batch before Ry came calling for their morning run.

He got back to work, at peace once again, just him and the

dish he'd soon share with his family. That was almost as good as the cooking, the sharing. It was why he opened his own shop, to connect with everyone in town. It kept him from feeling alone like his mother had always said she felt. He knew he took after her—sensitive and introverted—it was why he was careful never to be alone for too long.

Food was life and connection. It was everything.

Shane had just taken a bite of muffin, the lemon zest worked perfectly with the blueberry, when he heard someone leaning on his doorbell upstairs. He went out the back door to tell his brother to knock it off.

"Oh, you're up." Ry rubbed his hands together and smiled. "Come on. Let's get some endorphins going."

Shane muttered some choice obscenities about morning people. Ever since Ry had gotten on a regular schedule with his job as a cop, he'd become unbearably cheerful in the morning. He liked it better when his brother slept until noon in his old job as a private investigator and never checked up on him until the afternoon.

They set off at a jog. The town was quiet except for the occasional delivery truck passing through. Mostly it was just the birds and the crazy joggers.

Ry picked up the pace, and Shane kept up. Five days of running and he got nothing but tired and sweaty from it. After what felt like twenty miles, but was probably only two, Shane stopped. "When do I get that runner's high?"

"Just keep going, bud, you'll get there," Ry said, jogging in place. "You have to build up some endurance first."

They kept going.

Shane finally broke the silence. "Rachel and I are business partners."

"Seriously?"

"Yeah."

"Doing what?"

"We're opening a café next to Book It. I do the food and

coffee; she runs the shop."

"Shane…"

He sucked in some air as they went up that damn hill to the high school again. "What?"

"Do you really think she's going to go out with you if you go into business together?"

He pushed himself hard up that hill. He'd conquer it today. "No," he wheezed.

Obviously not or he wouldn't be meeting Janelle tonight for drinks at Garner's. He still couldn't believe Rachel had set him up with a friend. He hadn't wanted to hurt Janelle's feelings when she called last night and invited him, so he'd agreed to meet her. He'd never given Janelle a second glance at Book It, always being focused on Rachel, but she was cute. A little young, but not too young, he'd checked. She was twenty-four.

Ry beat him up the hill. Shane joined him and took a moment to catch his breath, enjoying the view in the early morning sunshine over Clover Park. The trees in their full greenery, the tall white steeple of the Methodist church, the shops downtown, houses nestled in a grid.

"It's just business," Shane said.

Ry fixed him with a pitying look.

"Shut up."

"I didn't say anything. Race ya." And with that Ry took off downhill.

"You win!" Shane called and sat down to enjoy not running. He was happy to be starting a café. The idea invigorated him. He'd been wanting to try out some new recipes for scones and breads and danishes. A lot of stuff he hadn't had time to work on with the ice-cream business booming. This would be good. Even without Rachel in his bed. He shifted uncomfortably remembering the night he had been in her bed. And that towel dropping.

He stood and raced downhill, trailing behind his brother.

Ry stopped and turned, jogging in place. "Winners never quit, bud. Good to see you remembered that."

Shane didn't have the breath to tell his big bro to shut it, so he merely nodded and ran, determined to catch up to Ry. He wouldn't quit on Rachel. He couldn't. He was in deep in too many ways.

Rachel closed Book It on Friday and headed downstairs to the back parking lot, where her sister was picking her up for the short drive to their parents' house for their family Shabbat dinner. The ritual was the one time her family seemed in perfect harmony. She'd often wondered why. Maybe it was because her mom had converted to Judaism and made a big effort to make the night special and all that effort reminded her dad of his wife's good intentions.

Maybe it was just the wine.

The beige minivan pulled up with its three rows of seating and multiple car seats. Sarah's husband, Mark, drove. Rachel squeezed into the backseat between baby Jacob and three-year-old Olivia. Leah, age five, and David, age seven, were in the row behind them.

"Shabbat shalom, everybody," Rachel said.

"Shabbat shalom," they chorused back.

"How's the ankle?" Mark asked.

"Doing okay," Rachel said. "I do these exercises the doctor gave me every day, and the swelling is finally gone. Still need the Ace bandage and hiking boots, but I'm getting there."

"Good." Then Mark barked out suddenly, "I'm with my family. Make it quick."

Sarah pointed to her ear, indicating he was on his Bluetooth headset.

"I do exercises every day too, Aunt Rachel," David piped up. "Wanna see?"

"Not now, sweetie," Sarah said. "Wait for grandma's house."

"I'm not happy with that," Mark said. "Run the numbers again. Call me back when you've got something workable."

"Daddy's mad," Leah said.

"It's just work stuff," Mark said. "Not you guys. You're

angels."

"I'm the best angel," Leah said.

"Me!" Olivia screamed.

"You're both stupidheads," David said. "The biggest is always the best. That's me."

A chorus of insults were hurled back and forth. Someone from the way back seat tossed a shoe, hitting the baby's arm, who started to wail. Rachel cringed, caught in the middle of kiddie chaos.

"Everybody quiet!" Sarah hollered, sounding very much the general in charge of the unruly brigade. "I don't want to hear a *peep* until we get to Grandma and Grandpa's house."

The car went silent, even the baby seemed startled into silence.

"Bet you can't wait to have some of your own, huh, Rach?" Mark asked, glancing at her in the rearview mirror.

"Oh, yeah," Rachel said. "The more, the better."

"It really is lovely to be a mom," Sarah said. "We love you guys."

The kids remained silent. Sarah turned around. "You can talk if you have loving things to say."

Rachel glanced behind her. Leah shook her head and crossed her arms. Olivia copied her sister. Then somebody finally spoke.

"Peep."

Then louder, "Peep!"

Rachel giggled. That set the kids off.

"Peep!"

"Peep-peep!"

"Pee-pee-pee-peeeeeep!"

By the time they arrived at their parents' house, the kids had moved on to chicken clucks and rooster calls, and Rachel joined in with a donkey hee-haw that had the kids in hysterics.

"Shabbat shalom, everyone!" her mom called, greeting them at the door. "Give Grandma a kiss." She reached out and hugged and kissed each grandchild as they went inside. David wiped off his kiss as soon as he got inside.

The house smelled of brisket and potatoes. Rachel had brought a strawberry and rhubarb pie she'd picked up at Garner's. Sarah and Mark brought the wine.

"How're my girls?" her dad asked.

Rachel bit back a sarcastic reply. They were "his girls" exactly one night of the week. Otherwise, he was all work, all the time, the hell with the rest of them. Her dad was the CFO of a major investment firm.

"Good," Sarah said, hugging him. "How are you, Dad?"

"Can't complain."

Rachel hugged her dad too. "How're the Yanks doing?"

It was literally the only topic he would talk about besides finance. He'd grown up in Brooklyn and was a die-hard Yankees fan. Rachel could've cared less about baseball, but hearing him go off about work stuff was worse.

"They're hanging in there," her dad said. "Forty-two and forty. Here, have a seat on my chair. We'll recline it so you can elevate your ankle."

"It's not necessary. I'm fine," Rachel said.

"I insist," he said.

"Just do it," her mom said, "or we'll never hear the end of it."

"I'm just looking out for our daughter," her dad said with a tight smile.

"She says she's fine," her mom sniped.

"Clearly she's not fine, *honey*," her dad said pleasantly. Though honey sounded more like *you irritating shrew*. "Rachel wouldn't be hobbling around if she was fine."

"I'm not hobbling," Rachel said, sitting in the stupid chair just to avoid hearing them get into it again. Their fights flared and then quickly moved to a sullen, tense silence. Rachel had enough of that growing up; she didn't want to hear it on the one night they usually all got along.

The kids got into a spirited game of Candy Land while Sarah took baby Jacob with her to keep their mom company in the kitchen. Then Mark stepped out to the backyard to take a call, so it was just Rachel and her dad.

Her dad turned on the TV and flipped to the Yankees

game. Rachel pulled the lever on the recliner to put her feet up and closed her eyes. She still couldn't believe she was actually going to open a café. If it hadn't been for Shane, her dream would've been dead in the water. He was such a good friend. She'd make sure he didn't regret his investment.

"How's Book It?" her dad asked, startling her out of her thoughts. "In the black?"

It was always about the bottom line for her dad. He'd tried to talk her out of opening Book It. He'd said bookstores were dying and she should stick with accounting. It was like he didn't even know her. She glanced at the TV. A commercial was on. She spoke fast, knowing he'd go back to the TV as soon as the Yanks came on no matter what was going on in her life.

"Book It's good. I'm going to open a café soon next door. I'm hoping that'll make Book It the place where people hang out and buy more books."

He cocked his head. "You really think it's wise to expand? You're barely breaking even."

Thanks for the support, Dad. Always could count on you to be in my corner.

"I think of it more as a diversification," she said tightly.

Rachel stole that diversification idea from Shane, but thought it sounded pretty good.

"How much did you have to borrow?" her dad asked.

"Actually I got an investor. Shane. He's more like a partner. He does food; I run the store."

He shook his head. "Bad idea. I'd never borrow money from family or friends. Or lend it. Here's why—" he ticked off the reasons on his fingers "—the person investing the money always wants to know what you're doing with it, they always want to know if you're being smart about the way you run things, and they keep checking up to see if you're spending too much."

"Shane's not like that. Anyway, he said…" She stopped. He was already back to the game.

She blew out a breath. Why did she keep expecting more from him? When would she learn? She never should have told him about her latest venture. It felt like he'd dropped an ice-cold bucket of harsh reality on her still-fragile dream.

"It's time to light the candles," her mom called.

Her dad set the game to record and headed to the dining room. She followed behind, joining everyone around the dining room table set with a white tablecloth and their best china and crystal. Even the kids would be drinking out of crystal goblets. Her dad turned off the lights, and everyone quieted as her mom lit two candles in her dad's great-grandmother's silver candlesticks. Her mom waved her hands over the candles to welcome the Sabbath, then covered her eyes with her hands while she recited the blessing. She uncovered her eyes and looked at the candles, signaling the beginning of their Sabbath celebration. Her dad recited the Kiddush prayer while holding a full glass of wine. Next her dad removed the cover from the challah—two sweet braided loaves of bread—lifted the bread and said a blessing before passing it around for everyone to tear a piece off. Rachel loved challah bread.

They sat down for the meal. Her parents sat on opposite ends of the table, at the head and foot, while everyone else filled in between. The scary thing was, even when no one was here to join them for a meal, her parents still sat at opposite ends of the kitchen table. Her dad ate while reading the newspaper in front of his face. Her mom stared at the newspaper from afar, perpetually angry over the noncommunication but refusing to break the silence. It was downright creepy. Would it kill them to talk about it rather than live in tense silence day after day?

Rachel didn't envy Sarah and Mark's marriage either. Oh, they got along okay, but Mark was always working, and Sarah spent her days and nights elbow deep in diapers, runny noses, and noise. Her sister had been on the corporate fast-track before kids. It wasn't that Rachel didn't like kids, she was crazy about her nieces and nephews, but she certainly didn't want to feel like a single mother doing all the hard work by herself. Sarah didn't seem to mind having a workaholic husband, but Rachel steered clear of that type.

She wanted someone who was dashing, brooding, arrogant, with barely suppressed passion just waiting for the perfect woman to bring him to heel with her love.

She wanted Mr. Darcy.

She sighed. There were so few of those to go around. *Pride and Prejudice* was her go-to comfort read, and she fell in love with Mr. Darcy all over again every time she read it.

The meal passed pleasantly. The kids took off to watch TV in the pajamas Sarah had brought along while the adults lingered over wine. The wine made her think of Shane and Janelle. Right about now they'd be meeting for drinks at Garner's. Janelle had told her earlier today. Would they get a little tipsy and move things over to Shane's place just down the block? Rachel suddenly felt sick and set her wine down.

Shane was free to see whoever he wanted. In fact, the sooner he was part of a couple, the better for their business.

The dinner conversation turned to the stock market, but all Rachel could think about was Janelle and her so-called seduction spell. What the hell did she do anyway? Rachel had never set out to seduce. Things just sort of went that way naturally after dating for a while. She'd never cast a spell. Was Shane vulnerable to that? Would he put out on the first date?

Rachel pushed up from the table. "I'll get dessert."

"Thanks, honey," her mom said. "I'll help."

"Me too," Sarah said.

They made short work of clearing the table. Rachel opened the pie box and sliced the pie. Sarah got out some dessert plates.

"So you and Shane in business together, huh?" her mom said.

"Dad told you?" Rachel was shocked. Her parents hardly ever talked. She always had to tell them news twice, once for her dad's benefit and once for her mom's.

"I overheard," her mom said. "He's a very nice young man." She smiled her mysterious I've-got-some-ideas-about-that smile.

"Oooh!" Sarah sang. "I sense some matchmaking."

Her mom turned. "It worked for you, didn't it?"

Sarah grinned and kissed her mom on the cheek. "It sure did."

Mark was the nice Jewish boy, the son of her parents' friends from college, that her mom had set her up with. Sarah, being a pragmatic woman, had decided at twenty-seven that it was time she married and had kids. They met, got along, and married one year later. Sarah had been popping out kids ever since. Rachel didn't need that kind of help.

"Shane is very nice," Rachel said calmly. "So am I. That's why we'll be good *business* partners."

"Maybe business plus something else," her mom suggested.

"Business plus," Sarah chimed in. "I like it."

"It's just business," Rachel said through her teeth. "Nothing else."

Sarah shook her head. "The stubborner they are, the harder they fall."

"I'm not stubborn," Rachel said. "We're friends."

"Friends with benefits maybe?" her mom asked hopefully.

Rachel's eyes widened. "Mom! Do you know what that is?"

"Yeah, a good time," her mom said.

They cracked up.

"I wouldn't mind another grandchild," her mom said. "Hint, hint."

"Four's not enough?" Rachel asked.

Sarah planted her hands on her hips. "Yeah, you've already got four fabulous grandkids."

"I don't have a redhead," her mom said with a pointed look at Rachel.

Maybe Janelle will have a redheaded child.

Rachel sliced a big chunk of pie for herself.

"Do you think Shane would be willing to raise the children Jewish?" her mom asked.

Rachel's head snapped up. "I don't know, Mom. We never talked about what religion we'd raise our children on account of *we're not a couple.*"

Her mother tsked. "I guess it doesn't matter. The mother carries the religion."

Her mother had been raised Catholic and was now more into being Jewish than her father, who was born to it. She really got into all the rituals and holidays that went along with it. Rachel could take or leave all that. She didn't know about Shane...why was she even thinking about all this? They were friends, period, end stop, forever and ever.

"You won't get a redhead out of me," Sarah said, setting pie slices on the plates. "Mark's whole family are brunettes."

"Our family is too," her mom said.

They both turned to Rachel. Rachel held up a hand in the universal sign for stop. She worked for calm, irritated beyond reason, knowing Shane was with Janelle right this very minute. "This whole conversation is a moot point."

She grabbed the dessert plates and made a break for it.

"You know Mr. Darcy was fiction, right?" Sarah called.

Rachel stiffened. How dare Sarah mention her favorite book like it was a joke! She bit her tongue on the snappy comeback she wanted to say: Not everyone has to settle like you and Mom. She knew her family thought she was lost in some fantasy world half the time, but that wasn't what books were to her. Yes, they were an escape, but when she came back, life was richer, more meaningful. No one ever got that about her. Even Liz called her egg because she thought she was too much in her head. Shane was the only one that never teased her about her obsession with books. He was so nonjudgmental. It was one of the things she loved most about him.

Loved as in friendship type of love. Why was she thinking about Shane again? She blamed her mom and sister with all their teasing. They couldn't understand being just friends with a guy. Shane was not her Mr. Darcy. That much she knew for sure. He was her rock—a steady, calm presence in her life. And when her Mr. Darcy did sweep into her life, she knew she could count on Shane to help her make good choices and not give her heart too soon. He would keep her grounded and safe like a best friend should.

7

Rachel tried to read while she waited at Book It on Saturday night for Shane, but it was hard. She kept checking the street for the sight of him, pizza in hand, as promised for their planned business meeting. According to Janelle, things had gone well last night and drinks had turned into dinner. Janelle didn't share any more details, and Rachel hadn't asked.

Rachel played with the end of her braid. *This is good. Things are right where they should be between you and Shane—two good, no* best, *friends starting a business together.*

She was happy for her friend. And Shane too. Of course she was happy for him; it was her idea to get them together. A flash of red hair caught her eye, and because he was interested in Janelle now, she let herself look, really look.

And what she saw was the sexiest best friend she'd ever had.

He'd shed the belly he'd gained from taste-testing ice cream. Now he was all trim and muscled and buff as he crossed the street toward her. She couldn't tear her gaze away.

Blue eyes with gold flecks.

That strong jaw.

Dimples.

Her heart started pounding. How was she going to pretend she didn't notice he was a grade-A hottie now that her eyes had been opened?

Omigod, he was here. She quickly stuck her nose back in her book.

The bell jingled as he let himself in. "Got the pizza. Half pepperoni, half olive."

He set the pizza and a paper bag on the counter, and then he stuck his hand on top of her book right where she was pretending to read. She looked up. He smiled, and she got a hot flash. Was she premenopausal? No, she was way too young for that.

Omigod, she was hot for Shane.

"Hey, partner," he said, still smiling that adorable dimpled smile.

"Hey," she managed.

He remembers I only like olives on my pizza. They hadn't even shared a pizza in months. He was so freaking thoughtful.

His blue eyes with gold flecks looked at her in concern. "You okay, Rach?"

She swallowed hard and wished for a cold splash of water to bring her back from this overheated place. Maybe she was even, embarrassingly enough, blushing. She almost never blushed. It was a point of pride for her. She'd been blushing way too much in front of Shane. It was like he'd contaminated her with his own bad habit.

"My blood sugar's low," she snapped. "It took you forever to get here."

He raised a brow. She snatched a slice of pizza and took a bite. *Hot!* She spit the scalding cheese into her hand and immediately regretted it. "Ah!"

She dropped the scalding blob of cheese on the counter. Wasn't she such a catch? Check out my spit-out food!

Shane pulled a napkin from the bag and handed it to her. "Slow down. That's fresh from the oven."

She hid the cheese in the napkin while she chugged the water, her eyes tearing from the pain of her poor scalded tongue. She swore she burned off half her taste buds with that idiot move.

Shane set out paper plates and napkins from the bag. "There was a long line for takeout. That's why I was a little late." He opened the box and pulled off a slice of pepperoni, leaving it to cool in the box. "Saturdays are busy for Joey's Pizza just like for the rest of us."

Unfortunately Saturday was not busy for Book It. They'd sold exactly three books today. People were too busy in the summer going to the beach and stopping for pizza and ice cream on the way home. No one wanted to hang out in her store, but now with a café, that would all change.

He joined her behind the counter and pulled up a cushioned stool. "How's the ankle?"

"Better. The swelling's gone."

He smiled. "Good."

She watched him pick up the slice and take a bite. He inclined his head for her to eat too. She picked up the slice from hell and took a careful bite. Cooler. Too bad she couldn't taste it with her taste buds gone, but…whatever.

Business, Rachel. Keep your head in the game.

"Did you have a chance to read the business plan?" she asked. "I mean, I know you were busy with Janelle last night."

Shut up! It's none of your business.

He tilted his head to the side, studying her. "I squeezed it in. It looks great. You covered all the bases, except the product, but that's why you have me."

She smiled. She'd planned to ask him to help with the menu, but this was even better, having him on board as an equal partner. She loved his baking. Everything he made was sinfully delicious.

"Do you think we should have sandwiches and wraps or just baked stuff?" Rachel asked.

"To start, we should stay small. Sandwiches and wraps would take more staff, more inventory, and more refrigerated cases."

"I do have a glass refrigerated case the previous owners left behind."

"Good. We'll keep snacks and desserts in it. Small impulse buys like apple tarts, blueberry scones, sweet breads that change with the seasons, brownies, cookies, mini-cupcakes, biscotti. Maybe some cheese danishes."

She nodded and took another bite of pizza, suddenly starving with the idea of all that mouth-watering goodness. After she chewed, she said, "Do I get to sample the food before we decide what to sell?"

"Absolutely."

He opened up a bottled water, and she watched his Adam's apple go up and down.

She cleared her throat. Might as well deal with the elephant in her head. "Janelle said she had a good time at dinner last night."

"Yeah, it was nice."

"Nice," she echoed. What did that mean? Nice as in, let's hop in bed together, nice as in, it was okay once, but let's not see each other again? Nice could mean anything!

Shane continued eating, unperturbed.

"Are you going to see her again?" she asked as she concentrated on folding her napkin into perfect squares.

"She said you invited her to the barbecue on Sunday, so I guess I'll see her then."

Rachel barely resisted smacking her forehead. She'd forgotten she'd invited Janelle to the O'Hare family barbeque before she'd pawned her off on Shane for a date. "Good, that's good. Fantastic. So...yeah."

She shoved more pizza in her mouth. *Shut up, Rachel. You sound like an idiot.*

"I've got a good supplier for appliances," Shane said. "I'll bring my espresso machine, coffee brewer, and a couple of grinders from my shop, but I think we should have another coffee brewer and grinder for flavored coffees."

That was a good savings right there, using the machines that Shane already had. "Do we have to have flavored stuff? It would be great to keep our expenses super low."

"Believe me, you'll want the flavored stuff. A lot of people asked for it at my shop, but I just didn't have the space for another machine. Now we can go big. Do it right."

"I defer to your beverage wisdom."

He grinned. "Have you checked the electrical and plumbing in the space?"

"I wouldn't even know what I was looking at. I did sign the lease yesterday. We've got ninety days rent-free to get us going."

"That's great!"

"It's only because the realtor was desperate to get someone into that space. I was the only interest they had in the four months it was on the market. And they know I always pay my rent on time."

"You got the keys?"

"I do."

"Let's check it out when we're done eating."

"Okay."

He lifted his bottled water in a toast and gave her a dazzling smile. "To tasty adventures to come."

Tasty! And did he put special emphasis on come? She squirmed in her seat. It definitely sounded dirty. She met his eyes dancing with laughter, and for the first time ever with Shane, felt a little off-center and out of her depth. He didn't feel like her rock; right now he felt like a buzzing light and she was the moth. But, if she got too close, zap! Game over.

Moth, really, Rach? The literary symbolism was not lost on her. Metamorphosis, transformation, yada, yada, yada. She still wasn't going to sleep with him no matter how hot he'd recently become. Hmm...maybe he was the one transformed. Maybe Shane was the moth. Augh!

She hastily lifted her water bottle and bumped it with his. "To tasty adventures," she blustered.

He drank and watched her over his bottled water.

She went back to her pizza, ignoring the unsettling feeling of being watched. He was interested in Janelle. Building a business together would only work with solid, rock-hard, um, boundaries. With that thought firmly in mind, she launched into a long, detailed description of projected income and expenses for the café that would've made most people's eyes glaze over, but Shane kept up surprisingly well. He even added expenses she hadn't thought about, like flooring that wouldn't stain, tables that were easy to clean, and lighting that was both decorative and inviting.

They finished eating and walked next door to the abandoned deli that would soon be their café. She unlocked the door and flipped on the lights. Not much to look at, but it was a start. A long counter with a deli case, a cooler for drinks, six small square wood tables with wood chairs.

Shane walked behind the counter and looked around. "We need more voltage to run the machines. I'll call an electrician." He squatted down and opened up some cabinets. "Gonna need a plumber. I want in-line water for a direct feed to the brewing machines." He opened the rest of the cabinets. "We need a water softener too. We've got hard water around here, and it makes a big difference in the flavor of the coffee. Plus you don't want mineral deposits clogging the espresso machine."

Dollar signs tallied in Rachel's mind. She wasn't going to argue. Shane knew what he was doing, and she didn't want to be penny wise, dollar foolish. They had to invest in the beginning for it to pay off in the long run.

Shane continued. "I want a good flow for the customers and the staff working behind the counter. We'll extend the counter and wrap all the way around to here." He gestured where he wanted the L-shaped counter.

More dollar signs.

"That seems unnecessary," she said. "We already have a perfectly good counter. It worked for the deli."

"No, it didn't work for them. They went out of business. It'll look better if we just add an all-new counter. Laminate is best so it doesn't absorb stains. Or maybe granite. And we need part of it to be lower to accommodate the disabled."

"A granite counter!" she exclaimed.

He ignored this. "We're also going to need two sinks behind the counter. One against the wall for hand-washing and the other up front for a quick rinse or anything else we might need."

"More expensive plumbing," she muttered.

He planted his hands on his hips. "We'll need more cabinets, more shelf space. All this stuff matters. You have to be organized in the prep area to keep inventory fresh and your staff efficient. The more efficient the staff, the more people you can get through here ordering food and drinks."

She blinked. Bossy Shane was making a reappearance. So, okay, food was his domain, but they were equal partners, and she didn't want to spend unnecessarily. She went behind the counter and took in all the cabinets. "We've got plenty of cabinet space. We don't need more."

"We do need more." He opened a few cabinets. "Look at this. Just one big space. No shelves at all. We need shelves. And more cabinets. I know what will work and what won't. And this won't."

She tensed, not liking the way Shane was taking over with all his opinions that would cost them serious money. It killed her not to have the upper hand, being inexperienced in the food business. This whole thing would be a huge adjustment for her, being partners, being indebted to him. She was used to doing everything herself and paying her own way. She couldn't wait to pay him back for her half of the partnership. But he'd signed the papers. They *were* partners. He wasn't the boss. She was done with bosses.

He regarded her steadily. She took a deep breath and nodded once, letting him have this one.

She walked out from behind the counter and looked around the space. The walls had tan wallpaper, the floors a dinged-up linoleum. She imagined a literary theme. Some book cover posters on the walls. The walls would be a deep red with floating shelves featuring first editions and the classics. Some golden sconces and a pair of cushioned leather reading chairs thrown in with the existing square tables. Maybe some comfortable cushioned chairs to go with the tables instead of those hard, wood chairs.

Shane joined her in the center of their would-be café. "I'm thinking a deep red paint on the walls."

She turned, eyes wide. "Me too."

He smiled and threw an arm over her shoulders. "All right, partner."

She caught herself smiling, all cozy with his arm around her. She shifted away. "My ankle's bugging me. I'd better sit down."

She sat down at a table, and he joined her.

"I'm torn between a laminate wood floor or black and white ceramic tiles," he said. "What do you think?"

"Ooh, a dark laminate floor. That would be nice. And some framed posters of book covers of all the great classics."

He smiled. "I like it."

"And hanging lights with pretty sconces."

"Maybe some gold tones."

"Yes!"

They smiled at each other. Their eyes locked, and she found herself unable to look away.

Shane stopped smiling. "Rach?"

She swallowed hard. "Yeah?"

He leaned forward and lowered his voice, though they were alone. His large, warm hand covered hers, and heat rushed through her. "If you don't want me to see Janelle again, I won't."

She pulled her hand away and quickly removed her glasses, cleaning them on the bottom of her shirt. "Don't be silly. You can see whoever you want. Janelle likes you. Go for it."

He leaned back and crossed his arms. His newly muscular, sculpted arms. They were a little out of focus, but they were there, right in front of her, taunting her.

"If that's what you want," he drawled.

She shoved her glasses back on. "I have nothing to do with it. That's between you and Janelle."

He shook his head. "You are so damn..." His mouth clamped shut.

Her eyes widened. He actually sounded mad at her. Shane hardly ever got mad. "So damn what?"

"Difficult." His chair scraped back as he stood. "I'm going to check out the back storage area."

"Okay." Rachel stayed right where she was. "I'm not trying to be difficult," she called after him.

She heard something slam in the back. He *was* mad.

Geez. She wasn't the one going out with Janelle. He could've said no. She traced a circle on the tabletop, and the image of petite, blond Janelle being carried in Shane's arms, smiling and laughing, came to her unwarranted. She stood abruptly, knocking over her chair.

"You okay?" Shane called.

"Everything's fine!" she hollered.

He stepped out to see for himself, glowered, and went back to the storage area.

Everything was fine. If Shane wanted to carry Janelle around, even though Janelle didn't even have a sprained ankle or any valid reason like that, Rachel certainly had no right to complain about it, now did she?

8

Shane was sweating, down by ten points in basketball against Ry, and wishing Trav was back from his honeymoon so he could take his place. Shane glanced at the patio, where Rachel, Liz, and Janelle were sitting under a patio umbrella talking to Gran at their Sunday family barbecue at Ry's place. Yup, Rachel sitting there was the only reason he'd even attempted the game. He sucked at ball sports, something that always made him feel separate from the other boys as a kid, especially when his older brothers were such athletes. When word got out in town that he was the one baking all the delicious food at church events, he'd taken a lot of teasing from the boys at school. And when he said nothing in return, the teasing escalated to punching by one particularly nasty bully and his two mindless friends until one day Shane felt forced to fight back. Luckily, he was big enough to defend himself and Ry had taught him how. He hated fighting, but no one messed with him after he'd kicked the ass of the ringleader.

Ry sunk a three-pointer while Shane halfheartedly went for the rebound. Shane retrieved the ball, and Ry stole it right out from under him. Ry stopped suddenly, tucked the ball under his arm, and looked sideways at Shane. "I think they're talking about you."

Shane glanced over to where the women were giggling

and looking right at him. Janelle wiggled her fingers in a little wave.

"Great," he said between his teeth, waving back.

Ry handed him the ball. "Make a shot. Show 'em what you got. I won't even steal it."

Shane dribbled and headed toward the basket. Ry feigned a steal, letting him go past. Shane took the shot and watched it bounce off the rim and into the yard. He didn't turn around to see the women's reaction, but Gran's voice carried.

"He's never been good at sports, but boy, oh boy, can he cook. That's what you look for in a man, ladies."

Shane's ears burned. Ry chuckled and tossed him the ball. Why did Gran always sound like she was trying to convince women to give him a second look? He worked out now. Lost the belly. He didn't need a grandmotherly assist.

Ry inclined his head toward the basket. "Give it another go, bud."

"Maybe I should just whip up a batch of cookies," Shane said. "Maybe then the ladies will give me a chance."

Ry grinned. "That's just the Pillsbury Doughboy in you talking. Take the shot."

It was either that or face the women. Shane blew out a breath and dribbled toward the basket. Ry didn't even fake a steal, instead standing back with a smile. Shane took the shot. *Swish.*

Applause broke out behind him. He turned. The women were all smiles, only one woman making his day by it. He jogged over to talk to Rachel when Janelle intercepted, putting a hand on his arm.

"Nice basket," Janelle purred.

"I missed the first one," he muttered, glancing over her shoulder. Rachel quickly looked away, turning to talk to Liz.

"I had a good time on Friday night," Janelle said softly.

It had been nice. They'd talked about Book It and Clover Park and Janelle's part-time graduate work in anthropology. Drinks had quickly turned to dinner as the night wore on pleasantly. He always liked the food at Garner's. Comfort food at its best.

"It was a good dinner," he agreed.

She looked up at him under her lashes in that weird way some women did. "You want to stop by my place after this?"

He glanced at Rachel, who was now watching them with a stormy expression on her face. He looked at Janelle, all perky and young and cute. It struck him that Rachel was jealous, and while that was a very good sign for him, he didn't want to hurt Janelle. He'd only gone out with her to be polite. He had to let Janelle know he didn't feel that way about her. But now didn't seem like the right time in front of everyone. Maybe later he'd get a chance—

Her hand slid up his arm and stroked his shoulder. "So will you stop by? We can get to know each other without all these people around."

He didn't want Rachel to see Janelle's hands on him. He stepped out of her reach and walked over to the patio to get a drink from the cooler. Janelle followed him. He popped open a Sam Adams and took a long drink. "We can get to know each other here."

"Do I have to spell it out for you, sweetie?" She went up on tiptoe, rubbing her breasts against him as she did, and kissed his cheek.

He stepped back. Message received, loud and clear. But Shane had never been the type to jump into bed with a woman after one date. And he didn't want to be with someone who did that either. Besides, his heart was already taken.

"I'm all sweaty." He lifted the bottom of his shirt and wiped his face.

"I like a sweaty man. Think about it."

She walked off, hips swaying, and went into the house. Hagar bounded out of his confinement when the door opened and started running in circles around the yard, barking joyously. Ry picked up a tennis ball and threw it. Hagar took off like a shot.

Shane dropped into the chair next to Gran.

"I'm telling you, ladies," Gran said, nodding her head as she spoke, her big floppy hat nodding along. "He graduated from the Culinary Institute of America. You won't find a better chef, and he has other talents—"

Shane groaned, his cheeks burning again. "Stop bragging about me. It's embarrassing."

"If I can't brag about my own grandson, then what do I have to brag about?"

"Parasailing," Liz chimed in.

"Your lasagna," Shane said.

"Winning the seniors tango competition with Jorge," Rachel added.

"I heard my name," Jorge said, coming out of the house and crossing over to Gran. He kissed her tenderly. "How are you, my love?"

"I'm wonderful," Gran cooed. "Sit with us."

Gran and Jorge had been married almost a year now. It had happened fast, but as Gran liked to say, she wasn't getting any younger. She was seventy-three. Jorge was fifty-something. Age didn't matter to them. It was really nice to see his gran so happy. She'd been alone for a long time, ever since his grandfather died.

"Looks like things are going well with you and Janelle," Rachel said flatly.

Shane suppressed a smile at Rachel's carefully neutral tone. She *was* jealous. Even though she was the one who set him up with Janelle, it was eating away at her. As far as he was concerned, there was absolutely nothing keeping him and Rachel apart except her own damn stubbornness.

"She's all right," he said.

Rachel sat up straighter and looked around the table. "Shane and I have some great plans for Something's Brewing Café. We want you all to come to the grand opening." She turned to him. "How soon you think until we can open?"

He smiled. He'd rather talk about the café than Janelle any day.

"I'd love to open on Labor Day in time for the street fair," he said.

"Do you think you have enough time?" Liz asked.

Rachel considered this. "Six weeks. Maybe."

"If we can get the electrical and plumbing done quickly, it'll work," Shane said. "I'll place our equipment orders on Monday. The rest is just cosmetic."

"Well, cosmetics are pretty important," Rachel said.

"That won't take long," Shane replied. "I can jump in with the contractors. Move things along."

Rachel's face lit up. "*Veni, vidi, vici!*"

Liz wrinkled her nose. "Is that the—" she finger-quoted "—*we won* Latin?"

"We came, we saw, we won," Shane said.

Rachel turned, jaw dropped. "You remember my favorite Latin phrase?"

He lifted one shoulder up and down. "I listen. You could also say *aut viam inveniam aut faciam*."

"Shane!" Rachel exclaimed.

"What's that one?" Liz asked.

"I will either find a way or make one." He couldn't help but laugh at Rachel's shocked expression. "I told you I listen."

Rachel shook her head and smiled. "Six weeks to financial security!"

"Rach," Liz said gently. "I'm glad you're so positive, but I think it'll take a while for the money to roll in. Didn't you say there were a lot of start-up costs?"

Shane reached across the table and squeezed Rachel's hand. "We'll make it work, partner."

Rachel snatched her hand back and busied herself cleaning her glasses with the bottom of her shirt. "Of course we will," she muttered.

Liz and Gran exchanged a look.

Gran smiled widely. "Something's brewing between friends, I say."

Shane's cheeks and ears burned. He would never, ever pull off cool in front of his grandmother.

Rachel shoved her glasses back in place and stood stiffly. "That's right, Maggie. It's called coffee."

He watched Rachel stalk off to the house, stopping briefly to say hello to Janelle, who'd just stepped outside, and disappear inside.

"Gran, you made her uncomfortable," Shane said.

Gran shooed him away. "Then go make her feel better."

"I will."

He left his beer and walked straight by Janelle to catch up with Rachel inside.

～

Rachel headed back to the kitchen and poured herself a glass of ice water, pausing to take a few deep breaths. This whole thing was completely absurd. Jealous over Janelle. Suddenly noticing Shane's dimples, his body, his deep, rumbly voice, his Latin—

"Rach, you okay?"

She jumped and whirled around. The man needed some kind of early warning system—squeaky shoes, swishy corduroys, a spinning propeller hat that played "Yankee Doodle Dandy." Anything equally nerdy would do because these lusty ideas about her best friend and partner were wreaking havoc with her rational, professional business-woman side.

With firm boundaries. Don't forget that. Very firm.

She walked straight up to him, bravely looking him in the eye. It was time to put all these crazy ideas about Shane to rest once and for all. "You ever sleep with someone you worked with?"

He swallowed visibly. "No."

"You ever sleep with a friend and then go back to being friends?"

He gave her a slow smile that made something flutter low in her belly. "I kissed someone and went back to being friends."

He stepped closer, and she found she couldn't move. He smelled like sweaty male. That shouldn't be good, shouldn't make her weak in the knees. He took the glass from her hand and set it on the counter. One large hand cradled her face. "You want to give it a try?"

Don't be stupid! You're playing with fire!

She was all set with a firm *no,* but what came out was an embarrassingly weak, "Um…"

She caught his quick smile before he leaned down and kissed her, soft, so soft. His tongue traced her lips and then dipped inside. Someone sighed. That couldn't have been her. She wasn't the sighing type. Her hands went up to his chest, gripping his shirt as his mouth and tongue took over a thorough exploration. She pressed closer, nipping at his bottom lip. His hands slid to her bottom and pulled her close against what felt like a massive erection. *Cock-a-doodle-do-me.* Shane was hung. Someone let out a needy whimper. Her again. Shane growled. Wait, Shane growled?

Bark! Bark! Bark! They broke apart. Hagar was here, and apparently he didn't like what he saw.

"Sorry!" Liz called from the other room. "I just came in to get him some water. We didn't see anything."

Rachel dropped her head on Shane's chest and heard a low laugh rumbling there.

"Can I just get his water dish real quick?" Liz asked.

"Come in," Shane called, turning Rachel so her back was pressed against his front. He wrapped his arms loosely around her waist. She wanted to pull away, to give herself a chance to cool off and quell the rumors surely to follow through the family gossip mill, but something hard pressing into her hip told her Shane wasn't quite ready to let her go.

Liz beamed at them and filled the dog's water dish at the sink. "Come on, Hagar. We'll take this outside. Carry on!"

As soon as Liz left, Rachel stepped away from Shane and turned to face him. "That never happened."

Shane rubbed a hand over his face. "Why? Why can't it happen?"

She had to let him down easy. She knew he was sensitive, and she didn't want any hard feelings. *Hard feelings.* Her gaze fell to the front of his tented shorts, and she had the sudden urge to peel them down and see exactly what he had going on under there. Just one peek. She'd had no idea…not until he was pressed up against her. Not that size mattered. At least she didn't think so. She'd never been with anyone that was… above average. Jumbolicious. Giganto-screw.

"Rach?"

She heard the smile in his voice and snapped her attention back to his face. Her cheeks burned. She couldn't believe she was blushing again. That was Shane's thing. But he wasn't blushing now. He was giving her an unsettling, knowing look that said, *You want?*

Focus. She took a deep breath. "This can't happen because we're business partners and friends," she said firmly. "And, um, Janelle."

He took a step closer; she stepped back. He advanced on her with a determined look in his eyes that had her heart beating like crazy as she kept backing up until she felt the counter bump against her back. He boxed her in, one hand on either side of her hips.

She gulped. "I don't think—"

"Don't think," he said as his lips brushed hers, kissing one corner of her mouth gently, then the other corner. So gentle, so tender, it undid her. Her eyes closed on their own. He kissed the bow in her upper lip softly, luring her in; then he was kissing her long and slow and deep until she wrapped her arms around his neck and melted against him. His hand fisted in her hair, and the kiss turned hard, a dark promise of possession that had sparks shooting down low where there hadn't been sparks in a very long time. She moaned, unable to stand on the moral high ground with the sensations clouding her brain.

He pulled back long enough to say, "Let's get you off that ankle," then he was lifting her to the counter, nudging her legs apart as he pushed between them, his mouth claiming hers again. Her mind went blank, and there was just the hard planes of his back as her hands ran over him, the throbbing between her legs, and his mouth demanding on hers. His large hand slipped under her shirt and stroked up her back, then ran lightly down her spine, giving her a hot shiver. He pulled away and gazed into her eyes with a look so ravenous her heart actually kicked up. She'd never had a man look at her that way.

She would've swooned if she wasn't sitting down.

This was bad. Really bad. This was *Shane*. Somehow when he was kissing her, she could forget it was actually Shane she was wrapped up in, but one look at him and she was back to looking at her friend. They couldn't do this.

She loosened her grip on the back of his shirt and dropped her hands, focusing on a point just over his shoulder. He was still close, standing between her legs, his hands resting on her hips. She was surrounded with his scent, some combination of male sweat and fresh-scent deodorant and Shane that made her want to rip off his clothes. *Get a grip!* She pushed at his chest with both hands, suddenly needing him out of her personal space.

He didn't move. Instead he gently tucked a lock of hair that had fallen out of her braid behind her ear. "Do you like that, Rach?" he asked, his voice a whispered rumble in her ear. "Do you like when I kiss you?"

She opened her mouth to deny it, felt like a total hypocrite, and shut it again. Besides, he knew. She'd moaned loud enough. God, this was embarrassing. She should just shut this whole thing down right now. Say something snarky to really piss him off. But then he was cupping the back of her head, holding her there while he trailed hot, open-mouthed kisses down her neck. She swallowed hard, her mind and body at war with themselves. He licked and nipped at the soft dip of her collarbone, and she gasped. His mouth left a hot trail up her neck, skimming her jaw, coming up to the corner of her mouth. Her lips parted in anticipation. She might've sighed.

His lips brushed hers, once, twice. "Do you? Say it."

"No, I hate it."

And then she grabbed his head and kissed him again to prove it.

He took over the kiss, his tongue delving into her mouth. His hands slid under her bottom and pulled her tight against him. She wrapped her arms and legs around him, forgetting everything but this incredible need to get closer. She had to get closer. His hands were still gripping her ass when they heard a familiar voice. Female.

"Shane?" Janelle called.

Shane jerked away from her, and Rachel slammed to reality with a sickening crash. She suddenly felt shaky and cold from the loss of his body wrapped around hers.

Obviously he didn't want Janelle to see them together. Hurt sliced through her. She slid down from the counter and quietly slipped out the back door on shaky legs, leaving Shane and Janelle alone.

9

Shane headed for the street-fair meeting in the Clover Park library conference room the next day, wondering how Rachel would react when they saw each other. After they'd kissed at the barbecue, she'd kept her distance, always keeping at least one person between them. But after a scorching kiss like that, he had no plans to pretend he was only interested in her as a friend.

"Why, hello there, Shane," Miss Smith said as he passed her librarian desk. "Haven't seen you here in a while."

Shane couldn't remember the last time he'd borrowed a book. Whenever he wanted a new cookbook or mystery, he bought it at Rachel's store. He tried to keep Rachel in business. He didn't even need the cookbooks since he created his own recipes.

"Hi, Miss Smith. How are you?"

She smiled a rare smile and patted her gray hair in its usual bun. "I'm just fine. You're such a nice young man. If I were twenty years younger…"

Twenty? More like forty. He felt himself blush anyway from the compliment. Old women loved him for some reason. If only he had that effect on the younger generation.

"I'd better get to my meeting."

She shook her finger at him. "I want to see your face around here a lot more, Mr. O'Hare. Reading is still an important skill for all ages."

"I'll be here every Monday night for the street-fair meeting."

He headed to the conference room. Only one person here so far, his friend, Gabe Reynolds, wearing what he thought of as a casual outfit: a preppy polo shirt and khakis. Gabe had moved back to Clover Park only a month ago, shedding his expensive suits along with his fast-track job at his dad's law firm after his dad had died suddenly of a heart attack at age fifty-seven.

"Gabe," he said, pumping his hand, "they roped you into this, huh?"

Gabe held up his palms. "I'm giving back to the community. It's my new thing."

Shane laughed. Gabe had been like a shark with the sharp teeth of his law firm to back him up, so it was hard to picture him as a community volunteer. "What did Rachel promise you?"

"Nothing," Gabe said indignantly. "Can't a guy just do his part?"

Shane shook his head. "Well, I'm glad you're here. There's this new guy in charge of the street fair, Barry, from that fro-yo place, and I just know he's going to try to pull some crazy stunt that makes the street fair a total—"

"Hey, guys!" Barry Furnukle waved as he walked in wearing a loud, red Hawaiian shirt. "I brought coupons!"

He handed them each a ten percent off frozen yogurt coupon to his shop The Dancing Cow.

"Thanks," Gabe said.

Shane stared at it. He didn't believe in coupons. Quality food was not about a bargain.

Barry sat at the head of the table and rubbed his hands together. "Who else is coming?"

"Rachel," Shane said.

"That's it?" Barry asked.

"Whoever else she managed to rope into it," Gabe said.

"I knew it," Shane said under his breath.

"I get free coffee for life," Gabe whispered.

Shane grinned. He'd let that one go. He just hoped Rachel hadn't promised anyone else the same treatment or they'd never keep the café profitable. Gabe had always helped him with legal questions and paperwork and never charged him. They'd become fast friends after Shane had kicked the ass of that middle school bully. Turned out Gabe, a scrawny "late bloomer" as Gran liked to say, had been tortured by the kid too.

"It's a lot of work," Shane said to Barry. "A lot of business owners are busy in the summer."

Barry pulled a pen from his front shirt pocket along with a Dancing Cow napkin and set them on the table, presumably to take notes. "The more hands, the lighter the work."

Just then Rachel walked in with Liz and Janelle.

"I brought many hands," Rachel declared.

Shane went instantly hard. She wore a snug pink T-shirt that read Born to Read. Her black shorts showed lots of leg. He couldn't wait to get her in his arms again. He tried to catch her eye, but she avoided looking at him and walked to the far side of the table with Liz. She needed a little convincing, a little reminder of their kiss. After the meeting.

Liz waved. "Hi, everyone."

It was almost like a high school reunion. Shane had graduated with Liz, Rachel, and Gabe. He relaxed. This wouldn't be too bad.

Janelle slipped into the seat next to Shane and stuck her lip out. "I haven't heard from you."

Were they supposed to do something? He shifted closer to the table to hide his massive interest in Rachel.

"I, uh, just saw you yesterday," Shane said.

She put her hand on his arm and whispered in his ear, "Let's grab some drinks on Friday. That was fun."

"I'll let you know," he said noncommittally. He really needed to have that talk with her. He'd gotten distracted with Rachel yesterday. He'd never had to reject a woman before.

He'd wait until they were alone and explain that he was interested in someone else.

Janelle smiled at him. She pulled a notebook and pen out of her purse. "Rachel wanted me to take notes," she announced. "I'll email you all each week with the minutes so we don't forget what we agreed on."

"And here I thought the napkin would cover it," Barry said, waving it in the air.

Liz giggled and quickly slapped a hand over her mouth.

Rachel spoke up. "Barry, I just wanted to let you know what we've done in previous years. The street fair is always on Labor Day, and we close Main Street to cars. The sidewalks have sales from all the stores, and in the street we set up games for the kids like bean bag toss, fishing in a kiddy pool, sand art, and face painting. Last year we all went in on an inflatable bounce house."

"And of course, food," Shane chimed in. "We have a tent set up with burgers and hot dogs grilled by Garner's." He inclined his head toward Liz. She smiled. "And I have a small freezer set up for ice cream with more flavors offered in my shop."

"Ooh, this year we could offer iced coffee and iced tea from our café," Rachel said, meeting his eyes for the first time. Their gazes locked. It felt like an invisible thread drew them together even across a table in a room filled with people. This attraction was real and growing with every look, every touch. He wished they were alone right now. He couldn't wait for the meeting to be over. Her cheeks turned a pretty pink.

"Great idea," he said, but he meant *I want you so bad*.

Rachel quickly looked away and twirled the end of her braid. Was she really that freaked out by the idea of the two of them? They were good together. Friendship was a great foundation for a relationship, not a reason to avoid one.

Barry scribbled something on his napkin. "So the entire street fair's on Main Street?"

"That's where most of the businesses are in town," Rachel said.

"I'd like the fair to extend to the front of my shop too," Barry said.

"You're a mile away from downtown," Rachel said, her voice amping up a degree in irritation.

"And well worth the walk," Barry said cheerfully. "People will love cooling off in my spacious air-conditioned shop. And the kids will love seeing the dancing cow giving out wacky glasses."

"Don't forget how healthy the frozen yogurt is," Shane said, looking to get Rachel smiling with their favorite joke.

Barry nodded vigorously. "That too."

Rachel tipped her head and gave Shane a sideways look. "Why is that again?"

"Because of the pro-bee-otics, of course," Barry replied.

Shane and Rachel stifled a laugh.

"I should put that right on the sign out front so people will remember," Barry said. "You and Shane are always forgetting about the most important ingredient."

"You don't need a sign," Shane said, working hard not to crack up. "Just remind them. Much more effective that way."

He exchanged another amused look with Rachel across the table. She smiled, biting her lip. Her shoulders shook with suppressed laughter.

"You know it's actually pronounced—" Gabe started. He jolted as Shane kicked him under the table.

Rachel got herself back under control. "Barry, it's really too far of a walk. It doesn't make sense when you're the only one in the chamber of commerce out there."

"Don't forget Derek from Flying Leap Fitness," Barry said.

"Yes, but what are people going to do at his shop?" Rachel asked.

Barry made a nonexistent muscle. "Get fit."

"That's not the point of the street fair," Rachel said.

"Okay, let's just table this issue," Barry said, tapping the table. "Let's move on to the important stuff. Coupons."

Shane frowned.

"Coupons," Rachel repeated, looking like she wanted to throttle Barry. Shane would be happy to watch.

"I love coupons!" Janelle declared. She looked around. "Who doesn't love a good bargain?"

"Yes, but there's the paper and printing and distributing," Rachel said. "Not to mention cleaning up all the coupons that kids lose or throw on the ground."

Barry stood and walked around to Rachel's seat. He whipped a coupon out of his shirt pocket. How much did he manage to fit in that pocket? "I present to you ten percent off a frozen yogurt. Come into my shop, try it, and then tell me how you feel about coupons."

Rachel gingerly took the coupon. "Uh, okay."

Barry nodded and gamely returned to his seat. "What else? Someone to make balloon animals? Pony rides? Maybe a carousel?"

"There's not that much room on Main Street," Gabe said.

"There is if we push it all the way out to my shop," Barry said. "I'll host the pony rides in my parking lot."

Liz looked at Rachel. "That does sound like fun."

"It sounds expensive," Rachel said. "And we're not stretching the fair that far because there's nothing between downtown and your shop but houses." She threw her hands up. "It makes no sense!"

Shane intervened. "We should vote on it."

Rachel shot him a grateful look. No one would vote this in Barry's favor. He was the new guy, and he just didn't get how things worked around here.

"How many in favor of extending the fair out to The Dancing Cow?" Gabe asked.

Barry's hand shot up in the air. Everyone else sat hands down. Barry slowly put his hand down.

"The people have spoken." Barry frowned. "Guess I'll have to cancel the ponies," he muttered under his breath.

"Maybe for another occasion," Liz said. "It sounds like fun."

Barry had lots of ideas and lots of friends in the kiddie "entertainment" industry. The group decided to let him make some phone calls to get an idea of costs and then meet again the following Monday.

The meeting adjourned, and everyone stood and gathered their things. Shane waited outside the room for Rachel. He wanted to walk her back to her place, clear the air between them, and kiss her until she was soft and willing again.

Barry got to her first.

"Allow me," Barry said, holding out an arm to Rachel.

"I can walk," Rachel said. "I know I've got this ankle thing, but I'm managing fine."

"You'd be doing me a favor," Barry said with a smile. "I haven't had a beautiful woman on my arm since, well, I can't remember when." He looked at her sheepishly, with an aren't-I-so-adorable look that made Shane want to puke.

Rachel fell for it. "When you put it that way."

She took his arm, and they walked out together. Barry was telling her all about frozen yogurt and its many flavors and healthful benefits.

A rare temper flared in Shane as they walked right by him. What was Rachel doing? They liked to make fun of this guy. She looked genuinely interested in what he was saying.

Liz placed a hand on his arm. "Why don't we all get some ice cream at your shop?"

"Sure," he said, knowing she was just trying to distract him from Rachel leaving with the fro-yo guy.

"Sounds great!" Janelle chirped.

"You got any of that salted caramel left?" Gabe asked.

"Yup, let's go." Shane left with Janelle talking his ear off, Liz and Gabe trailing behind.

When they got outside, he saw Rachel getting into Barry's Honda Accord. Shane stopped right there on the sidewalk to watch. The bright blue car had a huge Dancing Cow magnet on both sides. There was a loudspeaker mounted on top that actually mooed. They always made fun of that stupid car, and now Rachel was driving around in the thing?

Janelle pulled at his arm. "Come on. I'm hungry."

He stayed rooted to the sidewalk. The cowmobile drove past Book It and continued down Main Street. Was Rachel taking Barry up on his offer? Was she choosing fro-yo over the far superior ice cream he offered? Really? Fucking Barry the dancing cow?

Shane marched across the street to his shop. Janelle hurried to keep up with him. He gestured to the group. "Tell Mike what you want. On the house."

Then without another word, he went straight out the back door and went for a drive.

Rachel didn't know what made her agree to go to Barry's shop. Maybe it was the compliment he gave her. Maybe it was the jealous stab of watching Janelle sitting so close to Shane.

Maybe it was just to avoid Shane. She knew they had to keep things strictly business, but when she saw him again today sitting in that library conference room, she got another one of those ridiculous hot flashes. And the way he looked at her. Like he wanted to eat her for breakfast. That was way more than a hot flash, more like an inferno that would consume them both and spit out the cold, dead bones of their friendship.

So here she was in the cowmobile. If Shane couldn't reach her, she couldn't cave. It was dumb and temporary, given that they had to get the café off the ground, but it was the best she could do the day after their make-out session in Liz's kitchen. All day she'd been reliving that kiss.

Her mind flashed to that incredible heat. The pull she'd felt, like she wanted to climb inside and somehow merge with him. She went damp at the memory of his hardness pressing between her legs. It couldn't happen again. Kissing was a slippery slope to the end of their friendship. And she'd do anything to keep Shane as a friend. He was the only man she could ever truly count on. Boyfriends didn't last. Friends were forever.

A sudden moo startled her and snapped her attention back to Barry. He grinned as he pressed the button to make the loudspeaker on top of the car moo again. "The kids love it," he told her.

She sank further down into the seat. "I bet they do."

Barry told her all about his plans for making his fro-yo shop a hit, and she found she could relate. Here was an enthusiastic businessman willing to work hard and try new things to make his business a success. She wanted Book It and Something's Brewing Café to succeed something fierce.

They pulled into The Dancing Cow parking lot.

"We're here, my lady," Barry said. And before she could say *I'm not your lady*, he'd leaped out of the car and run over to her side to open the door.

"Thank you."

He offered his arm again and led her into his shop. She looked around, studying it carefully, very interested in the setup now that she was getting into the food business. The floor was white with black speckles—good for quick clean up —there were several lime green melamine tables with pink cushioned chairs plus a long counter with bright yellow stools. The walls were painted with farm scenes of rolling hills dotted by cows. Frozen yogurt machines lined one wall, boasting eight flavors of frozen yogurt that you could dispense yourself and pile on the toppings at the toppings bar. The whole thing was self-serve, so Barry only needed staff to keep things neat and ring up the purchases.

Several families were already here enjoying their healthy frozen yogurt covered in toppings. The gummi bears seemed especially popular.

"Help yourself," Barry said. "I'll be behind the counter, waiting to check you out with your coupon." He smiled and laugh lines formed around his eyes. He really was a nice guy. She knew Shane saw him as enemy number one on account of the frozen yogurt-ice cream competition, but maybe Shane could learn something from him.

She smiled back. "Thanks."

She grabbed the smaller size paper bowl, which was still very large, and pulled the lever for a swirl of peach. Then she added piña colada and watermelon on top of that. Next the toppings bar. This was kinda fun doing it yourself. She had just reached for the bin of Nerds when the lights started flashing and a disco ball she hadn't noticed before started spinning. She froze, wondering if this was the part with the dancing cow.

Sure enough, a dancing cow appeared doing a little Irish jig in the center of the store. It was Barry. She couldn't help but laugh. Maybe Shane couldn't learn anything from Barry. The idea of Shane dancing a jig in front of customers made her laugh even harder. Barry produced several pairs of wacky glasses—black rimmed with big blue eyes on the lenses—and danced around the shop, giving them to delighted kids.

"Have a moo-tastic day!" Barry said to one. The girl, five at the most, looked thrilled as she put the glasses on.

"These are fresh from my udder!" Barry told a little boy.

"What's an udder?" the boy asked.

"It's where my udderly delicious fro-yo comes from!" Barry replied.

Some parents groaned good-naturedly. The boy laughed.

"Remember, fro-yo is healthy because of the pro-bee-otics!" Barry sang. He gave out more wacky glasses, patting kids on the head and dancing silly in front of them.

He made his way over to her. "For my lady." He tipped the glasses back and forth, showing her how the eyes blinked.

"I'm not…" She trailed off as he slipped the glasses on over her own glasses. It was silly, but it was also kinda fun. Barry smiled before dancing away.

She pushed the glasses to the top of her head and finished piling candy onto her yogurt, topping it with a maraschino cherry. While she waited in line to pay, she looked around the shop. Everyone was happy and smiling. Barry did that. He was funny and strange and annoying, but his heart was in the right place.

She made it to the cash register, where Barry placed her fro-yo bowl on a scale. The price rang up by the pound. "Coupon?"

"Oh, yeah." She pulled it out from her purse and handed it to him.

Barry rang up her purchase. "That would've cost eight dollars and twenty-three cents, but with the coupon, you saved eighty-two cents. Doesn't that feel good?"

Eight dollars for yogurt? Barry must be making a fortune. It was so easy to fill up those huge bowls. How much did the bowl weigh anyway?

"Yeah, okay." She pulled out the money and handed it to him. At least at Shane's shop the prices were reasonable. You never left feeling like you were ripped off. "I'll take this to the patio."

"Great." He waved to a customer. "Let me know when you're done, and I'll drive you home."

"Okay." She turned and walked out to the patio, which had a few empty tables on this hot July night. Most people wanted the air-conditioned inside tables. She felt someone staring at her and turned, nearly dropping her fro-yo to see Shane sitting at a table with an angry look that she'd never, ever seen directed at her.

She actually felt guilty, eating the enemy's fro-yo, even if she did save eighty-two cents. She sat across from him. "What are you doing here?"

He crossed his arms. "What are *you* doing here?"

"It's not like it looks," she said, trying for a light tone. "I had a coupon."

"A coupon. A fricking coupon. I can't believe—" He stopped and clenched his jaw.

She wasn't going to apologize for eating eight-dollar fro-yo. Wasn't it bad enough she got ripped off?

He lowered his voice. "We always make fun of this place, yet here you are."

She tried the yogurt. It was...cold. Not much in the flavor department. No creamy texture. Kind of a chalky aftertaste. "It's not very good," she told him.

He looked somewhat mollified. "Frozen yogurt is made with a thin, low-fat base. It could never have the mouthfeel of fresh-made ice cream."

"Absolutely."

"Let me try."

She handed him the spoon, and he took a small sample. "Blech." He handed her back the spoon. "At least I know I have him beat on quality. This tastes like it was made from a mix."

He could tell that from one sample?

"The product's just okay," Rachel said, "but I think we can learn something from Barry."

"Like what?" Shane huffed. "How to dress up like a cow and dance around?"

She gestured inside the store. "Look at all the families in there. They're smiling and happy. They don't care that they just spent ten bucks a pop for fro-yo from a mix. He makes it fun. The shop is fun with its bright colors. The cow's cute."

"The cow is cute!"

"Yeah, and he dances and hands out party favors. Don't you remember getting glasses like these when you were a kid?"

She took the glasses off the top of her head and tilted them back and forth to show him. He glowered at the glasses.

She slipped them on, scooped up some Nerds, and spoke around the candy in her mouth. "Plus, the coupon makes you feel less like a dope for spending so much."

"What's wrong with having reasonable prices to start?" Shane asked. "I can't lower my prices any more or I'll go out of business." He scowled. "I'm not gonna jack up my prices just so I can hand out stupid coupons."

She took off the wacky glasses. "Okay, okay, relax. You guys have two different approaches to frozen desserts. Nothing wrong with that. You do your thing; he does his thing."

Shane fixed her with a steely look that instantly put her on edge. "I'm driving you home, not Barry."

She set her spoon down. "Is that so?"

He raised his chin, his eyes full of challenge. "Yeah, that is so."

"You might have to fight Barry for that privilege."

"I will gladly kick his ass," Shane growled.

"Shane! That's not like you." She stared at his frowning face. "You're a lover, not a fighter," she teased.

He gazed into her eyes. "Remember that."

She felt a jolt at the heated promise in those eyes, but she had no time to come up with a snappy comeback because Barry caused a fervor of excitement when he made an appearance on the patio still wearing the cow costume.

Shane rolled his eyes. Barry handed out his coupons to all the parents outside. He stopped by Shane and Rachel's table.

"How is everything?" Barry asked. "Can I get you some fro-yo, Shane? You're looking a little overheated. Hot night, isn't it?"

"No, thanks," Shane said tersely.

Barry handed them both coupons. Shane dropped his to the table.

"Let me get out of this cow suit, and then I'll be ready to drive you home," Barry said to her. "No rush, of course. Finish up all that delicious, healthy fro-yo. The more you eat, the more pro-bee-otics will boost your health." He smiled widely.

Rachel bit back a laugh and turned to a very pissed-off-looking Shane. Geez, not even pro-bee-otics were funny anymore.

"Sure thing, Barry," Rachel said. "I'll be inside in a bit." Barry left, and Rachel smiled at Shane. "So I guess that settles the car-ride thing."

A muscle ticked in his jaw, and if she was the kind of woman who knew when to stop talking, she might've known that was a red flag.

"Barry's all set to drive me." She poked around in the cup, looking for more gummi worms. "I'll see you tomorrow for our business meeting."

"Say good-bye, Rach."

"Good-bye?" She snapped her head up and saw him approach, a hard glint in his eye. "Why would I say —ohhh!"

He plucked her off the seat like she weighed nothing,

carrying her cradled in his arms. She tried to see over his shoulder. "My fro-yo!"

"Barry can toss it in the trash where it belongs."

He carried her down the patio steps over to his car, unlocked it, and slid her into the passenger seat. She watched him stomp around to the driver's side and hid a smile. She had to admit, despite all her misgivings, some part of her liked this new caveman side of Shane. Me want woman. Me take woman.

He turned the ignition, and they peeled out of the lot.

"Where to, partner?" Rachel asked.

Shane was silent, tension radiating off him.

She exhaled sharply. "It's not like I betrayed you. It's fro-yo. I was just checking the place out. I wanted to see what made his place so popular. I think there're some lessons that could help both our shops."

A beat passed in silence.

"You got into the cowmobile," Shane ground out.

"It's just a Honda. I hate to break it to you, but Barry's not the devil."

"You hung onto his arm," Shane accused.

"He was being a gentleman. And hello! You and I are business partners. I can hang onto as many arms as I want."

Shane went silent. Fine by her. Geez, where did he get off after the way Janelle was all over him at that meeting? She didn't see him pushing Janelle away. They rode the rest of the way home in tense silence. Shane pulled into the parking lot behind her shop and turned off the car.

She waited for him to tell her off or demand she never eat that crappy fro-yo again, both of which she could've handled, but instead he leaned toward her, his hand reaching out, eyes at half mast. She sucked in a breath. Were they going to have an angry, passionate make-out session? Some part of her was on board with that. A very important part that remembered all too well the make-out session from last night.

Her heart thudded in her chest. They shared a breath as his mouth hovered near hers, but he didn't move, just waited. She had a moment of indecision between pulling back and leaning forward when he made the decision for her, saying simply, "Good night, Rachel," and pushed open her car door.

She straightened and exited the car. "Good night," she said sharply and headed inside her apartment.

She sighed, a little relieved, a lot disappointed. She really should get a cat. Or four. Do this spinster thing up right.

10

Rachel had been planning on shopping online for some of the furniture and decorations she and Shane had talked about for the café, but after checking out a restaurant supply warehouse website over breakfast, she started thinking it would be better to go there in person. The warehouse was in the Bronx, about an hour away. She didn't absolutely need Shane to come with her. She could ask Liz to drive her. Besides, Shane was in charge of food; she was in charge of the shop. He'd already given her a debit card for direct access to the funds for the café.

He was probably way too busy.

She walked across the street to Shane's Scoops anyway. Just for some caffeine. It was already open and serving up coffee. Shane was behind the counter in his blue and white striped apron along with his part-timer Matt.

"Coffee?" Shane asked. His tone was terse. He was still pissed about her "horrible" misstep in trying Barry's fro-yo. Geez, get over it.

"Yes, please," she replied. "You got time to drive over to Sal's Restaurant Warehouse? I thought it'd be good to look at stuff in person."

He looked over her shoulder at the line that had formed

behind her. "If we leave around ten that should work. Morning coffee rush will be over, and there's a lull before afternoon ice cream."

"I got this, boss," Matt said.

Shane looked at Matt, looked at the line of four people waiting for coffee. "Okay, thanks, Matt." He turned to Rachel. "Give me fifteen minutes to wrap things up."

"Okay." She sat on a stool by the side counter and sent Janelle a text that she'd be in late today. Janelle had the keys and had opened and closed the shop many times for Rachel. She watched Shane greet the customers, smiling at each of them, locals who were regulars. She realized people came here as much for Shane's warm friendliness as for the coffee. If only she could clone him for the café. She smiled at customers, sure, but she knew she didn't project that kind of warmth. Now if the occasion called for snark, she was all set.

A short while later, Shane took off his apron and gestured for her to follow out the back exit. She got into his car, and they headed out of town. He was still irritated with her, she could tell, but he was going shopping at her request, so she ignored it. He wasn't the kind to hold a grudge for long.

Besides, dealing with his anger was a hell of a lot easier than dealing with this palpable *thing* sparking in the air between them at the strangest times. Just from a look or a shared smile. It was horrible.

"How do you do that whole warm and friendly thing with everyone that comes in?" she asked.

He didn't even glance in her direction. She was the enemy, the betrayer of ice cream.

"What warm and friendly thing?" he asked. "I just say good morning and take their order."

"No, it's more than that. You're smiling, and your voice is so warm."

He lifted one shoulder up and down. "I like the people who come in. I guess that shows."

Might as well get the fro-yo thing out of the way.

"I guess Barry never comes in," she said casually.

He tensed and slowed for a stop sign, turning to hit her full-on with what she'd come to think of as the alpha Shane look. Must be related to his above-average package. Testosterone levels or something. She fidgeted in her seat as a hot flash ran through her from alpha Shane. Where the hell did that hidden alpha come from anyway?

"You're trying to push my buttons," he said.

She bit back a smile. "Who, me?"

He hit the accelerator. "You and Barry would have such beautiful cow babies."

She snort-laughed, glad he was back to joking around with her. "They would be udderly delightful and full of pro-bee-otics!"

He smiled, just a little.

"It's too bad you can't work at the café too," Rachel said. "You know I don't give off that people-friendly vibe."

His voice dropped to a husky tone. "You're pretty friendly with me."

She felt herself flush, remembering all too well exactly how friendly they'd gotten in Liz's kitchen.

"I'm bitter and jaded," she informed him.

"You are?"

"I'm practicing to be a spinster with ten cats."

He laughed.

"I'm serious. I'll die alone, and the cats will eat my eyeballs."

He shook his head. "That's ridiculous. Cats don't eat eyeballs. They'd just bat them around for a while."

She smiled, feeling more relaxed as they segued into easy conversation. They went over what they would shop for. Shane told her his ideas for using the undercounter space efficiently and the importance of a good inventory system. Geez, she was glad she'd gone into business with him. The workflow of food and coffee preparation and the constantly revolving inventory to keep everything fresh would not have occurred to her. Things were much simpler with books: scan the price, take the money, stick the book in a bag. Done.

They got to the warehouse, a huge place with separate areas for seating, flooring, appliances, lighting, and even framed artwork. What they showed on their website was a fraction of their inventory.

"Whoa," Rachel said, completely overwhelmed.

"I've been here before," Shane said, hands on his hips. "It's great. Let's start with tables and seating and work from there. The seating left over from the deli is not gonna cut it."

"Lead the way."

They checked out square tables, round tables, and rectangle tables with a variety of surfaces. Rachel was feeling dizzy from all the choices and the prices. "Maybe I should just stick with picking out the books to display and the artwork."

Shane grabbed her hand and pulled her along. "Come on. You have to actually sit in some of the chairs."

They sat in a bunch of chairs, and a lot of them seemed good.

"Let's just order the cheapest ones," she said.

"You want people to hang around, right?" Shane moved to another set of chairs. "So they spend a lot of time next to Book It and wander over."

"Well, yeah," she said from a chair that looked great and felt comfortable. She leaned over to see the tag: two hundred dollars. Each. She jumped up. "I also wanted some reading chairs. Maybe I could look for those in a regular furniture store. On sale."

"Sure. Hey, these are pretty comfortable." He indicated for her to try the square wooden chair next to him. "It's got good back support."

She sat. "It's okay, but I was thinking something with a cushion."

"You know they're gonna spill coffee. You have to get something spill proof. I like the wood more than plastic or metal. It's warm."

She looked at the price tag. One hundred dollars, on sale for seventy-seven. "Sold. So dark wood chairs, dark wood floor, deep red on the walls. I want full-color book cover posters on the wall."

"I have no idea what book covers to choose. I'll leave that to you."

"Sounds good." She liked the way they complemented each other. What she didn't know, he did. And vice versa. She turned to him. "I'm glad we're partners."

He smiled warmly. "Me too."

She found herself basking in that warm smile. A flash of something else crossed his expression, something hungry. Butterflies danced in her belly, which was absolutely ridiculous sitting here in the middle of Sal's Restaurant Warehouse with her best friend.

"Stop that," she told him.

"Stop what?" he asked, the picture of innocence. He didn't fool her. He knew very well he was giving her the hungry eyes just to get her all flustered.

She stood abruptly. "You know what."

He stood next to her. "No, I don't. Tell me."

She looked over to the table section and answered out of the side of her mouth, "Stop giving me that look."

His hand settled on the back of her neck and squeezed. The gesture, at once possessive and not at all kosher between friends, made her whole body turn to mush. His voice rumbled in her ear. "I'm not looking at you any different than I always do."

She suppressed a shiver. He was, but she couldn't talk about it anymore without embarrassing herself.

"On to tables," she said, extricating herself from his hold.

Several hours later, they'd placed an order for tables that could seat two, four, and six people along with the chairs. They also put in an order for flooring and checked out the mini-refrigerators. Shane wanted one under the counter for easy access to milk, cream, and whipped cream.

They stopped for lunch at a Mexican restaurant. Shane knew the place and requested a booth in the back. He slid in next to her on the bench seat.

"What are you doing?" she asked, scooting closer to the

wall. He moved with her. It was so intimate having him next to her. The lights were dim. A fountain nearby muffled the sound of the other customers, making it feel like they were in their own private oasis. She could feel the heat of his leg through his athletic shorts on the bare skin of her leg. Actually she could feel the heat of the entire side of his body. Her whole body was in heated overload.

His hand settled on her shoulder, his thumb rubbing the back of her neck. He leaned close, his breath hot on her ear. "I'm letting you get used to having me close."

She swallowed hard and debated crawling under the table to sit on the other side. She was between him and the wall, and there was no way he'd make it easy and let her out to sit across from him.

"I'm used to you," she hissed. But she wasn't. Far from it. Not with him invading her personal space. She studied the menu, holding it up in a desperate attempt to hide her burning cheeks.

"Are you?" His lips pressed on the side of her neck, and hot tingles raced through her. "Good."

"What a cute couple!" someone exclaimed.

Startled, Rachel dropped the menu. A perky waitress stood at their table, smiling at them.

"We're not a couple," Rachel said.

Shane's hand stroked Rachel's back while he smiled at the waitress. "Thank you."

Miss Perky smiled some more. "It's so cute the way you guys sit on the same side of the booth. How long have you been together?"

"How long has it been, honey?" Shane asked. "Feels like only a couple of days."

"Too long," Rachel said, elbowing him hard. He shifted his arm off her back and blocked her from further jabbing.

"You guys are *so* funny," Miss Perky said. "What can I get you to drink?"

After they ordered drinks and the waitress left to fetch them chips, Rachel turned to Shane. "What the—"

He shut her up with a hard, fast kiss that zinged through

her and just as quickly released her. And then that arrogant man, looking entirely too pleased with himself, gave her a raised eyebrow, daring her to retaliate. Except she was speechless.

And wanted another kiss.

He grinned and took her hand, entwining their fingers together. She let him because she couldn't think of one damn thing to say that would make him back off.

Maybe she didn't want him to back off. That scared her most of all.

∿

It was late afternoon by the time they got back, and Rachel realized Shane should've been back earlier to help with the afternoon rush at his shop.

"I've kept you too long," she said as they drove down Main Street.

"It's fine. To tell you the truth, I've got a great staff that can run the shop without me. In fact, I make enough from restaurant orders that I don't even need the shop. I just like being part of downtown."

"Really? So the shop is just so you can hang out with everyone?"

He smiled. "It's a little more than hanging out. I'm offering homemade ice cream with the best, freshest ingredients. I'm keeping local dairies and farms in business. Food is everything, Rach. It's life, it's community. Everything."

She actually got chills hearing the way he spoke about his passion for food. "Shane, that was beautiful. Like poetry."

He blushed. "Stop."

"I'm not teasing," Rachel said. "I actually understand. That's how I feel about books. Life is hard, and books can lift you up. They can give you an escape when you need it, let you know you're not alone, help you dream of better things."

"Now you're the poet." He pulled into the small parking lot behind her store. "I want to check out the café space again.

Take some measurements. I've got a few more ideas for behind the counter."

"Okay, I'm going to look into the posters and order some floating shelves and reading chairs."

"Sounds like a plan."

She put her hand on the door handle, stopped, and turned back to him. "Thank you. I don't know what I would've done if you hadn't gotten on board with the café. I just had this idea." She gestured wildly with her hands. "A café to save the bookstore! But I really had no clue how to put that plan into action. I was just following along in my *Nitwit's Guide*."

"Nitwit." He chuckled. "You would've figured things out. But I'm glad it worked out this way too."

He smiled his dimpled smile that was really just too adorable.

"You know you have dimples? Like right here." She indicated the sides of her mouth.

"I do look in the mirror occasionally," he said dryly.

She was the nitwit. She grabbed her purse and got out of the car. They headed for the café, and she unlocked the door for him. "I'd better get back to work." And then because she needed to remind them both of the boundaries of their business relationship, she added, "Janelle's been alone there all day. How're things with you two anyway?"

"She wants to meet for drinks again on Friday night—"

"Have a good time."

She turned to go, and he grabbed her arm, turning her back to face him. "I didn't say I would go. I want *you*."

Her hand flew to her throat, where her pulse was beating wildly. Shane had never pushed the issue like he had today. First the restaurant and now just baldly stating that he wanted her. It was too much. *Boyfriends don't last.*

"I should go." She looked down at his hand still gripping her arm. "Shane, please."

"Please, what? You want me to pretend we're just friends? That's your game. I'm done playing it."

She stared at his hand, and he dropped it. "I told you I value your friendship." She avoided his eyes and forced the words out over the lump in her throat. "That's not a game. Far from it. You're the best thing in my life."

He tipped her chin up and held it, forcing her to look at him. "Then let me in."

Her breath caught at the heated look in his eyes. "You're in. You couldn't be more in."

His jaw clenched, and he dropped his hand. "You know what I mean."

Anger flared within her. He meant sex. She wasn't going to throw their friendship away just for a quick lay. She tamped her anger down. Fighting wouldn't help anything.

"Look, it's been a while for you," she said gently. He hissed out a breath. "I get it, but just because we have some kind of weird chemistry doesn't mean we have to be stupid and throw away our friendship."

"I'm not talking about throwing anything away!"

She grimaced. He sounded like a wounded bear. She must've hurt his ego reminding him it'd been a while. Even if it was true. As far as she knew, Janelle was the first person he'd gone out with in a long time.

She tried again. "You can't sleep with someone and still be friends. It's just not possible."

"I wasn't trying to—" He stopped himself. "It wouldn't be…"

And while he struggled for the perfect words to make her believe they could actually stay friends while sleeping together, she slipped away.

When she got inside Book It, she found Janelle sitting at the register, reading her anthropology text. Something about the Incas.

"Hey, Janelle. How was it here today?"

Janelle grimaced. "Slow. Only one person came in, and they didn't buy anything."

Rachel's mood sank even lower as her previous excitement over shopping and setting up a new business deflated in the face of this sobering reality. If this café didn't work, she would not only lose Book It, she'd let Shane down who had put up all the money. Business with a friend was tricky. What if he blamed her for the café's failure? She suddenly felt ill. This café just had to work out.

"How was your day shopping with Shane?" Janelle asked.

"Good. We made a lot of progress setting up the café."

"Did he mention me?"

Actually I mentioned you. Stupidly.

Rachel booted up her laptop. "No."

"Oh. I told him to meet me at Garner's on Friday for drinks."

"Did he say he's going?"

"He said he had to check his calendar."

Rachel bit her lip. Shane was trying to let Janelle down easy. She felt bad for ever bringing Janelle into this mess with Shane. Now her friend was going to get hurt.

"I'm going on break," Janelle said.

"Sure, take as long as you need," Rachel said.

Janelle left. Rachel clicked on an art poster website and found herself staring at it blankly. Things with Shane were all tangled up with the money and the business. Sex would only complicate things. There were plenty of other men she could hook up with just to satisfy those basic, sadly neglected needs. And there was always Neal, her vibrator. He understood her needs and never asked for more than she could give.

She could hear Shane next door doing whatever it was he did with measuring stuff and checking on wiring and plumbing. What would happen if she gave in to her newfound lust? To what he so clearly wanted. Maybe they'd have a good time and then what? They'd still have to work together every day. They already saw each other all the time with their shops and apartments across the street from each other. It would be awkward at best.

At worst? A failed business. A destroyed friendship. A broken heart.

She dropped her head in her hands. Why now? After months of perfectly companionable platonic friendship, all those times they'd spent hanging out at his place and her place, going to family barbecues, holiday parties. All that time it was just Shane. He'd kept a safe distance, and if she occasionally wondered what it would be like to be in his arms, she'd never been stupid enough to risk their friendship by acting on it. Too much was at stake now.

What was she going to do?

11

_____

As it turned out, all of Rachel's hand-wringing over the Shane situation turned out to be for nothing. He was merely friendly while he worked on demo at the café with the help of Ryan and Gabe. They'd knocked down the wall between her bookstore and the deli and installed a pull-across grille to lock up when needed. Now they were working over by the counter.

Shane caught her watching.

"We're making good progress here," he called with a wave before using a crowbar to peel off the old counter. Rippling, sweaty muscles flexed with the effort. The display of muscular prowess did nothing for her. His brother Ryan was just as strong, working at his side. So was Gabe. Three sweaty, muscular men next door. One of them making her tingle all over.

Rachel had to move to her office.

She sat in there updating her inventory spreadsheet, wondering if she was going insane. He'd flat-out said he wanted her. Had kissed her multiple times. And now, nothing. She'd been all set to fend Shane off with firm boundaries and phrases such as, "You mean so much to me; let's keep this professional," and, "I don't like to mix business with pleasure," that even to her ears sounded like dialogue from a

B movie, but Shane had slipped easily back to friendship mode.

She blew out a breath. It was disconcerting to say the least. Disappointing. Disheartening. Disillusioning. *One giant dis on her is what it added up to. The big jerk.* Getting her riled up and then no follow-up. Nothing. So when Janelle invited her to have a drink after work on day two of not watching Shane's sweaty, rippling muscles, she went gladly.

They headed across the street to Garner's Sports Bar & Grill and sat at the bar, sharing a plate of nachos. They ordered margaritas and chatted amiably about Book It and the café until Janelle suddenly waved to someone over Rachel's shoulder.

"Dean, over here!" Janelle called.

Rachel turned to see a twenty-something guy wearing a T-shirt emblazoned with a piñata and the phrase I'd Hit That. His gray shorts hung low enough to show off his boxers with red hearts. His hair hung long and greasy, a perfect complement to his untrimmed beard and mustache.

Janelle jumped up and hugged him. "Rachel, this is Dean Lehrman. He's studying anthropology with me. Dean, Rachel."

Dean inclined his head. "Hey."

He sat next to Rachel and helped himself to some nachos.

"Rach, I think you and Dean have a lot in common. You both love the classics." She leaned close to whisper in Rachel's ear. "Have fun. Don't do anything I wouldn't do."

And with those ominous words of what had obviously been a setup buzzing in her head, Janelle left. Rachel looked at Dean, who was now guzzling down the margarita Janelle had left behind, and had to wonder if this was payback or simply returning the favor of a setup the way she had set up Janelle with Shane. Either way, it sucked.

"Hey, babe," Dean said. "Think you could pay for your drinks? I'm a little low on funds. My parents cut me off after I got a D in stats."

"No problem." She liked paying her own way on dates,

especially blind dates she had no idea she was about to have. "Just call me Rachel, okay?"

"Whatev," he muttered as he inhaled the nachos. Rachel lost her appetite.

She glanced around the bar, hoping for someone she knew. Nope. "So what made you interested in anthropology?" she asked, gamely trying for conversation.

Cheese dripped down onto his beard, but he didn't notice. Rachel gestured to his chin. He patted his beard with his greasy fingers and accomplished exactly nothing. No way was Rachel touching it. She tried not to look at it.

"Easy A," he said. "I'm only in grad school to put off the real world a little longer. Know what I mean? *Love* the college life."

"I liked school too. But it gets expensive just to keep going to school and not, you know, working."

"That's what parents are for."

Rachel was speechless.

"Mind if we get some potato skins and beer?" Dean asked.

Rachel didn't think she could bear to sit through another round of food with this guy. She was just about to say so when Barry appeared at her side. She'd never been so glad to see a familiar face in her life.

"Barry, hi!" she said.

"Nice to see you, Rachel," Barry said, sitting next to her. "Is this your younger brother?"

"No, he's my…" She couldn't say it. Couldn't say blind date. Definitely not a friend.

"I'm her date, so take off," Dean said.

Barry's eyes widened.

"No, no." Rachel grabbed Barry's arm. "Stay right here. He's not my date. We just met."

Barry nodded and, thankfully, talked enough for all three of them. Rachel began to relax as Barry told them the story of the little boy who showed up at his shop wearing his own cow costume from last Halloween and how they'd danced together. It was sweet. Really sweet. Rachel felt bad for mocking Barry so much behind his back with Shane.

The food arrived along with Dean's beer. Dean dug into his pocket and produced a five-dollar bill. "Rachel, could you spot me? I'm a little short."

Yes, you are. Short in many, many ways.

"Sure," she said between her teeth. *Janelle, you will pay for this.* She opened her wallet.

"I got this," Barry said.

"Hey, thanks, man," Dean said around a mouthful of potato skins. "You're all right."

It got worse.

Dean went through three beers in record time and stood. "I gotta take a piss."

Rachel let out a breath of relief when he left. Barry asked her about her plans for the café, and she was just telling him about some of the first edition books she'd found online for display when there was a commotion by the bathroom. A woman screamed, and then Dean took off like a shot through the back door.

"He stole my purse!" the woman hollered.

Barry ran after him. He came back empty-handed a few minutes later. "He drove off."

Rachel went to talk to the woman, telling her what she knew about Dean so she could file a report to the police. She texted Janelle to find out where Dean lived. Unfortunately, as Chief Bailey explained when he arrived on the scene, since Dean lived just across the border in New York, the Connecticut police couldn't easily cross over to arrest him for a case of theft. Something about different jurisdictions.

When the chief left, Rachel turned to a somber Barry. "Drink?" she asked.

Barry's eyes brightened. "With me?"

"Yeah, with you."

"Great!"

They settled back at the bar and spent the rest of the night reliving the shady Dean incident, with Barry doing a very good impression of Dean being completely obnoxious on their "date." They laughed, they drank, and Rachel felt more relaxed than she had in a very long time. Barry was a decent guy. He was goofy, but nice. If she'd felt even one spark between them, she would've called this the beginning of some kind of date.

"We're ba-a-ack!" a voice called behind her. She turned to see Liz's older sister, Daisy, and her new husband, Trav, holding their son, Bryce. They looked tan and happy, fresh from their honeymoon. The cousins surely to come from Liz would probably grow up close as siblings. Rachel felt a pang of envy and quickly dismissed it. She stood and hugged Daisy.

Rachel smiled at the two of them. "How was Bermuda?"

Daisy beamed her sunny smile. "It was everything I dreamed of."

Trav kissed Daisy's hair. "Well, there was a little sand in uncomfortable places."

Daisy elbowed him, and Trav laughed. He set Bryce down, and he toddled straight into his grandma's arms with a delighted squeal.

"There's my angel baby," Mrs. Garner said. She must have come out from the kitchen when she heard them arrive.

"Hey, Barry," Trav said, shaking his hand. "Are we interrupting something?" He pointed between the two of them.

"Oh, no." Rachel shook her head. "It's not like that. We're just friends."

"Well, so far," Barry said with a smile.

Uh-oh.

Trav raised his brows. "Go back to what you were doing."

"See you soon, Rach!" Daisy called before walking off with Trav to greet some of the staff. Daisy used to work as a waitress at her parents' restaurant.

Rachel returned to her seat next to Barry. "I hope you know—"

Her reply was cut off with his mouth covering hers. It was a loose, sloppy kiss, and she recoiled. She wiped her mouth with the back of her hand. "Don't do that again!"

She stood, slapped down a twenty, and headed for the door.

Barry followed her. "Rachel, wait! I'm sorry! Sometimes I

get carried away. We were having so much fun. Please stay." He handed back her twenty. "Drinks are on me for the rest of the night."

She crossed her arms.

"Please, I really am sorry." He looked at his shoes. "I don't have many friends in town. Just stay a little longer."

Oh, geez. Now she was feeling sorry for him.

"No more kissing," she said.

He held up two fingers. "Scout's honor."

"Were you really a Boy Scout?"

He nodded vigorously. "I made Eagle Scout. The highest honor."

She exhaled sharply. "Okay, fine."

She rejoined him at the bar, and between the chardonnay that Barry kept refilling for her and his easygoing nature, the evening passed with no further problems. She left late that night, declining Barry's kind invitation to walk her home. It was just across the street. It was nice to know that some guys could be just your friend without kissing you and making things all complicated and weird, she thought, as she made her way on wobbly legs back to her apartment.

Wait, Barry did kiss you. Duh!

But everything was fine and dandy now. Yes, sirree. Maybe Shane could learn a little from Barry's fine example. She stopped in front of Book It and turned to look at Shane's apartment above Shane's Scoops. The lights were out. He must be sleeping. That didn't stop her from reminding him of something very, very important.

"We're just friends!" she hollered.

She hoped Shane got the message. They had a good friendship, and now that they were business partners, that was the way it would stay. No matter how many times he kissed her on kitchen counters. Or in Mexican restaurants. So there. She nodded for emphasis. Then she turned and walked into a wall.

Not a wall. Shane.

She jumped back and nearly toppled over. He righted her.

She socked him in the chest. "What are you doing here? You scared the bejeezus out of me!"

"Trav texted me and said you went drinking with Barry. I wanted to make sure you got home all right."

She eyed him, taking in his alpha Shane look that made her overheated and cranky. "That's creepy. You know that, right?"

He made no response. She stopped to consider the ramifications of Shane being here now after the setup from hell, and the sloppy Barry kiss, and way too many glasses of chardonnay. Her brain was too muddled to figure it all out, so she focused on the thing that was bugging her most. Shane being here.

"Trav texted you?" she barked. "Ridiculous! You've got spies!"

She veered around him and stopped for a moment, feeling a little lightheaded.

He put an arm around her shoulders and guided her toward her apartment. "What's up with Barry?"

"What's up with Janelle?" she fired back.

He chuckled. "You put up a good fight. Just let go."

"Let go of what? I'm *not* fighting." She stopped and jabbed a finger in the air. "You're the one at fault here. You haven't even tried to kiss me all week."

His lips twitched. "I'm giving you space. I know you, Rach. If I push, you'll put up all those prickly defenses you're so good at. It's your move. I'm not going anywhere."

Shane was so confusing. Her move? She didn't have any moves. She was moveless. But having him here so solid, so kind brought something home to her. Shane was better than any guy she might ever get set up with. He really was. She should tell him—

Oh, no. She hurried over to a bush and puked. She stood unsteadily and lifted her chin. "Good night, kind sir."

Shane stared at her. She made her way to the back entrance of her apartment. Shane followed at a distance. She successfully unlocked the door and went inside, vaguely disappointed Shane hadn't pulled the prince carrying the princess act up the stairs. She supposed she slipped down a notch on the attractiveness scale after puking. She never could hold her liquor.

She walked straight to the bedroom and flopped down on the bed, dumping her purse on the nightstand. Her cell rang. She dug around in her purse and answered it. "Princess speaking."

"Just wanted to make sure you got in okay," Shane said. "Good night, princess."

"Good night to you, sir."

He chuckled, and she hung up. She hugged the phone and fell asleep.

Shane thought about the progress on the café as he walked to the library for the second street-fair meeting. Things were going well. The plumber came last Friday and installed the in-line water feeds he wanted for the espresso and coffee machines, as well as ran the pipe for two sinks he wanted by the prep areas behind the counter. The water softener went in today. The electrician was due on Wednesday, and the painter was scheduled for Friday. The painter promised to work into the weekend in exchange for Shane giving out sports water bottles with the painter's logo at the street fair.

He walked by the ancient librarian on his way to the conference room. "Hi, Miss Smith, how are you?"

"I'm just fine, Shane. How lovely to see you again." She lowered her cat's-eye glasses and gave him a once-over that made him feel a little dirty. "Let me know if I can help you with anything."

"Thanks," he said over his shoulder as he picked up the pace.

Everyone was already seated and talking when he got there.

"Hey, sorry I'm a little late," Shane said. "Big crush at the shop. The travel baseball team made it to the semifinals, and they were celebrating."

"No problem, mate," Barry said.

Mate? Shane raised his hand in greeting to Gabe, Liz, Janelle, and Rachel. He noticed an empty seat between Janelle and Rachel. He took it.

Big mistake.

"Your boyfriend's here," Janelle hissed over him to Rachel.

"He's not my boyfriend," Rachel snapped.

Shane leaned back to get out of the line of fire.

"He said he couldn't meet me for drinks because he had feelings for someone else. You, obviously."

Shane felt his cheeks burn. That was a private conversation. Gabe raised a brow, clearly getting a kick out of this little scene.

"So that's why you set me up with that thieving asshole?" Rachel asked.

Set her up? What? He bolted upright, looking from Rachel to Janelle.

"I told you he seemed nice," Janelle said. "He reads Dostoyevsky in class. I thought you guys would have literature in common."

"Let me guess, *Crime and Punishment*?" Rachel asked.

Janelle's eyes widened. "How'd you know?"

Rachel leaned over him, her eyes shooting fire at Janelle. "Oh, I don't know, wild guess?" Her voice rose in agitation. "He stole a woman's purse!" she hollered.

"Now, ladies," Barry started.

Shane held up his hand to Barry and turned to Rachel. "Wait, you went on a date, and Barry was there too?"

"Janelle set it up," Rachel said. "Without telling me!" She shot Janelle a lethal look.

"Luckily, it turned out all right," Barry said. "Rachel and I had a good time despite that thief. Right?"

Shane glared at Barry, who merely smiled, unaware of the treacherous ground he was stepping into. He turned to Rachel. "You go out with a thief, then go drinking with Barry? What the hell are you doing?"

Rachel glared at him, mutinously silent.

"Shane, let's take a breather," Gabe said.

"Maybe we should get back to the meeting agenda," Liz suggested. "We still haven't confirmed exactly the location of the street fair."

"Yes, let's get back to business," Barry said, tapping his pink Dancing Cow pen on his Dancing Cow napkin.

Janelle leaned over Shane and turned accusing eyes at Rachel. "Boy, you get around."

Rachel gasped. "I do not get around!"

Janelle tossed her pen and notepad at Rachel. "Take your own damn minutes. And don't expect me at work tomorrow. I quit."

"Janelle, don't quit!" Rachel cried. "I need you. You're my only employee."

"You should've thought of that before you started messing with my love life, pawning me off on the guy you really wanted for yourself." She stood and looked down her nose at Rachel. "I only took this job because it was so slow I could study at the same time. I'd rather work at a fucking library!"

Miss Smith peered around the corner. "Excuse me, young lady, you'll have to keep your voice down. This is a library."

"I know it's a library!" Janelle hollered.

Miss Smith's eyes narrowed behind her cat's-eye frames. "Exit the premises immediately."

"I was leaving anyway!" Janelle stomped off.

Rachel took off after her as fast as she could given her ankle still slowed her down.

The room went quiet.

"Last meeting we talked about kiddie entertainment," Barry said into the awkward silence. "I know a clown who will do balloon animals for five dollars a balloon."

"Who pays the five dollars?" Gabe asked. "Us or the kids?"

"Us," Barry said.

"That's too expensive," Shane said. "Tons of families show up for this thing."

He peered out into the hallway, looking for signs of Rachel. She'd left her purse here, so he knew she'd be back. What the hell was she doing? Kissing him and then going out with someone else—a thief no less—and then drinking with Barry. She'd rather go out with a thief and this ridiculous dancing-cow guy than him?

"What would you suggest for entertainment?" Barry asked.

"Why not invite the thief for fro-yo?" Shane said. "That sounded very entertaining. Or maybe you could have drinks with Rachel again."

Gabe inclined his head to the door. "Shane, let's go for a walk."

Shane shook him off. "No, I want to hear exactly what happened that night."

"I think we're getting off the agenda?" Barry said, tapping his pen like crazy.

Shane crossed his arms and went silent. Liz jumped in, and the three of them worked out some plans for entertainment. Something about tricycle races and a peewee run. Shane only half listened as he waited for Rachel to come back.

Finally Rachel slipped into the room, looking serious. Probably worried about losing an employee. She was better off without Janelle if Janelle was mad at her and goofing off all the time, studying instead of paying attention to the customers.

"Sorry about that," Rachel said quietly. "What'd I miss?"

Barry filled her in.

"Sounds good," Rachel said. "Why don't we start the peewee race at The Dancing Cow? Then you could give out coupons and wacky glasses. That would encourage them to return later for fro-yo, and the glasses would make for some great photo ops."

"Excellent idea!" Barry exclaimed.

Shane seethed. Rachel had clearly shifted into the Barry camp. The meeting adjourned. Shane waited outside for Rachel, trying to get a hold of his temper. It took a lot to make him mad, and Rachel had pushed him just far enough.

"I'll walk you home," he said when Rachel emerged from the library with Liz.

Rachel stared at him. "I'm walking with—"

"We'll talk later, egg," Liz said.

Rachel scowled as Liz walked on ahead of them. "Chicken!" she called after Liz.

Shane couldn't hold it in any longer. "You'd rather go out with a thief than me? With a dancing-cow guy? What the hell?"

Rachel regarded him steadily. "You're my business partner."

"So?"

Rachel walked as quickly as she could. She probably would've run if she didn't have a sprained ankle.

"So that's it," she said. "That's the answer. That's *always* the answer. We are business partners. The end."

"You kissed me," he said, holding on to his temper, barely. That fire between them hadn't been one-sided. He knew it like he knew a good sauce and exactly when it was hot enough to boil over. That was how their kiss in Ry's kitchen had been—a near boil, barely contained.

She didn't say anything, just kept walking.

"What's with you and Barry?" he asked.

"We're friends. He's a nice guy."

So was he. That's what nice guys got. The *friend* treatment.

"What happened between you and Janelle?" he asked.

She stopped and glared at him. "You. You happened."

"What did I do?"

"Apparently she wants you, and you don't want her, and somehow I'm to blame."

He put a hand on the small of her back. "Rach—"

She looked away. "Business partners. The end."

He dropped his hand, torn between carrying her off and showing her how much more they were than that, and pulling back and giving her exactly what she claimed she wanted. He'd wanted to give her space, but now hearing about the two guys she'd seen in one night, he was finding it very hard to do. He'd dropped Janelle after one dinner, hadn't even kissed her, and here Rachel had gone out with two guys. Two guys!

Barry pulled up in his cowmobile and mooed. "Stop by for free fro-yo any time you want, Rachel!"

She smiled. "Thanks, Barry."

Barry waved and drove off. Shane couldn't stand one more minute watching these two. He wasn't in the same category of friend as Barry. How could she pretend that he was?

He walked Rachel to her place in tense silence. She wanted to be just business partners, then fine, that's what she'd get. He wasn't going to put himself out there only to have her stomp on his heart all over again.

They arrived at her apartment door.

"Night, partner," he said coolly. He turned on his heel and walked back to his place.

"Night," she said softly.

He picked up the pace, ignoring that soft tone that made him want to carry her off to bed and never let her go. He went for a run, hoping sheer physical exhaustion would get Rachel out of his head. All he got for his trouble was tired.

12

Rachel was super busy at Book It the next couple of weeks on account of being the only employee. She'd roped Liz into subbing a few hours here and there so Rachel could keep working on the café with Shane. Things were going perfectly there. Shane supervised the contractors, and they'd already completed plumbing, electric, and painted the walls. Now they were installing the cabinets and counter that Shane had ordered. She should've been on top of the world. Everything was going so smoothly. Except Shane was so distant.

Gone were the warm looks she'd grown accustomed to. No more sweet, dimpled smiles just for her. No more alpha looks giving her hot flashes. He was professional, polite, considerate. The perfect business partner.

She hated it.

She put up a sign on the front window of her shop announcing she'd be back in fifteen minutes and headed across the street to Shane's Scoops for the only decent coffee in the area. At least until their café opened.

She got in line. Shane and Matt were working.

"Hi, guys," she said. "Can I get a latte?"

"Hey," Shane said. He inclined his head to Matt.

"Coming right up," Matt said.

Shane busied himself rinsing out a pitcher.

"What's up?" she asked.

He stopped and met her eyes, no warmth in those blue eyes, just a blank expression. "We should get the coffee brewing machine and grinder delivered tomorrow."

"Awesome! We should try them out. Do some taste tests."

He nodded. No warmth. No enthusiasm. Rachel's stomach dropped a notch lower into the beginnings of despair. She was losing him, losing his friendship, the one thing she wanted to keep more than anything.

"Aren't you excited?" she asked, hating the way her voice came out small. "We're almost there." Matt handed her the latte. "Thanks."

"I'm excited," he said flatly.

He didn't sound excited. He sounded like he barely cared about the café, barely cared about her.

She took a step back, hurt by his withdrawal. She still wanted him in her life. She missed hanging out like they used to. He used to pop by for lunch whenever he had a chance, two or three times a week. They never binge-watched Brit comedy like they used to. They used to laugh themselves silly watching shows like *The IT Crowd* while eating popcorn at her place.

"You busy tonight?" she asked.

"Yeah, I've got a lot of work to catch up on. Accounting stuff." He didn't meet her eyes.

She knew when she was getting the brush-off. "Okay, well, if you need a break, stop by. I just got *Not Going Out* seasons one, two, and three. It's supposed to be really funny."

"Maybe."

She gestured for him to walk over to the side, away from Matt, for a private conversation. "Are you mad at me? I thought we were friends."

He crossed his arms. "We are."

"Friends hang out."

He said nothing, but his body language clearly said: *Back off.*

She swallowed hard over the lump in her throat. "I miss you."

He shifted from one foot to the other. "We see each other all the time. We're working together. Speaking of which, I have to get back to work."

He went behind the counter again, not waiting for her response. Which was fine. She had no idea what to say.

She hurried back to her store and flipped the sign back to Open. Not like anyone was waiting in line to get into her store. She missed Janelle, even forgave her for that sneaky revenge setup. She never should've used Janelle as a buffer between her and Shane. That backfired big time. Now Janelle was out of the picture, and there was a bigger wall between her and Shane than there'd ever been.

She pulled out her battered copy of *Pride and Prejudice* and let herself slip into that world again, sorely needing an escape from this one.

∾

The next day Rachel saw the coffee machine being delivered for the café, followed close behind by Shane supervising the installation. The new countertop was in, a warm brown and black speckled granite that Shane had insisted was worth the price for the looks and resistance to heat and stains. She wandered over, not hard to do now that the wall was down between the two spaces.

She smiled at Shane. "This is exciting."

He glanced at her. "Yeah. It'll take a little while to set up and get everything working. I don't know if we'll get any coffee out of it for a few hours."

"Need any help?"

"Nope. I'll let you know when it's ready." He turned from her and unpacked a coffee grinder from its box.

"Oh."

He was telling her to leave. She wandered back to the register in her shop, her throat tight. She wasn't a crier. She couldn't even remember the last time she'd cried, but she was dangerously close. This distance between them sucked.

Thank goodness Liz came in just then. She needed a distraction fast.

"Hey, Rach, need any help today?" Liz asked, breezing in.

"No, but it's good to see you." She hugged her friend tightly.

Liz pulled back, looking at her with concern. "You okay, egg?"

Rachel sniffled. "Don't call me egg. I stopped calling you chicken."

"Okay," Liz said gently. "What's wrong?"

"It's stupid." She glanced over to the café. "It's probably all in my head. I'm blowing things out of proportion. Forget it."

Liz glanced over to the café at Shane. "Guy trouble."

"Actually no trouble at all. Everything's effing perfect."

Liz raised a brow and called over to the source of Rachel's misery. "Hey, Shane!"

Shane waved and smiled. Rachel hadn't seen that smile directed at her in weeks.

"I'm going to check out your café," Liz said.

Rachel stayed behind while Liz went over to check it out. She kept her nose in her book, ignoring the friendly conversation between Liz and Shane. He was definitely giving Rachel the cold shoulder. It was subtle, but she felt that distance big time. A short while later Liz returned.

"You guys are doing a great job," Liz said, taking a seat behind the counter next to Rachel. "I love the wall color."

Rachel managed a smile. "Thanks, I picked it."

"Nice. So what do you need to do still? The floors and maybe something for the walls?"

"Yup. Shane ordered another refrigerated case for the baked goods and a small refrigerator for under the counter."

"Did you pick out tables and chairs or are you going to use what's in there?"

Rachel warmed to the topic. "We've got stuff coming, but we want the floors in first."

"I love the cute hanging light fixtures."

Rachel smiled. "I picked those out too. Shane's going to

put up some floating shelves for the first editions I want to display. I've already got some book cover posters waiting in my apartment. We'll put those up last."

"So you're décor, and he's food and drink," Liz said.

"Basically. Though we did shop together for a lot of stuff. But once it opens, he's the food and drink supplier, and I run the place."

"Sounds like the perfect partnership," Liz said.

"Yup, perfect," Rachel said. Somehow the words deflated her.

"But…" Liz prompted.

Liz knew her inside out, and there was no use hiding anything from her. Rachel took off her glasses and cleaned them on the bottom of her shirt. Some things were easier to talk about without the sharp focus of eye contact.

"Shane's been really distant," Rachel whispered. "Like really distant. I don't even think he wants to be friends anymore."

"I'm sure that's not true. I've never known Shane to just drop a friend. He's still friends with people he knew back in New Jersey from when he was in sixth grade. I think he's even still friends with all of his ex-girlfriends."

Well, *that* was comforting. Rachel slid her glasses back on. "So it's just me."

Liz looked over and watched Shane help set up a huge coffee machine. "Shane doesn't have a mean bone in his body. If he's distant, I don't think he's doing it to hurt you."

"Why else would he do it?"

"Did you ask him for space? Tell him to back off?"

Rachel squirmed. "Kind of. I told him we were business partners, end of conversation."

Liz cringed. "Now don't take this the wrong way—"

"Nothing good can follow those words."

"You can be a little…harsh sometimes."

"I didn't say it harsh! I just said it like a fact." Rachel threw her hands up. "It is a fact!"

Liz lowered her hand for Rachel to keep it down. "I think you hurt him. You know he cares about you. But you basically told him to back off. I think he's just doing what you want."

His words came back to her: *It's your move. I'm not going anywhere.*

But Rachel didn't want to make a move. She wanted things back like they used to be. She twisted her hands around and looked over at Shane. "I want us to be friends again. How can I fix this?"

"Just give him time. He never holds a grudge. I'm sure he'll warm up again."

"Rach, come check this bad boy out," Shane called.

"See?" Liz said. "He's not being mean."

"I never said he was mean," Rachel muttered as she headed over to the café. It was more like a cool distance. Rachel joined him to admire the new coffee-brewing wonder. It was shiny silver and black with a lot of buttons and switches. "Wow."

"Yeah. Let me show you how it works. First we have to grind the beans." He opened a bag of coffee beans. "I ordered several for us to try before we finalize the menu. These are from Peru, medium roast." He sniffed the beans and nodded in approval before holding out the bag for her to smell. She did.

"They smell a little like berries," she said.

He smiled, seeming pleased with her remark. "Very good. A lot of the Latin American beans smell like berries. The beans from Ethiopia are more like lemongrass. You'll see. It depends where they're grown. I want to try out a few beans before we decide on some unique blends and flavors for the shop."

"Okay."

"So next we grind the beans. They go in here." He measured and poured some into the grinder. "We want to only grind small batches just before we're ready to brew the coffee. It's really important that everything is fresh for the best flavor."

He kept talking, explaining the process from beans to grounds to brew, and Rachel's spirits lifted. She really should be taking notes or committing it to memory, but all she could hear was the enthusiasm in his voice. She soaked in the way his blue eyes lit up, his passion clear for the tools and techniques that led to great coffee. She'd missed this relaxed vibe between them.

"Pretty cool," Rachel said when he'd wound down. She smiled brightly. "How soon until we get to try it?"

His expression shut down. "Still a way off," he muttered. "I want to run it through a few test cycles." He turned his attention back to the machine, seeming to remember the wall he'd put between them.

"Okay," she said. "I'll be here."

She drooped back to her store. Somehow in trying to hang onto their friendship, she'd ruined it.

Shane spent the rest of the afternoon testing the brewer, a higher-end model than he had in his own shop, making up small batches of coffee in the thermal carafes he'd ordered. He'd have to teach Rachel how to operate the espresso machine and his older coffee brewer once he moved them over here from his shop. He set out a series of coffee mugs for their coffee tasting and headed over to Book It.

Rachel had her head bent over a book, sitting alone at the counter. She played with the end of her braid, a sure sign she was deep into the story. He toyed with the idea of sneaking up behind her—it was a perfect scare setup when she had her nose in a book—but he didn't want her to topple off the stool and hurt her ankle again. He settled for his old standby and placed his hand over the page she was reading.

Her head snapped up, eyes wide. He smiled. He'd surprised her just by existing. The way she got lost in a book was the way he got lost in a good cooking groove.

"Shane, hi," she said, her voice a near squeak. "I didn't hear you."

"I know, I know. You always say I'm like a cat, but really I think you're just lost in..." He lifted the book to read the title. "*Pride and Prejudice* again, huh?"

"It's a classic," she said defensively.

He took her hand and tugged. "Come on. It's time. Get it while it's at its peak."

She stiffened. "That sounds dirty."

He stopped, intrigued. "What sounds dirty?"

She blushed and waved her hand. "Never mind. It smells wonderful."

They headed to the café, and he stepped behind the counter to pour the cups. She stayed on the other side of the counter.

"This is called cupping," he said.

She narrowed her eyes. "Why does everything that comes out of your mouth sound dirty? Are you doing that on purpose?"

He grinned, getting a big kick out of where her mind obviously was. He'd only said two things that she'd misinterpreted. "That's all you. You're hearing what you want to hear."

She put her hands on her hips. "It most certainly is not me. You said cupping." She cupped a hand in front of her that might have been cupping a man. Intimately. The message went straight to his groin. He shifted closer to the counter to hide the evidence.

He cleared his throat and focused on the coffee mugs. "Cupping is coffee tasting. So we've got a light roast, medium, dark, and a hazelnut. This is just straight up, no cream, no sugar, no foam. It's pretty strong so don't drink the whole cup. Just a sip." He started pouring from the thermal carafes he'd prepared ahead of time. "First, take a big whiff to get the aroma, then a loud slurp so the coffee goes to the back of your tongue. Pay attention to the mouthfeel, the texture as it runs over your tongue. Notice the flavor, the aftertaste."

He glanced up to find Rachel staring at him, lips parted. It took everything he had not to reach across the counter and answer that look in her eyes. She shook her head and stared at the counter. "You're doing it again."

"What?"

"You keep talking about mouthfeel and flavor and taste," she told the counter.

He tipped her chin up and gazed into her chocolate brown eyes. "That's what food is all about. Are you ready to get started?"

The question hung in the air between them. This time he'd fully intended the double meaning. He wanted to know if she was ready to start things between them. Their kiss before had been a taste. He wanted to feast on her and savor all the flavors in between.

She said nothing, merely picked up a cup of coffee and breathed it in. Dammit. He had his answer. Not ready.

He picked up the mug next to hers and took a whiff. "This is the light roast. It packs a wallop of caffeine. Taste it. Just one slurping sip."

They both slurped. It had a slight, grainy flavor that was pleasant, not overwhelming.

"Tastes a little bit like malt or barley," Rachel said.

Shane smiled and inclined his head, glad she was attuned to the subtleties of flavor. He'd enjoy cooking for her.

"I like the mouthfeel," he told her, lowering his voice a notch just to tease her. "Rich body, some flowery notes in the aftertaste."

She squirmed and focused on the mug in her hand. "Yes, I agree. Next!"

He chuckled and poured them both a glass of water. "Here, take a drink to cleanse your palate."

She watched him over the rim of her glass. He was tempted, very tempted. In three short weeks the café would open. Then he'd go back to working at his shop and just be the supplier to the café. Maybe then, she'd drop all this nonsense about them keeping things strictly business between them. They wouldn't be working together in the same space. He could wait. He'd waited months to make a move in the first place. Thinking again of that move, that damned kiss that replayed in his mind on a daily and nightly basis, he handed Rachel the next mug, letting his fingers brush her hand.

She blushed but didn't meet his eyes or say a word. Stubborn woman.

They finished tasting the coffee and decided all of them were good, except for the dark roast. It was too bitter. He'd look for another dark roast through his coffee-bean supplier, and they'd try again.

"I've got a different kind of taste-testing planned for Thursday night," Shane said. He was starting to enjoy teasing her. He loved seeing her blush, something she did rarely, as nothing seemed to faze her. "You in?"

She pursed her lips and eyed him suspiciously. "What kind of taste-testing?"

You.

God, he wished he could just say that and follow through. Like now. He busied himself rinsing the mugs in the sink. "I always do a practice run on my family before anything hits the menu. We're all meeting at Gran's house to try out the baked goods I've been working on."

He glanced up. Her mouth formed what he'd call a pout on anyone else, except he'd never, ever seen Rachel pout. Was she hoping for a different answer?

"Oh," she said softly.

He considered her disappointment a good sign. Teasing Rachel was a little like setting a pot to boil and then watching it. The progress was excruciatingly slow, but she'd get there just the same. He just hoped the resulting boilover was in his favor. He was flying without a net here, something he normally didn't like to do, but with Rachel he hadn't found a better way. The direct approach hadn't worked. At all.

She took off her glasses and cleaned them on the bottom of her "Reader Love" T-shirt, exposing a glimpse of the smooth, olive skin of her midriff. His mouth went dry, and he took a long drink of water.

She shoved her glasses back on. "Sure, I'll be there."

"Great. Do you want to invite your family too? It's always good to have a variety of opinions."

She made a face. "Your family is plenty."

"Too much, huh?"

"No, your family is great. Mine's just better in small doses. Like once a week."

He shrugged. He'd met her family plenty of times around town and in his shop; they were nice. Rachel probably had something or another that bugged her about them. Most people did bug her, but not him. Least not until he'd started teasing her.

"Help me load these mugs into the dishwasher in back," he said, gathering up some mugs. "I'll show you how the machine works."

"Sure." She grabbed some mugs, and they headed to the back storage area, where a commercial dishwasher sat. They loaded them in.

"It's pretty simple," Shane said. "The detergent, sanitizer, and rinse aid are already in the pumps. Back here." He pulled the control panel forward to show her, then closed it. "Then you just shut the door and hit on."

"Easy enough," Rachel said, peering closely at the dishwasher, seemingly unaware of how close she was to him. He could feel her heat and breathed in her flowery scent.

Don't do it. Do not kiss her. It has to be her move.

She met his eyes and jumped back, her hand going to her throat. "I guess we're good here. I'd better get back to the shop."

She walked away as fast as she could.

"Busy over there?" he called, knowing she wasn't. He was calling her out on avoiding him whenever they got too close. This attraction between them wasn't going away no matter how much she danced around it.

She gave him the finger over her shoulder.

He shook his head, smiling to himself. For once he didn't have to tiptoe around a woman and worry about upsetting her, taking care of her tender feelings. Rachel gave as good as she got. He couldn't wait to see exactly how much she'd give when he finally got her to cross that line in the sand she'd drawn. It would happen soon. He could feel it.

13

Rachel got to Maggie's house a little early on Thursday night and quickly realized her mistake. It was just her, Maggie, and Shane. The older woman took the opportunity to do what she did best—butt in.

"Rachel, I'm so glad you're here to get a taste of Shane's stuff." Maggie waggled her eyebrows. The brow waggle paired with her outfit—a pink knitted tube top and matching knitted beret—would have been comical if Rachel wasn't on guard against further matchmaking.

"Gran," Shane warned. He was setting out platters of baked goods on the dining room table—scones, sweet breads, muffins, danishes, tarts, mini-pies.

"He's a great cook," Rachel said, refusing to rise to the bait.

"And how are things going with the café?" Maggie asked. "What was the name again?" She tapped her chin. "Something's brewing between friends?"

"Ha-ha," Rachel said.

Maggie pinned her with a sharp gaze. "So what's stopping you, girl? My Shane is a catch. And he's not getting any younger. Thirty-one is plenty old enough to settle down."

Rachel glanced at a blushing Shane, who was looking at

the ceiling, probably praying for strength to deal with his grandmother.

"I'll fetch some drinks from the kitchen," Rachel said, hurrying away. Shane's voice rumbled in reply to his grandmother, and she heard Maggie's snappy reply loud and clear.

"Make your move. You could cut the sexual tension with a knife!"

Shane rumbled something that sounded distinctly annoyed. Rachel stayed hidden in the kitchen, praying for the doorbell to ring. Instead Maggie joined her.

"It seems *some people*—" Maggie called loudly in Shane's direction "—think I've overstepped my bounds. Sorry."

Only she didn't sound sorry. At all.

"That's okay," Rachel said.

Maggie grabbed some plates and forks. "Did I ever tell you about when Shane first started baking in seventh grade? He came to me after his mother died, so sad and nearly mute. In fact, he *was* mute at school."

Rachel remembered him as quiet. She hadn't realized he *never* spoke.

Maggie went on. "We spent hours right here in this very kitchen. Cooking healed him. Everything he makes he pours his heart and soul into, so when you sample one of his recipes, just know that it comes from love."

Rachel blinked rapidly. "Um, okay."

Maggie exhaled sharply and lowered her voice. "He's not much of a fighter. Oh, he'll kick ass if he has to, but he'd rather get along." She wagged her finger. "Just remember that. If you push him too far away, he might not come back."

"I'm not pushing—"

The doorbell rang. *Thank you!*

Maggie dropped off the plates and forks on the dining room table and went to answer the door. Rachel gathered the glasses and set them on the table.

"Don't listen to Gran," Shane said. "She's always playing matchmaker."

"I'm sure you get a lot of women that way," Rachel said with a smirk.

Shane set down the platter he'd been holding with a clatter and headed straight for her, a determined glint in his eye. She squeaked and escaped to the living room, where Liz and Ryan, Shane's oldest brother, stood.

"Chicken!" Shane called.

Liz grinned at Rachel. "Doesn't he know you're egg?"

"Oh, shut it." Rachel hugged her friend and whispered, "I'm so glad you're here. Maggie was trying to play matchmaker."

Liz pulled back and grinned at Maggie. "No. I'm shocked. Maggie matchmaking?"

"I was not matchmaking," Maggie huffed. "I was merely pointing out Shane's finer qualities when he got all persnickety."

"Hey, Rach," Ryan said. "Anything good to eat in there?"

"Definitely. Hope you skipped dinner."

The door opened again, and Maggie's husband, Jorge, walked in. "Mmm, something smells good. Hello, everyone."

A chorus of greetings went around. They all gathered around the dining room table.

"How long do we have to wait for Trav?" Ry asked. "Turtle's always late."

"So is Daisy," Liz put in.

Trav and Daisy were newlyweds with a toddler, so Rachel figured they were often late.

"They live across the street," Ry said. "How hard can it be to get here on time?"

"It's not easy to get out the door quickly when you have a little one," Maggie said with a pointed look. "I'm sure you'll know all about that soon enough."

Ry sent a longing look to Liz, who busied herself with her napkin. It was no secret that Ry wanted to get started on a family while Liz dragged her feet. Taking care of her colicky nephew Bryce had scared Liz straight.

"I say we wait," Maggie said. "Shane wants the full effect of everyone's feedback all at once. Right, my single, eligible, bachelor grandson?"

Shane looked to the ceiling, but still couldn't prevent the blush that stained his cheeks. "We'll wait."

They chatted about the summer Little League team that Ry was coaching with pint-size kids full of attitude, until they heard the front door open followed by Bryce's toddler squeal. "Na-na!"

Maggie beamed and stood. "Bryce!"

The boy ran straight for her, wrapping his arms around one leg. She ruffled his hair. Trav lifted him up, and Maggie rubbed noses with Bryce. Then he was off, running into the kitchen. Trav followed at his heels. "Hi all! Be right back."

"Sorry we're late," Daisy said. "Just when you think you're out the door you have to come back in for a diaper change. Never fails." She took in the table full of food. "Shane, you outdid yourself. Wow. Just wow."

"Thanks," he muttered, blushing again.

Rachel used to think it was funny how much Shane blushed, but now that she'd been doing so much blushing of her own, she could sympathize. It was bad enough to be embarrassed, but then to have the world know it was even worse. Trav returned with Bryce on his shoulders holding a sippy cup with monkeys on it.

"Hang onto that cup, Bryce," Trav said. "If you throw it, you're done."

Bryce just kept sipping, one hand tangled in Trav's hair.

Ry rubbed his hands together. "Let's get started."

"Wait!" Shane ordered. "We're starting with the fruits and working our way up to the super sweet." Shane grabbed a notepad and pen he'd stashed nearby. "First up, corn muffins with blueberries. Remember, one bite, savor, then tell me the first thing that comes to mind. Thumbs up or down for adding it to the menu."

"No brownies?" Trav asked, scanning the table.

"I skipped the brownies and chocolate chip cookies because I already know you guys like them."

"Aw, no cookies?" Ry asked, looking disappointed. "Just fruity stuff? I come here for sinful desserts."

"You come here for your brother," Maggie said.

"I love you, man," Ry said, pounding his chest and pointing at Shane. Shane smiled and pointed back.

Maggie grinned. "That's more like it. Trav?"

Trav snorted. "What is this, a lovefest?"

As if on cue, the sippy cup slammed into his head. "Ow!" He pulled Bryce off his shoulders and set him on the floor. "I love you too, little bro. Can we eat?"

"I love you all too," Liz said, smiling at everyone.

"I'm so happy to be part of this family," Jorge chimed in.

"Now you know I love you all," Maggie said.

"Me too," Daisy said with a loving look at Trav.

Rachel stayed quiet, uncomfortable with all the open affection going on. She couldn't remember the last time anyone in her family had said I love you.

"All right, all right," Shane said. "Everyone eat."

Platters were passed around as everyone took one of everything. Rachel wondered how often they got together for taste tests. Once they got started, they moved like clockwork, passing dishes, savoring, reporting on initial reactions. The food was fabulous, everything fresh and in season. They were lucky it was August and the blueberries, peaches, and raspberries were all at their peak. The blueberries in the corn muffins burst with flavor in her mouth. The peach mini-pies were velvety and delicious. And the raspberry scones were so good she couldn't stop with just one bite. Their café was going to be so popular.

"Shane, this is amazing," Rachel said, halfway through. "People are going to be lining up out the door just for the baked stuff."

Conversation stopped as all eyes went to Shane.

"Thank you," he said. "That means a lot to me."

They smiled at each other. Rachel suddenly realized no one was eating. She looked around the group, who were looking at her and Shane. They were all smiles.

"The coffee's great too," she said uneasily.

"I'm sure it is, dear," Maggie said with a knowing smile. "We'll be the first ones in line."

They went back to eating. Lemon cookies, chocolate cupcakes with raspberry filling, éclairs.

"Yes to éclairs!" Rachel exclaimed, overwhelmed with the delectable dessert. It was heavenly, a thick chocolate ganache on top, sweet cream inside. "This is the best thing I've ever tasted!"

Shane grinned.

Maggie held up an éclair, which suddenly looked very, very phallic. "I told you it's the love!"

Rachel blushed furiously. Everyone laughed.

"Shane's got a lot to love," Trav quipped.

Now Shane blushed furiously. "Moving on," he grumbled.

They finished the taste-testing with a lot of moans and groans over eating too much. There wasn't a dud in the bunch.

"It sounds like I should keep everything and just rotate the items," Shane said. "Rach, keep track of the top-selling items, and we'll keep those on the menu permanently."

"Sure," she said.

Shane addressed the group. "In the fall, we'll have another taste-testing for pumpkin, apple, pear, and cranberry flavors."

Everyone moaned and groaned good-naturedly.

Shane started gathering up the platters.

"I have to wonder, bro," Trav drawled, "why you'd become business partners instead of just taking the easy way and asking her out."

Rachel stiffened.

"Shut it," Shane snapped.

"Would that really be the easy way?" Maggie asked. "What if he asked her out and then she said no, then that's that."

"I told him going into business together wasn't going to help his case," Ry said.

"But now that they're working together, he has lots of chances to ask her out," Daisy pointed out.

This launched a big debate over whether going into business together was the easy way or the hard way for two people to get together. Face flaming, Rachel looked to Shane for help, but he'd gone back to gathering dishes, seemingly fine with his entire family teasing them. Liz shot her a sympathetic look.

"It was more than just an investment, you know," Maggie said. "It was a sacrifice on Shane's part."

Shane's attention snapped to Maggie, clearly surprised. "Don't," he warned.

"What sacrifice?" Ry asked.

Rachel's stomach dropped. "Shane?"

He shook his head. "Don't listen to her."

"You should tell her," Maggie urged.

"What's going on?" Trav asked.

Everyone stared at Shane.

"Nothing," Shane said. "It's nothing. I dug deep for the cash, but we'll make it back. No problem."

Rachel stared at him. "Tell me what you did to get that money."

He shook his head.

Rachel went hot and cold. She had a very bad feeling about this. "Tell me!" she demanded.

His eyes were steely in their resolve. "No."

Rachel jumped up from the table and rushed from the room. Something was very wrong here. What did Shane do? What did he sacrifice? *Shit.* She went outside, taking a deep, calming breath of the nighttime air. She walked down the front path, needing to get away from the crowd. She heard the voices in the house rising in volume, followed by some catcalls, and then Shane was heading her way.

"What's Maggie talking about?" she asked once he reached her side. "What did you do to get that money?"

Shane's mouth formed a grim line. "She must've talked to my dad. I never told anyone."

"Told them what!"

"I sold the Shelby."

"What's a Shelby?"

He ran a hand through his hair. "It's a car. A very expensive, highly collectible classic car. It was a '67 Shelby Mustang GT 500 I inherited from my dad. He got it from his dad."

Her brows scrunched in confusion. "I never saw you drive a Mustang."

He lifted one shoulder up and down. "I kept it at my dad's house because I didn't want my brothers to be hurt that he gave the Shelby to me and not them. My dad gave it to me as a thank you for spending time with him. We spent a lot of time fixing it up on the weekends."

Rachel suddenly felt shaky. She knew Shane had only recently started spending time with his dad after his dad had abandoned him as a kid. Her hand went to her mouth, and she took a step back, hitting air where the sidewalk should've been. Shane caught her and held her.

"Why would you do that?" she asked.

He gazed into her eyes. "I did it for you."

"How much?" she whispered.

"How much what?"

"How much did you sell the car for?"

"I was going to sell it at auction, but the guy who owned the garage I took it to bought it from me on the spot for ninety-five thousand."

Rachel gasped. Shane had given up this car that was worth so much money just to help her start the café? This car that had been in his family for generations? That he'd bonded with his dad over?

Omigod.

Her ears had a weird ringing to them, and she felt light-headed. "I need to sit down."

She sank to the ground, and he sat on the curb next to her.

"I'll pay you back right away" she told him. "We'll get the car back."

"No, it's a done deal."

"I'll find another investor. You're not losing your inheritance because of me." She gripped her hands tightly. "I'll fix this."

He snagged her chin and turned her to face him. "You don't have to fix this. It's fine."

"Shane...what your family said back there. Were they right? You did all this just to..." She couldn't say it, but it was there. Shane went into business with her to sleep with her. "Just tell me why you wanted to be business partners. What's the real reason?"

His mouth formed a tight line. Rachel got the unsettling feeling that his intentions were exactly what his family had said.

"Just say it," she said.

He ran a hand through his hair, and the humidity made it stay rumpled. She quickly smoothed it back into its usual side part, not able to deal with a rumpled, sexy look right now.

He watched her warily. "I told you, to diversify against that idiot Barry."

"That's the only reason? Honestly?"

He paused, finally saying, "It was a plus that it helped you out."

"And?"

"And what?"

She stared him down. "What did you expect in return? To get me into bed?"

"You think I'm paying to sleep with you?" His voice was dangerously low, and she felt the first inkling that maybe she'd pushed him too far. "I've never paid for sex in my life!"

"Forget it," she muttered. She stood and turned to go. She'd fix this and soon. She'd find another investor and pay him back all that money he'd lost. She'd make sure he got his car back.

He stepped in front of her, blocking her way. "Say what you're thinking."

She tried not to get turned on by the return of alpha Shane. She wasn't going to argue with him over the money. She'd take care of it, and that was that. Still, his aggressive stance riled her up.

She raised her chin. "We've been friends for months, and you never kissed me, I mean, *really* kissed me until *after* we were business partners."

One corner of his mouth quirked up. "That wasn't why I kissed you."

He stepped closer, and she eased back a step, trying not to

look like she was running. She wasn't. She was just preserving her personal space. He closed the gap, and she stopped, taken in by his scent, his reassuring presence, so close after keeping his distance these past weeks.

He ran a fingertip over her exposed collarbone, and she swallowed, flushing with warmth. "Think about it, Rach. Think real hard. Why did I kiss you?"

She shook her head. "I don't know. It makes no sense. We were friends. We had just signed a contract."

His hand slid into her hair, and she thought, *I should go*, but then his mouth was near her ear, and his voice was low and silky, and she couldn't move. Not one inch.

"Think about it tonight when you're alone in your bed," he said. "When you reach for Neal—"

She gasped, horrified at the mention of her vibrator. She shoved him away with both hands, face flaming. He just smiled and stayed feet planted in front of her. Why had she confided so much in Shane? He was such a good listener she'd let her mouth get away from her. Now he would use everything he knew against her. This was just one more reason why you should never hook up with your best friend.

He nodded. "Oh, yeah, I remember. Think about me tonight when you're about to—"

"I shouldn't have told you that," she muttered. She exhaled sharply and stared at his chest. "Just shut up. I'm embarrassed enough just from hanging out with your family. Now you. Is that what you wanted?"

"You know what I want."

Her head snapped up. Their eyes met for a crackling moment. He reached out, one warm hand cradling her face as he leaned slowly toward her. She forgot to breathe. *Okay, just one kiss*, she told herself. They'd get this out of their system and move on. She closed her eyes.

Then nothing.

He pulled away, and she stared at him as disappointment swamped her.

"I think we want the same thing," he said.

Then he turned and walked back to the house. She stood

there fuming, unsure whether to lash out at him or her own stupid self for wanting what she knew she couldn't have. Shouldn't have.

He turned, hand on the knob. "Like I said, it's your move."

"Aargh!" The man was simultaneously devastating in his generosity and unforgivably withholding.

Rachel turned and walked home in a daze. One thing was for certain. She would *not* be spending time with Neal tonight thinking of Shane. She wouldn't give Shane the satisfaction of being right.

14

The next day Rachel was sitting at the front register of her store, still lost in thought, trying to figure out where she'd find another investor for the café when Barry walked in.

"Good morning!" he called cheerfully.

"Morning," she replied.

He stopped at the counter, and his brows drew together. "Everything okay?"

She forced a smile. "Yes, sure. What can I help you with today?"

"Got any recommendations for a beach read?"

"Sure. I just got a celebrity tell-all that might be fun." She led him to the memoir and biography section and handed him the book.

He glanced at it. "Thanks."

She went back to the register to ring him up, still lost in a dark cloud. She couldn't believe what Shane had sacrificed for her. Why would he do that and never say a word about it? Who does that?

"You sure you're okay?" Barry asked.

She rubbed her forehead. "I just had a bit of a shock."

He handed over his credit card. "Want to talk about it?"

She shook her head. "Not unless you know someone who wants to invest in my café."

He grinned. "As a matter of fact, I do. I'll invest."

Her mouth dropped open in shock. "But you just opened your own shop. How could you possibly afford—"

"You didn't think I always worked at fro-yo, did you? I had a windfall. I've got money invested in quite a few places."

She stared at him, confused. "What do you mean?"

He grinned. "You know Giggle Snap?"

Giggle Snap was a social media phenomenon focused on sharing sounds—laughter, conversation, weird sound effects. "That was you?"

"Yup. I sold it to one of the big guys. Then I started the fro-yo shop just for kicks. Mom was so proud I finally did something she could enjoy." He grinned. "So what do I get as an investor?"

She blinked. "Don't you want to know how much?"

He looked over at the café, shrewdly taking in the place. "I'm guessing a hundred, hundred fifty grand."

"Yes, a hundred grand would work just fine."

This was amazing. She could buy Shane out and get his inheritance back. He would go back to being just the supplier. Things would go back to normal. She wouldn't be in debt to him anymore. Sure, she'd be in debt to Barry, but he was such an easygoing guy, she couldn't imagine that being a problem.

Barry held out his hand to shake on it. She raised a palm, holding him off. "You'd get a fifty-percent share in the profits," she said, "but I run the place. You'd be a silent partner."

"Sounds perfect! Cash or check?"

"Um, check is fine."

Barry had that kind of cash lying around? They shook on it.

"I'll have my accountant cut a check," Barry said. "You should get the money on Monday."

Relief rushed through her. "Thank you, thank you so much. It's very generous."

He smiled. "I know a good investment when I see it."

Now she just had to tell Shane. She decided not to mention Barry by name, seeing as how Shane still saw him as annoying at best, the enemy at worst. She'd just tell him he would be getting his investment back and he could reclaim his inheritance.

Shane smiled as Rachel stopped by his shop. His shop was empty, the lull between morning coffee and afternoon ice cream. He wasn't sure she'd come to him after the way they'd left things last night with him reminding her it was her move, but she had. He wouldn't make this difficult. It was enough that she came to him.

"Hey," he said. "Long time no see. How are you?"

She played with the end of her braid, a sure sign she was nervous. "I'm okay." She bit her lip. "Got a minute to talk?"

His stomach twisted. He had a feeling this wouldn't be the good kind of talk.

He untied his apron and came out from behind the counter. She took a seat at a table near the front window. Did she want witnesses?

"What's up?" he asked.

"I just wanted you to know I found an investor."

"You did?"

"Yes. And I'll have the money on Monday. Enough to buy you out and pay off the loan you gave me for my share. You can get the Shelby back."

He crossed his arms. "What if I don't want to sell my share?"

She turned pleading eyes to him. "Please let me do this."

"Why?"

"I don't want to owe you. I don't want you to sacrifice. It's too much."

"Rach, I'm okay with it."

She gripped her hands tightly together. "It's your inheritance. I want you to get it back."

"I'm not buying back the Shelby," he said. "And I don't give a shit about the money."

She stiffened. "Please don't make this harder than it is. Just take the damn money!"

Something wasn't sitting right with him. She was pushing him away.

"Just tell me this…" He paused, almost afraid to hear the answer. "Are you trying to push me out of the café or out of your life?"

"The café," she said gently. "I just don't want you to invest. Besides, I miss you. I miss our friendship. We never hang out anymore."

Back to that again? Friends?

"You're scared," he said. "Scared to give a real relationship a chance. I'm not one of those loser guys you have to endlessly discuss with your friends, trying to figure out how to fix them and send them on their merry way."

Her eyes narrowed. She stood. "Barry's accountant will cut the check, and then you'll have your money."

He jumped up so fast the chair went flying out from under him. "Barry? Barry from The Dancing Cow? Are you fucking kidding me?"

She gave a quick nod and stepped carefully away.

"I'm not selling out to Barry!" he roared.

"I'm sending you the money either way," she said, and then she left the shop, leaving him furious and ready to destroy Barry and his stupid dancing cow.

He closed up shop and got in his car, determined to end this deal right now.

Late on Monday, with no small amount of trepidation, Rachel crossed the street to Shane's shop to give him the check she'd received from Barry. She'd asked that it be made out to Shane. She also brought the paperwork canceling her debt to Shane and naming Barry as silent partner in the shop. Gabe had helped with the paperwork while shaking his head at her. She hadn't appreciated the reminder. She knew Shane wouldn't be happy. But this was the only way to fix things.

She hadn't called Shane to give him the heads-up, too afraid she'd lose her nerve. Instead she'd waited until just before Shane's shop closed for the day before rushing across the street to catch him.

"Hi, Shane," she called.

He was closing up the register. He eyed her. "Hello, Rachel," he said flatly.

She swallowed and approached him. "Can we talk? About the business."

He indicated a chair, and she sat. Her hands were shaking. Geez, what was she so worked up about? This was business, and she was just doing what needed to be done. He joined her a few minutes later, making her wait just long enough to consider running out of the shop.

She handed him the check. "It's enough to buy out your share and cancel my debt."

He stared at it. The check said Barry Furnukle Enterprises in bold right on top. "I told Barry I wasn't selling."

"I know. I told him it wasn't up to you."

His jaw tightened.

She pushed the other papers and a pen toward him. "I just need you to sign off that I paid my debt and, um, sign here that you're not a partner."

He signed off on the debt. She breathed a sigh of relief.

Then he took the check and ripped it into tiny pieces.

"Shane! What are you doing?" She gathered up all the pieces.

"I'm not taking Barry's money, and I'm not selling."

Rachel was feeling positively desperate. "I'm trying to help you! I'm trying to fix things!" She tried to piece the check back together, thinking maybe she could tape it, but the pieces were just too small. She gave up and stared down at the mess. "Now I'm going to have to get another check," she muttered.

She met his eyes. He stared back, his expression fierce, and an unwelcome frisson of desire ran through her. She pushed back from the table.

He watched her as she stood and gathered the papers.

"We're not finished," she said. "I'll be back soon with a new check."

She headed for the door. He grabbed her arm and whirled her around. She gasped. She hadn't even heard him get up.

"You've got one thing right," he said, invading her personal space. She took a step back, but his hand was suddenly at the small of her back, keeping her close. "We're not finished."

His mouth met hers in a hard kiss. She put her hands up to his chest, pushing him away, but then he gentled the kiss, and her hands weren't pushing anymore, instead roaming over the hard planes of his warm chest. He took his time, slow and tender, and she surrendered to it, wrapping her arms around his waist and leaning into him.

He pulled back to gaze into her eyes. His arms still held her close in a loose embrace. "Rach, I'm all-in."

She swallowed hard. "I-I don't want you to have to do this."

"I'm *in*. The question is, do you have the guts to go all-in too?"

Her heart pounded in her ears. "I'll try my best to make the café work, but I still feel—"

"That's not what I meant, and you know it."

"Shane, please. You're making this very difficult."

His expression shuttered closed, and he dropped his arms, releasing her from his embrace. "Yeah, well, you're no picnic either."

He turned and left out the back door of his shop.

Rachel stood there for a minute, speechless.

Was Shane right? Was she too scared to give a relationship a chance? She'd never had a serious relationship. Was that why she'd hooked up with losers in the past? She'd thought she'd just been unlucky. Cursed. But now...

Shit. He was right.

She was scared. Very scared. But what was worse? Her fear of a real relationship and all the possible ways things could go wrong or her fear of losing Shane?

⚚

Rachel had a restless night, thinking of Shane and his sacrifice. His question ran on repeat through her head: *do you have the guts to go all-in too?* When she finally dragged herself out of bed, she had no good answer.

Mid-morning, he stopped by to check on the café, and she walked over, needing to talk. She found him in the back assembling shelves.

"Were you ever going to tell me about selling the Shelby?" she asked.

He looked up, still holding a shelf in place. "No. I didn't do it for any thanks. It means more when you do something without needing to take credit. Know what I mean?"

She'd never known anyone who went around doing good deeds anonymously.

"I guess," she said.

He tapped the shelf into place with a mallet. "When I finish here, come back to my shop and I'll teach you how to work the espresso machine."

"Okay."

A short while later, she followed Shane across the street, determined to make the best of their partnership and make their café a success. It was the least she could do for all that he'd sacrificed. They started with the espresso grinder to grind a fresh batch of Mexican dark roast beans.

"You want a very fine grind for the espresso," he said before he poured the beans in. "That's why I have a separate grinder for it."

She caught herself checking out his very firm ass and forced her gaze back to the grinder. It was the lack of sleep. It made her weak.

"Good to know," Rachel said, her voice coming out all breathy and Marilyn Monroe-like.

Get a hold of yourself! He's trying to teach you something very important!

Shane raised a brow, and any further conversation was

stopped by the loud noise of the grinder. He took the container of espresso grounds and showed her.

"Take a pinch," he told her, doing the same. "Slide it between your fingers. We want it to feel like grains of sand. If it feels like sugar, it's too coarse. Flour-feel is also no good."

Rachel slid it between her fingers. "Definitely sand."

He nodded. "You'll grind the next batch and keep doing it until you know exactly how long it takes in the grinder to get sand."

"Okay," she breathed. She gave herself a quick mental slap. She sounded like she'd been running a marathon instead of standing in his shop learning about espresso. She focused on the ice-cream menu, trying to cool it. She caught his efficient movements out of the corner of her eye as he moved over to the espresso machine. Shane standing there in a T-shirt, athletic shorts, and apron was disturbingly sexy.

It wasn't her fault she was feeling lusty. He was the one that kissed her. Twice long, twice quick. She often thought of those long kisses.

"C'mere," he said, to which she responded by rushing over in a lust-filled haze.

"I measured out the grounds," he said. "So now we put it into the portafilter and we tamp the grounds." He picked up a wooden mushroom-shaped tool and set the portafilter on a steel plate on the back countertop. Then he pounded the grounds down, twisting the tamper to flatten them further. Rachel's eyes shifted from the tool in his hand to the play of muscles through his biceps and the corded muscle running down his forearm. He stopped and turned to her. She dragged her gaze back to his face.

He smiled, almost a smirk. She smiled back, forgiving his arrogance in light of the male beauty he presented before her. She really did appreciate his trips to the gym now.

He handed her the tool and gave the portafilter a shake. "Give it a try. We want to pack it down so it has good resistance to the hot water pouring through."

She slammed the tamper down and nearly knocked the whole thing over.

"Easy," he said, coming up behind her and placing his hands over hers. "We're tamping it, not killing it."

She nodded vigorously, enfolded in his warmth. She loosened her grip and let him guide her to the proper tamp. Heat ran through her as she remembered their kiss from yesterday. Just when she thought she might have the courage to turn in his arms and make her move, he stopped and pulled away.

"Looks good," he said. "Now we attach it to the group, where the hot water comes out. Make sure it's in there firmly; otherwise the water pressure will push everything out the sides of the portafilter and make a mess. Believe me, I know."

"Firmly," she repeated on a sigh. He attached the portafilter to the machine, and Rachel breathed in the scent of espresso and clean, sexy male. She leaned closer, up on tiptoe; even his hair smelled good.

He froze. "Are you smelling my hair?"

She jolted backward. "No. I was smelling the espresso."

He gave her a suspicious look. "Sure seemed like you were smelling my hair."

"Nope." She played with the end of her braid. "So what's next?"

"We've got to brew quickly, like now, or the espresso grounds will start to deteriorate." He pressed a button and spoke over the noise of the machine. "It's delicate." A moment later, he stopped and showed her the cup of espresso. "Twenty seconds of brewing is ideal. Check out the foam, that's the crema where the sugar is concentrated. We want it a quarter-inch thick and lasting about a minute before it breaks apart."

Rachel pretended to watch the foam while she pondered how to make a move without being too obvious. Maybe she'd pull out her braid and shake out her hair. Or slide her shirt off one shoulder. No, lick her lips. They always did that in the movies.

"There it is," he said. "Perfect." He gave it a sip and handed the cup to her. "Try it."

She licked her lips, but Shane just stood there waiting for her to sip. She took a sip. "It's good."

He nodded. "Next we dump out the grounds and clean the machine. We'll keep the portafilter in the group so it stays warm." She watched and sipped the espresso as he efficiently prepared the machine for the next shot.

She felt jittery and a little giddy. She must be hepped up on caffeine. Or Shane. He was her business partner. She shouldn't let her appreciation for his good deed color her feelings for him. Yet she couldn't seem to help it. Her eyes trailed down to his firm ass. It was a very nice ass.

He turned. "Eyes up here."

She blushed furiously. "I wasn't...I was just lost in thought, and you happened to be in my line of vision."

"Uh-huh. You're next."

Her heart started pounding. "For what?"

He raised his brows. "What do you think?"

She wiped her suddenly clammy hands on her shorts. "I-I don't know."

He gave her a strange look. "Are you feeling okay? You're all flushed and pink." He put the back of his hand on her forehead. "You feel a little hot."

I am. I'm way too hot for you.

She stepped away from his hand. Yes, she was hot for him, but she was getting major nerves just thinking about acting on that. Was she ready for what that would open up between them? She knew Shane didn't do casual. Maybe that's what had scared her off him in the first place. In high school, he'd dated Kerry Habinowski for three years until she left for college. She'd heard he'd dated a woman from the culinary school for five years. The entire time she'd been back in Clover Park, she hadn't heard of him dating anyone. Except that one date with Janelle. She had a feeling one hookup wouldn't cut it for Shane with someone he really cared about.

With her.

Her pulse raced. Did she have the guts to go all-in?

Would she end up losing him?

He smiled and said gently, "It's your turn to make an espresso."

"Oh! Okay." She turned to the espresso grinder and found

she couldn't remember a single thing he'd just taught her. She hadn't been paying attention to anything but the play of his muscles as he worked and her debate over whether or not to make a move. God, she was pathetic. She turned to him. "Little hint here?"

He smiled. "Yup."

He spent hours going over and over the process with her until she could have made the perfect espresso in her sleep. Not that sleep would come anytime soon from all the caffeine she drank. She spent another restless night thinking of Shane. Neal was a very poor substitute.

15

Shane headed for the street-fair meeting at the library at the end of what had turned out to be a great day. The café was looking fantastic. He'd been prepared for the inevitable bumps along the way of working with various contractors and product delivery, but everything had been going smoothly. Today the flooring guys showed up on time and finished the floor in one day. The dark laminate wood really made the red of the walls pop. The furniture would be delivered Thursday morning.

"Hey there, handsome," Miss Smith called with a wiggle of her fingers. She'd gone from friendly to blatant flirting as he'd been at the library every Monday night this summer.

He blushed anyway. *Dammit.* "Hi, Miss Smith, how are you?"

"I'm very well, thank you." She craned her neck as he passed, clearly checking him out from behind.

What could he do? He was senior-citizen eye candy. He smiled to himself, remembering how he'd caught Rachel doing the same thing last week when he'd taught her to make espresso. Rachel was definitely warming up to the idea of moving things to the next level. She'd been smiling at him more ever since she found out he'd sold the Shelby. If he'd known it would get this kind of reaction, he might have mentioned it sooner. All this week she'd been touching his arm a lot, and he'd caught her watching him as he worked at the café with the workmen. Good signs, but not enough. He wanted her all-in, plain and simple. No more of this two steps forward, one step back.

He headed to the conference room where Rachel and Liz sat, relieved to see Barry hadn't arrived yet.

"Hey, Shane," Liz said. "Rachel told me the flooring went in. You guys are so close now!"

Shane grinned. "It looks awesome. Tomorrow we get the furniture. Rach, stop by after the furniture goes in and show me where you want the floating shelves and book posters, and I'll put them up."

"Great!" Rachel smiled warmly.

Shane smiled back, soaking all that warmth in.

"One more week," Shane said.

"Are you guys ready?" Liz asked.

"I think so," Rachel said. "The place is nearly done. All the kitchen stuff is in. Shane's training the barista I hired this week."

Shane nodded. "I came up with some iced coffee and iced tea recipes with different flavored syrups since it's still blazing hot out."

"Hello, hello!" Barry called as he walked in. He unfurled a large banner across the conference table. "I made a sign."

It read Clover Park Summer Street Fair. And then in pink neon letters underneath that: Sponsored by The Dancing Cow!

"Oh, hell no," Shane said.

"No," Rachel said.

Barry frowned. "What's wrong?"

"I don't think this will work," Rachel said gently. "This is an event to boost all the businesses, not just yours. Besides, you didn't sponsor the fair. We don't even have sponsors."

"I contributed the kiddie entertainment and negotiated a good savings," Barry said.

"No deal," Shane said.

"How much would a sponsorship cost?" Barry asked.

Gabe arrived, took one look at the banner, and chortled. "Shane, you should have sponsored too, then your name could be on there. Maybe in sparkly purple."

"We don't have sponsors," Shane said between his teeth.

"Now, wait a minute," Rachel said. She turned to Barry. "How much would you like to contribute?"

"Rach!" Shane protested.

"Five thousand dollars," Barry said.

"Five thousand dollars!" Shane exclaimed.

Gabe whistled under his breath. "Let the man sponsor it. None of you have that kind of money."

Rachel turned to Barry. "Thank you, Barry."

Barry beamed. The man looked like a lovesick cow. Pathetic. Shane realized with a start, he probably looked the same way when he looked at Rachel. She *was* an amazing woman.

Liz looked around the table. "I think it's a good idea. With that money, we could do a lot of advertising to draw people from all over. Not to mention, any extra could go into future chamber of commerce events. Maybe a trick-or-treating party, or a holiday stroll with carolers and horse-drawn carriages. There's a lot you could do with five thousand dollars."

Rachel leaned over to Barry to shake his hand. "Sold."

Shane gritted his teeth. Enough touching already.

Barry pulled a hat out of a tote bag. "I had these hats made up too." He gave them each a baseball cap that read We're Street People. "It's for the business owners so people know who to come to with questions."

"Oh my," Liz muttered.

Gabe put his cap on and grinned. "I'm street people."

Shane refused to even touch the stupid hat. "You realize this sounds like we're all homeless people living on the street, not professional business owners."

Barry's eyebrows scrunched together in confusion. "Yeah?" He studied the hat from all angles. "No problem. I'll have another batch made and add 'fair' to it. We're Street Fair People."

"I'm not wearing that," Shane said.

"Come on, buddy," Gabe said. "Where's your sense of style?"

Shane snorted.

"How about just Clover Park Street Fair?" Liz asked.

"Yeah?" Barry asked. "You don't think that's too on the nose?"

"Not at all," Liz said.

"Okay then!" Barry took out a pen and wrote the new phrase on a Dancing Cow napkin he pulled from the front pocket of his green Hawaiian shirt.

"I'm so glad the street fair's next week," Shane muttered under his breath to Rachel.

She patted his leg, and he was extra glad they were a week away from opening. Then she couldn't pretend that working together was a reason not to be together.

"Now, now," Rachel scolded quietly.

"Next order of business," Barry said. "Tricycles. Anyone know where we could borrow some?"

Shane inwardly groaned. Liz came up with that solution through her network of parents she knew from teaching at Clover Park Elementary. The meeting finally wrapped up.

He walked out with Rachel. "Come and see the flooring."

She smiled. "Sure."

"Oh, can I see too?" Liz asked.

"Me too," Gabe said.

"Wait up, guys!" Barry said.

And so it was that Shane led the entire group to the café, giving up his idea of getting Rachel alone and letting her flirt with him.

At Shane's orders, Rachel had taken the afternoon off while the sign for the café and the furniture was delivered. He wanted to surprise her with the "full effect" once everything was in place. Liz was working the register at Book It, and business had picked up now that it was September. Families had returned from vacation and stopped by to pick up books for the long Labor Day weekend before school started.

She spent the afternoon at her sister, Sarah's place playing treasure hunt in the backyard with the three oldest kids, David, Leah, and Olivia, while her sister napped with baby Jacob. After an hour nap, Sarah came out of the house, baby monitor in hand. "Thank you. I needed that nap."

"No problem."

"Mommy!" Olivia yelled, coming out from under the deck. She wrapped her arms around Sarah's legs, leaving a muddy mess on her sister's pale pink pajama pants. Sarah pressed Olivia close. "What are you doing under there?"

Olivia giggled. "Hiding."

"Okay, guys, next clue," Rachel said. "This tree has something that looks good to eat, but it's really sour." She made a face. "Bring me back one."

"Crab apple!" David exclaimed. The kids took off for the crab apple tree.

Sarah sat in the chaise lounge and leaned her head back. "You're so good with them, Rach. You'll be a good mom."

Rachel shook her head. "I nearly lost Olivia. She was hiding in the neighbor's doghouse."

Sarah waved that away. "I lose her too. But she's usually in the yard or next door."

The kids ran back, each with a crab apple in hand. Rachel took them. "Next clue, this is where secret clubs can meet. Bring me a flower from there."

The kids took off for the playset.

"How's things with you and Shane?" Sarah asked.

"Fine," Rachel said. "The café's almost ready. The sign and furniture goes in today. I'm supposed to go over there at five to see it. He wanted to surprise me."

Sarah smiled. "Good. But you know that's not what I'm asking. You ever think you two…"

Rachel's usual quick *no* didn't come out. This wasn't the first time Sarah had asked the question. Her sister thought it odd that Rachel had a cute guy she spent so much time with just as a friend. "Maybe," she allowed.

Her sister sat up and grinned. "Maybe? Maybe! Rach, this is so exciting!"

"Don't make a big deal." The kids came running back, panting and giggling, and handed her some buttercups. "Last clue, the big prize is hiding here...this is where the roses grow. But don't pick them!"

The kids took off for the side yard.

"So you finally found your Mr. Darcy," Sarah said.

Rachel shook her head. "He's not. He's just...he's good to me." She didn't want to share any more than that. Her feelings were still too raw, too new. "How're you and Mark?"

"Great!"

Rachel watched the kids running around, talking nonstop at top volume. She looked back to her sister in dirty pajamas, looking exhausted. "Doesn't it bother you that he's not around that much?"

"He's got a job in the city. I know the drill."

"I don't know how you do it. I'd be so mad having to do all the work at home by myself."

Sarah waved that away, smiling over at the kids. "He loves me, I love him. We're happy. Yes, I'd love to see him more, but when he's here, he's great with the kids."

"So you don't feel like a single mom?"

"No! I'm not a single mom. Mark's always here if I really need him." She grinned. "I can't wait for you and Shane to have kids."

Sarah said it like it was the most natural thing in the world, as if she and Shane were about to marry. Why was everyone pushing her to marry Shane? They'd only kissed four times! A very nice four times, but still.

At Rachel's silence, Sarah went on. "The cousins could grow up together. Wouldn't that be so nice?"

"Geez, Sarah, no offense, but if I were you, I'd be a wine-a-holic. It's just nonstop with the kids."

"It is, isn't it?" Sarah said, smiling serenely.

"I found it!" David hollered, emerging triumphant from the side yard. "Fifty cents!"

Leah and Olivia burst into tears.

"All right, everybody gets fifty cents because of the good teamwork," Rachel said.

The girls immediately stopped crying and held out their hands.

"You're a natural," Sarah said.

It was with some relief that Rachel made her way back to the café. She parked around the back of her store and walked to the front of the café to check it out. Shane was sitting out front in a wrought-iron chair.

She did a double take. Shane had created an outdoor seating area with several wrought-iron tables and chairs. "Where did these come from?"

He smiled his dimpled smile. "I ordered them. I wanted to surprise you. Do you like?"

She couldn't believe it. She hadn't even thought of outdoor seating. Though now that she saw it, she couldn't believe she'd overlooked it. "It's perfect! I love it!"

He stood and pulled her a short distance from the café, pointing upward. "Check it out."

She looked up at the sign. It was red with white raised letters: Something's Brewing Café. A coffee cup with steam coming out of it was painted on one side. It was gorgeous.

"I had them add the coffee mug," he said. "What do you think?"

She threw her arms around him. "I love it!"

He gave her a squeeze and put an arm around her shoulders. "Come inside. I want you to get the full effect." He opened the front door for her, and she stepped inside.

She'd seen the flooring and the counters, but now that all the furniture was in place, it looked like a real café. She slowly walked in, taking in the arrangement of the tables, a long table on one side, away from the counter, smaller tables near the front, a reading area with two leather chairs and a coffee table. She sat in one of the cushy leather chairs.

"This is perfect for reading." Her eye caught on the back wall, where Shane had hung a book cover poster. One she hadn't ordered. It was the *Just So Stories* by Rudyard Kipling with a red cover and black elephant. A kids' book.

She stood and got closer. "You ordered all this…" Her voice trailed off as she realized what he'd done. In the back corner, he'd set up a small blackboard easel with colored chalk, a kid-size wooden table with four chairs, and a small basket of picture books.

He joined her. "I was thinking of Bryce. Then I thought, maybe moms with little ones would like their kids to have a spot of their own."

She could just picture Daisy and Bryce here, Sarah with her brood. Her throat felt tight. She was *not* going to cry.

"Did I do the wrong thing?" he asked.

She shook her head. "No, it's perfect." She swallowed over the lump in her throat. "Just perfect."

He nodded. "Good. Now, you be the customer to get the full experience." He went behind the counter and put on an apron. It was red with white letters that matched the sign out front and embroidered with "Something's Brewing Café."

"You thought of everything!" Rachel exclaimed in wonder. "I can't believe you didn't tell me!"

"It's more fun to surprise you." He grinned. "How can I help you today?"

She looked at the menu, but she already had it memorized. "I'll take a cappuccino and a peach tart, please."

"Coming right up." She watched him prepare the drink, though after his thorough training, she could've done it herself. A few minutes later, he had served up two cappuccinos, a peach tart, and an apple muffin. The cappuccino had the perfect amount of foam with a decorative swirl that resembled a heart. God, he was so sweet. How could she compete with that?

She offered to pay.

"Are you kidding me?" he asked, feigning outrage. "Take a seat."

She picked up her drink and snack and chose a table by the front window. He joined her. She took a sip through the foam. "This is good cappuccino."

He sipped too. "It is."

She looked around. "The café is amazing, and you played

such a big part in making it that way. I don't know what I would've done without you. I probably would've made it like Book It, part two. But you took it to a whole new level. Thank you."

He took her hand and squeezed it. "We did this. Together."

She felt tears sting her eyes and turned away. Since when was she this emotional? The place was perfect. This was what they'd created together. This was their baby.

16

Rachel walked over to Daisy and Trav's place on Sunday for an end-of-summer barbecue. The café's grand opening was tomorrow, and she couldn't wait. She just knew it would be a hit. It had to be with Shane behind it. She followed the trail of balloons to the backyard, where several tables with folding chairs had been set up on the lawn near the patio. Bryce was splashing around in a kiddie pool, wearing a cute little polka-dotted sun hat and swim diaper. Hagar was alternating approaching the pool and dashing away as Bryce smacked the water, screaming, "Ha-ha!" Short for Hagar?

Shane and Trav sat in beach chairs next to the pool, both wearing sunglasses, looking *très* cool.

"Hi, Bryce!" Rachel approached the pool but kept a safe distance from the splash zone.

Bryce turned, looked at her briefly, then went back to the important work of pushing a plastic boat through the water.

"Hey, guys," she said, turning to the brothers.

"Hey, Rach," Trav said, rising to kiss her cheek. "Almost the big day, huh?"

"Yup! I'm psyched."

Shane smiled and stood to greet her. He kissed her cheek like his brother, but it left her wanting much more. He was wearing down her resolve with all his sacrifice and big gestures.

"Hey," he said. "Long time no see."

Rachel shook her finger at Shane. "Get back to work."

"Yeah, work never ends, does it?"

"Are you nervous about tomorrow?"

He gave her braid a playful tug. "Nah, we're all set. It'll be good."

"Ow!" Trav exclaimed. Rachel turned to see him rubbing his shin. "When do kids learn to stop being so rough?" He turned Bryce's boat in the other direction.

"Give him another couple years," Rachel said.

"I can't believe he's already one," Trav said, gazing at his son.

Rachel smiled. "I bet you can't wait to have another one."

Trav's chest puffed with pride. "I'd love to have two more just like him." His gaze wandered over to Daisy, who was laughing and talking to Maggie and Liz.

Rachel still remembered when Daisy had first had Bryce. She'd returned to Clover Park and shocked Trav with the news that he was the father. Now, here they were, married and happy. Something ached in her heart. It wasn't jealousy so much as...happiness for her friends. She shook off the uncomfortable feeling.

"You want to sit with us?" Shane asked. "I'll bring another chair."

"That's okay. I'm going to say hi to the ladies."

She approached the group on the patio and recognized Liz, Maggie, Jorge, and two of Daisy's friends, Amber and Zoe. "Hi, all! Daze, Trav was just telling me he wants to have two more kids just like Bryce."

Daisy shook her head, smiling. "He always says that. Bryce just barely turned one. I'm not ready to go through labor again." She made a comical face of exaggerated pain. "I was such a dope too; I didn't even realize I was in labor at first. I thought it was too soon and it must be those Braxton Hicks contractions. Remember, sis?"

Liz smiled. "I remember, and he came quickly too. That's

why she named him Bryce because he was in a hurry to get here. The nurse told her Bryce meant swift."

Amber laughed. "I didn't know that's why you named him Bryce."

Ryan came out of the house with a platter of hamburgers and hot dogs for the grill. "Hey, Rach, how're ya?"

"Good. How are you?" she asked.

He grinned. "Excellent." He smiled over at Liz, his heart in his eyes. Liz smiled back.

Rachel felt that odd ache again. It was just being surrounded by all these ridiculously in-love couples that was making her feel off.

Jack O'Hare arrived with his girlfriend, Gina. She wondered if he was upset about Shane selling the Shelby just to help her out, but he gave no indication, merely greeted her politely as he did everyone at their table. Rachel couldn't help but notice that Ryan treated his father and Gina politely, but coolly. In fact, Jack wasn't greeted warmly by anyone except Maggie and Shane. Rachel watched as Jack stayed to the sidelines, obviously not wanting to insert himself into his sons' domain. Shane ran interference, frequently talking to his dad, trying to include him with his brothers. Trav and Ry remained distant and clearly uncomfortable. She couldn't blame them, but she also couldn't help but think about the size of Shane's heart that he could forgive the man who had abandoned them, and then work so hard to bridge the gap in his family. The ache in her chest intensified until she finally had to tear her eyes away from Shane.

A short while later, after eating lunch and peach pie with Shane's awesome vanilla ice cream, the men played a game of horseshoes while the women gathered under the patio umbrella to talk. Rachel's gaze kept drifting to the men boisterously cheering whenever someone got a ringer. Bryce was on Shane's shoulders, his fists buried in Shane's hair. The two looked relaxed and happy together. Shane appeared to be talking to him because he'd occasionally look up toward Bryce.

"Trav brought me flowers this morning," Daisy confided,

her eyes lighting up. "He said it was just because he loved me."

"Awww," the women chorused.

"Ryan never brings me flowers," Liz pouted.

"He brought you a puppy," Rachel pointed out.

"True." Liz smiled dreamily, looked over at Ryan, and sighed.

Maggie piped up. "One time Jorge got me goggles and a snorkel and hidden inside the snorkel was a little piece of paper that said, 'Good for one trip to the Florida keys.'"

"Awww," the women chorused.

"Jack got me this cross," Gina said, holding out her necklace.

The women admired the necklace with a tiny diamond chip at its center.

"One time a guy gave me a singing telegram," Zoe said. "And p.s. the guy who showed up was a terrible singer."

They laughed.

"A guy once got a tattoo with my initials," Amber said. "Of course, Al was also his name so maybe not such a compliment."

"He totally lied," Daisy said. "That was all for him."

"How about you, Rachel?" Maggie said. "Any sweet or crazy thing a man ever did for you?" She looked over at Shane meaningfully.

Shane had invested in her café, but they knew that. Besides, it hadn't been a romantic gesture, more like a business decision. At least that's what he'd said. Besides that, she'd only gotten flowers and candy a few times from random ex-boyfriends on Valentine's Day.

She shrugged. "I guess guys don't get super creative with me. Just flowers and candy a few times."

She looked away. Why should that bother her now? She was a practical person. She didn't need someone on bended knee handing her a puppy or tattooing themselves.

She felt Liz looking at her and glanced over. Liz's eyes were filled with sympathy.

"It's no big deal," Rachel said. "Next topic!"

Liz lowered her voice. "Shane made a big gesture by investing in your café. He didn't have to do that."

"That's business," Rachel said defensively. "He needed to diversify."

"Don't forget when he scared her stalker away," Maggie said.

Rachel snapped her head around. "He what?"

"He didn't tell you," Maggie murmured. "Oh, dear, the cat's out of the bag now."

"I always suspected Ryan did that," Liz said.

They all looked over to Shane, who now held a sound-asleep Bryce cradled in his arms.

Rachel got chills. Shane—sweet, sensitive Shane—scared that psycho Drew away?

"I thought it was the restraining order," Rachel said.

"You didn't think Shane had it in him, huh?" Maggie cackled. "He's sweet, but I told you he'd kick ass when he had to." She turned to the group. "I was there when Drew followed Rachel into Shane's shop. Rachel, you went into the ladies' room, and Drew just sat there watching the door. Shane sat right down at that table and told him he knew Drew had a record and if he ever showed his face in Clover Park, he'd hunt him down and make sure he did hard time. He told him his brother was a cop." Maggie nodded for emphasis. "I remember the hunt-him-down part because he sounded just like Al Pacino, all menacing and quiet-like."

Rachel's mind flew. She thought back to when Drew had finally gone away. It had been January, more than a year and a half ago. She and Shane hadn't even been close friends then. Had he had feelings for her for that long? Enough to step in and help her like that? She'd been terrified of Drew, who'd seemed so nice at first only to turn violent. He'd punched her in the jaw when she was late to meet him one night for drinks. She'd run back to her car and drove straight to Liz's apartment.

Drew had stalked her for two months, even after she told him she never wanted to see him again. He left long messages professing his love on her voicemail and slipped notes under her door that said, "I will never let you go." He showed up at the oddest times at her apartment, at work, and at Shane's shop, where she liked to get coffee. She'd filed a restraining order. She'd become paranoid and swore she saw him around every corner. It had turned her into an insomniac, every noise in the old building made her think he was breaking in to get at her again.

He was not a lightweight either. He was stocky and strong. Shane could've been hurt. Because of her.

"Shane was just…" Rachel trailed off. "He was helping out a friend."

She swallowed hard, her brain racing through the times she'd been with Shane since moving back to Clover Park two years ago. How friendly he'd been when she'd come into his shop, the extra hot fudge he always gave her when she had a bad day, the many times he'd come into her shop and bought big, expensive cookbooks, which she now realized he didn't need; he created his own recipes. He remembered exactly how she liked her coffee, her favorite ice-cream flavor, her favorite pizza toppings.

Maggie knocked on Rachel's head. "What, is this made of wood? Open your eyes, girl. Shane does not like confrontation. Never has. For him to go up against your nutso stalker means he cares about you. A lot."

Rachel's heart started pounding as the shock wore off and the hard truth sank in. It was the most romantic, selfless gesture anyone had ever done for her.

"It's no puppy," Liz teased. "But I think Maggie's right."

Rachel felt a little sick. Then suddenly Shane was there, right next to her, holding a sleeping Bryce in his arms. She blinked rapidly as Shane morphed from the familiar guy she knew with the sweet, dimpled smile to fucking heroic. Hero with a big, glowing capital H. And he was holding a baby in a perfect cradle, so naturally, like he actually knew how to hold a baby. Her heart did an uncomfortable flip-flop.

"I'll tuck him into his crib," Shane told Daisy.

"I'll take him, thanks," Daisy said. Shane transferred Bryce to her arms. "I guess all the excitement wore him out."

Daisy left, and all the women smiled and stared at Shane. Rachel couldn't take her eyes off him. Hero with a fucking capital H.

He looked from one face to another. "What's going on?"

Maggie smiled widely. "We're just appreciating your studliness."

Shane turned scarlet. "Uh, okay. On that note…" He went back to the yard with the men.

The women burst out laughing, all except Rachel, who stared after him in wonder. Had Shane really had feelings for her for the past two years? All this time while she'd been going out with losers and telling him all about her dating disasters, all that time he'd had feelings for her? What took him so long to say anything?

She thought back to the way she'd responded when he'd asked her if she ever thought about being more than friends. She'd shot him down. And she'd told him to forget their kitchen counter kiss ever happened while she replayed it frequently in her head. The memory of his kisses came back to her at odd times, in the shower, just before she went to sleep at night, when she unexpectedly saw Shane come into the room.

Her gaze traveled back to him where he was playing horseshoes. He missed. Trav's friend Rico said something to him, and Shane laughed good-naturedly.

She had to talk to him. Thank him. Tell him how much it meant to her that he scared away her stalker. Wow. Just wow. Shane was…amazing.

～

As the party wound down, Shane found Rachel and offered to walk her home.

"Yeah, let's go," she said.

They headed down the sidewalk. The sun was nearly set, but the air was still warm. A perfect end-of-summer night.

"Was it nice to see your dad?" Rachel asked.

"Yeah, it was good."

"Your brothers weren't too keen on him."

"It'll take time."

She smiled and looked up at him. Just kept looking.

"What?"

"I heard something at the party that surprised me," she said.

He instantly felt wary. Now what had Gran told her? The woman was determined to embarrass him. "What?"

She stopped walking and looked at him with a strange, almost dreamy expression. "Maggie said you're the one that got Drew to stop stalking me. I-I didn't know, but thank you. Thank you so much."

He shook his head. "I told Gran to forget she ever witnessed that."

"I think she just wanted me to know that someone had done something really great for me. I can't thank you enough. Drew terrified me."

He regarded her steadily. "You have bad taste in men."

"I do," she said. "But not anymore."

And then she kissed him. Right there on the sidewalk. It was a soft, tentative kiss, and he let her take the lead, knowing if he did, he wouldn't be able to stop.

She pulled back. "How many other good deeds have you done behind my back?"

He grinned. "You'll never know."

"Shane!" She shook her head. "Now I have to come up with something to even the score."

"No objections here." He took her hand, entwining his fingers in hers. They walked in silence for a few moments. "Are you all-in now, Rach?"

She didn't respond at first, and his heart stuttered.

"I'm getting there," she finally said. "I just—"

He cut her off before she could make some lame-ass excuse. "No guts, no glory."

"Yeah, yeah," she muttered.

"Make your move after the grand opening, or I'm going to pull out all my best moves, and you won't know what hit you," he teased.

She didn't laugh. Instead she sounded dead serious. "Okay."

"Okay? For which one?"

"Both."

He grinned. "Okay, then. It's a date. Tomorrow night, there will be a move one way or the other."

"Just shut up about it," she said, sounding pained.

He wrapped an arm around her and kissed the top of her head. "You got it."

17

The morning of the street fair, Shane and Rachel got up early to set up at the café. Shane supervised as their new employee, Tanya, and Rachel prepared the first batch of coffee, iced coffee, and iced tea.

"We've got it, boss," Tanya said. "I was making coffee in my sleep from all the practice we did over the last week."

"I had a night like that too," Rachel muttered.

Shane nodded. "Good."

That was the secret to his employee training. He had them perform the task over and over, tasting as they went so they knew exactly when something was done to perfection.

Rachel bounced up and down on the balls of her feet. Her ankle was completely healed now. "Shane, I'm so nervous! I can't believe we did it in six weeks! It's here! The big day!" She frowned. "What if no one comes in?"

"They will. We've got a primo location." The fair was on the street centered right in front of the café.

"Ahh!" she squealed; then she hugged Tanya and hugged him. He hugged her back, wishing he could stay and hold her like that. He settled for breathing her flowery scent.

"I've gotta set up at my shop," he said, releasing her. "Break a leg!"

He worked with his trusted ice-cream guys, Manny and

Sam, to load up and move the ice-cream cart he'd rented into the street. Barry and Gabe had set up several white tents for shade. Liz and Daisy were tying festive balloons in front of each shop along Main Street. Barry had his staff setting up the kiddie games as well as an inflatable slide and bounce house. He glanced at the banner hanging across Main Street with The Dancing Cow in big letters and gritted his teeth.

The fair was a smashing success. They'd never had so many people come to check it out. Barry had gotten the word out in a big way. Shane spent the day scooping ice cream and greeting kids with their faces painted like lions and bears. He spotted a few wacky glasses, so he knew the kids must have been up by Barry's shop too. He saw a steady stream of families heading into the café, and even some people headed to Book It, where Liz was running the register for the day.

It seemed the iced coffees were a huge hit. A lot of parents sipped those as they walked around, helping their kids with the fishing in the kiddie pool game, the bean bag toss, the lollipop pull, and the inflatables. The tricycle race around a small track at the end of the street was a huge hit too.

"Three vanillas, please, Mr. Softee," Trav said, grinning at him. Bryce reached out for him, and Shane gave him a baby high-five.

"Hey, Bryce," Shane said. "Tell your dad to live a little with some more exotic flavors."

"Da-da," Bryce said.

Daisy joined them with Gran and Jorge, who wore wacky glasses with Hawaiian leis. Great. Another convert to the Barry camp.

"Shane, your new café looks great," Daisy said.

"It's fabulous!" Gran exclaimed.

"Thanks," Shane said. "It seems to be doing well."

"Of course it is," Gran said. "Everyone knows your food is the most delicious around. Can I get some of that new coffee ice cream?"

"I'll take chocolate mocha," Jorge said.

"You got it." Shane scooped up the ice cream for his family and handed them out.

Trav handed him a twenty. Shane shook his head. "On the house. Go buy some picture books for Bryce with that money."

Trav stuck it in the tip jar. "Buy yourself something pretty."

Shane shook his head. A few minutes later, Rachel's parents stood in front of him.

Mr. Miller greeted him jovially. "How's business?"

"Good, thanks," he said. "How are you guys?"

"Just fine," Mr. Miller said.

Mrs. Miller beamed at Shane.

"What can I get you?" Shane asked.

"Rachel's over the moon you two have a café together," Mrs. Miller said.

Mr. Miller turned to his wife. "I never heard her say that."

Mrs. Miller ignored that. "Over the moon. How do you feel about celebrating Jewish holidays?"

"Rita!" Mr. Miller chided.

"Uh, I like celebrating Jewish holidays?" Shane said. "I never have before, but I'm sure it would be good."

"Good," Mrs. Miller said, beaming at him. "*Very* good."

"I'll have chocolate in a cup," Mr. Miller said.

"I'll take *strawberry*," Mrs. Miller said with a huge smile.

Shane had no idea what Mrs. Miller was getting at with the special emphasis on strawberry, but he served them up just the same.

"Don't be a stranger," Mrs. Miller said. "We'd love to have you over for Friday night dinner."

"Sure, thanks," Shane said. After Rachel's parents left, he smiled to himself. At least he knew her family wouldn't stand in his way.

A short while later, Ry stopped by. "Large coffee ice cream. How's it going?"

Shane scooped some in a bowl. "Good. Lots of people stopping in the café. I've already replenished the ice-cream cart twice."

Ry looked around the crowded street. "I can't believe this turnout. How did you get so many people here this year?"

Shane handed him the bowl. "I guess Barry's good at P.R. or something."

Ry looked at the huge banner hanging over the street. "I'll say. I'll let you get back to work. Don't forget to take a break and check out the café. Rachel and Tanya are running around crazy busy."

A jolt of alarm went through Shane. He wanted them busy, but not frantic, that's how mistakes were made.

"I'll check it out," he said. He called his shop to get Manny to relieve him. After Manny arrived and took over the line, Shane stepped into the air-conditioned café. The line was moving along.

Tanya was serving up drinks while Rachel rang up the orders. They were busy for sure, moving quickly. He stepped behind the counter. "Hey, you guys need a hand?"

Rachel glanced at him, her hair falling out of its braid. "Can you help out Tanya?"

"You got it." He moved next to Tanya. "I'll get the more complicated orders. You just keep barreling through the straightforward ones."

Tanya smiled. "Sure thing, boss."

Funny how he never told his employees to call him boss, they just did. He and Tanya quickly got into a groove and served up a steady stream of people, with a huge peak in the afternoon as parents tired in the afternoon sun. The iced café mochas were really popular. Shane figured they must have sold at least two hundred cups in the first day. A fantastic start.

The fair finally ended, and Shane went to close up his shop and help put away the ice-cream cart and various tents. Rachel and Tanya closed up the café and got it ready for the next morning.

He headed back to the café to check in. The place was clean. Tanya had already left.

"How'd we do?" he asked Rachel.

She locked the door behind him and turned over the sign to Closed. She whooped and raised her fist in the air. "*Per aspera ad astra!*"

He grinned and pointed at her. "Through difficulties to the stars."

She beamed. "Yes! We sold four hundred cups of coffee today!"

"Wow." That was more than he'd even thought. He'd have to replenish the inventory faster than he'd originally planned.

"The baked goods were a huge success," she went on. "And Book It sold tons of picture books too!"

He grinned. "Awesome! We should celebrate."

She lifted a finger. "I'm way ahead of you. Just a minute." She went to the back room and returned a minute later with two coffee mugs and a bottle of champagne.

"Champagne in a coffee mug? No, no, no. That's gonna mess with the flavor."

She rolled her eyes. "Come on. I've got wineglasses at my place."

He followed her through Book It and out the back door, holding the champagne while she locked up. He tried not to think too much about being alone with Rachel in her apartment. He'd been there plenty of times before. He was already rock hard in anticipation. This was it. All their work paid off. And now it was time to play. They'd agreed. One of them was making a move. He was done waiting.

They went inside, and she reached up to pull two wineglasses from the kitchen cabinet. He forced himself to keep his hands to himself even as her T-shirt rode up, revealing the arch of her lower back. He wanted to taste her right there and a lot of other places too.

She turned and met his eyes, sucking in a breath, no doubt at the raw hunger she saw there. He couldn't hide it anymore.

She handed him the champagne. "Could you pop the cork? I always seem to make a mess of it."

"I'd love to," he said gruffly.

She sighed and, seeming to catch herself at it, shook her head, and laughed. "Get on with it!"

He opened the champagne, and the cork went flying into the living room with a loud pop.

"Mazel tov!" Rachel exclaimed.

"Mazel tov," he said with a smile, loving seeing Rachel excited and happy again. The summer had started out rough for her, but now things were good.

"I'll save the cork," she said, running into the living room to fetch it.

He carried everything into the living room, poured two glasses, and set the bottle on the coffee table next to the cork. They sat on the sofa.

Rachel clinked her glass to his. "To success!"

He smiled. "To success."

They drank.

Rachel smiled at him brilliantly. He hadn't seen her in this good a mood in a very long time.

She clinked her glass to his again. "To good coffee!"

He toasted her again, and they drank. He paced himself, only taking a sip, wanting to be completely in the moment when the moment came.

"To books!" she toasted and drained her glass.

"To books." He toasted again and took a sip. He held up her empty glass. "Slow down there, partner, or you're cut off."

She pursed her lips. "You wouldn't! We're celebrating."

"Exactly, I want you to remember every moment of our celebration." He refilled her glass and handed it to her. She made a face at him. He lifted his glass in a toast. "To good food. And sip this time!"

They clinked glasses and drank. He sipped and watched her over the rim of his glass. She took another long swallow in complete defiance of his warning. He took her glass and held it out of her reach, saw the moment she turned for his, and took that one too. He stood before she could grab his arm.

He held the glasses over her head. "You're gonna end up with this all over you if you fight me for it."

"Shane! I'm fine. I'm just a little tipsy. This isn't easy for me, you know."

He lowered the glasses. "What's not easy for you?"

She gestured up and down his body. "You know."

Relief coupled with triumph surged through him. She was just nervous, and he knew talking would calm her down. He set the glasses down on the end table out of her reach, then turned and took her hand, pulling her back to the sofa with him. He rubbed his thumb slowly back and forth over her palm. "Tell me about your day."

She stared at his hand holding hers and finally met his eyes. He waited. She began to talk, slowly relaxing and falling into the easy conversation they'd always shared as she told him about all the parents who'd come in first for morning coffee, then a second time in the afternoon for iced coffee and pastries. The crazy time she'd had keeping up with orders with Tanya. How Liz had sold so many picture books she knew were worthwhile children's literature from her experience as an elementary school teacher.

He gave her back the champagne, and she sipped. He did too as he told her about the street fair and the craziness that had ensued when Barry had joined the tricycle race and nearly run over the tent where they'd set up a kiddie pool to fish for plastic fish. They laughed.

His eyes locked on hers, and he raised his glass for another toast. "To friends."

"To friends," she said in a voice charged with so much more. He met her chocolate brown eyes, and he knew. Just knew.

She took a long drink, and this time he let her, knowing it was for courage. He set his drink down.

"To lovers," she said softly, setting her glass down.

He wanted to pull her into his arms right then, but he had to be sure it wasn't just the champagne talking. He wanted her to remember their first time. "Rach, are you drunk?"

She looped her hands around his neck and spoke so closely her lips brushed against his. "I'm only a little tipsy," she said, smiling against his mouth.

"Me too." He cradled her face with both hands and kissed her then, softly, gently. But that didn't last long because she threw herself on top of him, knocking him off balance. He fell back on the sofa and wrapped his arms around her. She stretched out on top of him, all of her soft curves hitting him in all the right places.

"Hello, lover," she said before kissing him hard.

Years of pent-up longing unfurled within him, and he quickly took over the kiss, his hand fisting in her hair, his tongue sweeping into her mouth, tasting champagne and a hint of espresso. He pulled the band from her hair, letting her braid free and running his fingers through the soft waves. They kissed for a long time, and Shane fought to keep things slow. With one hand on the back of her head, keeping her mouth fused to his, his other hand slipped under her T-shirt, freeing her bra.

She sat up and pulled off her shirt and the bra. She was so beautiful. Her breasts were even better than he'd imagined, full and lush. Her nipples perked up, and he had to taste. He leaned forward, suckling the pebbled peak of one breast. She moaned and arched her back, offering herself fully to him. He took his time, kissing, sucking, tasting. Luxuriating in the taste of her, a sweet honey lavender that made him greedy for more. He gave the same attention to the other breast and returned to her luscious lips. She was pulling at his shirt. He took the shirt off and pulled her close, the sensation of her soft skin on his was electric. She tugged at his shorts, trying to get them off.

He stood and pulled her up with him. Without a word, he scooped her up and carried her into the bedroom.

18

Rachel giggled as Shane carried her into the bedroom, giddy from the champagne and their smashing success with the café and this whole princess routine. He laid her gently on the bed. She wrapped her arms around his neck and kissed him again. He pulled back and gazed into her eyes.

"We're wearing too many clothes," she said. She stripped down, flinging her shorts and panties to the side.

"God, Rach, I can't wait to taste every inch of you."

Then he proceeded to do just that, nibbling, sucking, and tasting his way down her body, drawing soft moans from her as he made his way down, stopping to linger at a few places, the hollow of her throat, her breasts, he lingered a long time there, to her navel, dipping in to taste, then further down, just skimming past where she was already hot and wet and ready for him, to her inner thigh, down her legs, all the way to her toes.

Her hips rocked restlessly. "Shane, please, I—"

He flipped her over unexpectedly, and her breath left her in a whoosh.

"Shane?" she asked unsteadily.

"Every inch," he said, kissing and tasting his way up her ankles, her calves, the oh-so-sensitive backs of her knees. Who knew knees were sensitive? He kept going, placing a kiss and then a nip on her bottom that had her jolting. He soothed the spot with his hand, worked up the small of her back, lingering in the dip there, then up her spine. Her body tingled all over by the time he moved her hair to the side and nuzzled the back of her neck.

He rolled her over and smoothed her hair back from her face. "You taste delicious."

Her entire body was overheated and in need of the relief only he could give her. "You're still wearing too many clothes."

He stood and stripped off his shorts and briefs, and she took a moment to stare. She'd wanted to know what he looked like after feeling his size, and holy mother of amazeballs, she was speechless.

"We okay?" he asked.

She dragged her gaze back to his face. He was the picture of male cockiness. *Ha!* she thought deliriously. *Cockiness.*

She nodded slowly and couldn't help but take a second look. She swallowed. "Very okay."

He lowered himself over her and kissed her again. "I'll be gentle," he whispered in her ear.

"I'm not afraid of you," she said, wrapping her arms around him. They kissed until she truly did relax and became restless, needing him, wanting him inside her. She ran her hands up and down his back, urging him closer. He broke the kiss only to nuzzle the side of her neck again.

"Shane, please," she begged.

"I'm not done tasting," he told her, lowering himself down her body. He stopped at her breasts, teasing and suckling as she arched up, her hands tangling in his hair. When he'd taken his fill, he worked his way down her body with hot, open-mouthed kisses that had her quivering until his lips closed over her center. Her hips vaulted off the mattress. He took advantage of that, sliding his hands under her bottom. He gentled her with soft kisses until she relaxed again.

He lifted his head. "You taste like honey, and I want every last drop."

She shuddered, and he proceeded to claim her with his

mouth. He drove her crazy—sucking hard and alternating with a gentle mouthing.

"Please, please," she murmured. So close, she was so close.

He switched to the softest, gentlest tasting, and her body tightened with need, like a violin strung too tight. She fisted her hands in his hair, begging him silently to give her that release. He suckled her hard nub, and she broke in a sudden rush. He lapped at her, extracting every ounce of pleasure he could. Every last drop.

He rose up over her. His hand cupped her sex, and she cried out, still screamingly sensitive.

"Condom?" he asked.

"Medicine cabinet," she croaked.

He released her, and she sank into the mattress, feeling lost in a hazy, sensuous cloud. Then he was back, his body heating hers, and she wrapped her arms around him. He kissed her, thrusting his tongue in her mouth as he slowly pushed into her body. She arched, working to accommodate his size, wrapping her legs around him. He reached under her, angling her just right and sliding home. She'd never been filled so much in her life. He didn't move for a moment, and she felt him throb within her.

His lips brushed hers. "I've waited so long for this."

"I know."

He gazed into her eyes. "You're so beautiful."

She blinked. No one had ever called her beautiful. Pretty, cute, maybe, but never beautiful. "Thank you."

Then he was kissing her, so gently, so tenderly, she found herself unexpectedly choked with emotion. It was too much. She bit his bottom lip, and he surged within her. They found their rhythm and moved together urgently, their bodies long craving this union. She closed her eyes as she felt the sweet tension building again. His lips pressed to the side of her neck as he thrust harder and faster, and Rachel cried out as her body convulsed with her climax. She heard him rumble something that sounded like praise; then he grabbed her hips and drove into her, seeking his own release. He suddenly arched, letting out a guttural groan, and another orgasm shockingly ripped through her. She'd never been multi-orgasmic.

Holy Shane.

She woke the next morning on her stomach, naked. She rolled to her back, feeling lazy and relaxed. It was by far the best sex she'd ever had. She could hear Shane banging around in the kitchen. *I slept with Shane.* An uneasy feeling washed over her, nearly spoiling what should've been a very happy morning after. Now what? Shane was still her partner, friend, and now lover? The beginnings of panic invaded her brain. How many roles could he play before completely taking over her life?

She freshened up in the bathroom, tied a light cotton robe on, and slowly walked into the kitchen. She had to face him sooner or later.

"Mornin', sunshine," Shane said. He was barefoot in his Shane's Scoops T-shirt and basketball shorts from yesterday. He looked right at home in her kitchen. "Thought I'd let you sleep in a bit." He poured an egg mixture into a frying pan. "I'm making omelets."

She squinted at him, trying to reconcile the man she knew as friend with her lover from last night. Feeling raw and uncomfortable, she mumbled, "Thanks."

"I found an extra toothbrush in your bathroom. Hope that was okay. Coffee's ready. Unless you want to brew a cup downstairs." He meant at the café.

"This is fine." She sat at the table with her coffee. Her past history with men told her one thing for sure, she was great at letting them take over, not seeing red flags until well past the time when she should've gotten out. She couldn't let that happen with Shane. She had to stay true to herself.

A short while later, Shane set an omelet in front of her and sat at the table with his.

She stared at it. "I don't like omelets."

"Oh." He gave her a strange look. "Why didn't you say so

when I started cooking? I could've made you something else."

"I don't know." She stood and grabbed her usual granola bar. She held it up. "I like cardboard for breakfast."

He snorted. "Suit yourself."

They ate in silence, Rachel lost in her panicky thoughts. Her entire life was tied up with Shane's. This had been a mistake. Too much champagne, too much celebrating.

"Shane, I…"

He set his fork down and held her hand warmly in his. "Yes?"

"Last night was…" She groped for the right words. She didn't want to hurt his feelings. "Maybe we had too much champagne."

"You said you were only tipsy."

"I was."

"Do you remember it? Do you remember how I touched you?" His hand slipped to the back of her head, tugging her closer. She wanted to pull away, but some part of her wanted the reminder. He nipped her bottom lip, then kissed her gently. His lips barely grazed her bottom lip, another gentle graze over her top lip, and her mouth parted on a sigh. His mouth closed over hers in a slow, deep kiss, and she forgot all her qualms and surrendered to the sensation.

He pulled back, and she blinked.

He smiled. "You do remember."

"Yes," she said softly.

"Last night was special."

She shifted away from him.

He hooked a finger under her chin and turned her back. "Don't tell me you want to pretend *that* never happened."

She wished she could. She didn't think she could ever forget it. She twisted her granola bar wrapper. Everything was ruined. Every time she saw him she would be thinking of their night together. She wished they could always be friends. This would end like all of her relationships with a spectacular blowup, probably because of something she couldn't stop harping on, something she had to fix. All the guys had some one thing that she just knew if she could fix it, they'd be better off. She felt slightly nauseous. Shane didn't need to be fixed, and she had no idea what to do with him. She was in over her head, and she knew it.

At her silence, his jaw tightened. "Dammit, Rachel, do *not* tell me you want to pretend we're still just friends. Not after last night."

"I wish..." She stopped herself. She knew they couldn't go back, but she wasn't sure she wanted to go forward. Damn, this was awkward. "I need to take a shower and get to work. You can finish your omelet and, um, let yourself out. I'm sure you have to get to work too."

She felt his eyes on her as she rose from the table and left the room. She let out a breath of relief as she turned on the water for the shower and waited for it to warm up. She'd been afraid he would follow her and demand they talk this out. She didn't have the words to express the turmoil she was feeling. She remembered Kerri, Shane's girlfriend in high school, said they could never have a good fight. Shane always wanted to talk the thing to death. Rachel didn't want to hash this thing out. She felt raw and vulnerable and exceedingly foolish to boot. The one thing she said she wouldn't do, screw up their friendship, mess with their business relationship, accomplished in one fell swoop thanks to a celebratory night with champagne.

She grabbed a towel and washcloth from the small linen closet, tested the water, and dropped the robe. She stepped into the hot water and felt her whole body relax. Hopefully Shane would be gone by the time she got out. She lathered shampoo into her hair. Liz was going back to work today, so Rachel was needed at Book It, and she should probably peek in at—

"Ahhh!!!!" She let out a blood-curdling scream as the shower curtain was ripped aside. Shane's hand covered her mouth as he stepped into the shower naked with her.

Without her glasses, she could only see things that were very close, and Shane was very, very close. He looked serious, a man on a mission, and her heart galloped madly from the shock of his sudden appearance and from what she knew he could do to her with one touch. He said nothing, merely dropped his hand from her mouth and took over for her with the shampoo. His fingers felt wonderful as they massaged her scalp and stroked down her long hair. He finished the shampoo and tipped her head back for the rinse. Then he grabbed the washcloth and soaped it up.

"Shane, no," she said, her voice not entirely steady. "I can do that."

"This is what friends do," he said silkily. "They help each other."

"Not in the…" Her voice trailed off as he bathed her gently, down her neck, across her shoulders, paying special attention to her breasts, circling around them, spiraling in slowly. Her nipples tightened, and she moaned as the cloth rubbed back and forth across them. She gripped his shoulders, wanting him closer. Instead the washcloth trailed down, soaping her stomach, making a sharp turn to her hips. He knelt down to wash her legs, taking a trip back up her inner thigh. She braced herself for the rough cloth on her sensitive center; instead he was gentle, achingly gentle, then he dropped the cloth and replaced it with his mouth.

Her knees gave out, and he held her up, his hands on her bottom, holding her in place, using his tongue and lips and teeth to bring every nerve ending to life. She closed her eyes as the hot water ran over them, already on the brink.

He stopped and looked up at her. "Open your eyes, Rach. Look at what your friend is doing to you."

She shook her head and kept her eyes shut.

His lips grazed over her sensitive nub, and she jerked, her nerve endings raw. "No more unless you look."

She forced her eyes open. He smiled and returned to kissing her intimately. His red hair in stark contrast to her dark curls, his muscular arms holding her up. He sucked hard, and she saw stars, crying out his name. He kept going, wringing every last drop from her until she had absolutely nothing left.

He rose and kissed her then, and she clung limp and sated

to his warm body. He picked her up, set her outside the tub, and wrapped her in a towel.

"Stay right there," he said. "Wait for me."

She nodded and heard him whistling as he washed up in the shower. She stood in her towel, the small medicine cabinet mirror completely fogged up. She wiped the mirror off and put her glasses back on. Her hair hung in a wet, tangled clump. Her lips were rosy, cheeks flushed, eyes shining. To distract herself from why she was actually waiting in a towel, she took out a comb and eased the tangles out of her hair. Once finished, she leaned over the sink to wring the extra water from her hair.

The water in the shower shut off.

"Don't move," Shane ordered.

She froze, bent over the sink. "Uh, Shane?"

The towel was ripped from her body. She bolted upright and turned. Her eyes trailed down of their own accord. Her cry of protest died in her throat.

He dried himself with another towel. "I told you not to move."

He turned her and pushed her back in place, bent over the sink. She shivered at the vulnerability of the position, but still she waited.

He opened the medicine cabinet above her head and pulled out a condom. She heard the rustle of the wrapper and waited to feel the first hard thrust. Instead he banded his arm around her waist and pulled her upright.

"I've got a better idea," he said.

He lifted her, carrying her out of the bathroom and into the bedroom.

"Shane! You don't have to carry me everywhere. My ankle's fine."

"You like it."

She shut her mouth because she did. He knew her well, too well. She'd let him in, seeing her for who she was as a close friend, and now he was using it to his advantage in this new intimate territory. She'd never felt so vulnerable and yet so turned on. He set her down in front of the dresser with the full mirror mounted above it.

"Spread 'em," he said as he pushed her not ungently down over the dresser. And God help her, she did. He entered her slowly, letting her body adjust to him, and her breath caught at the sight of them in the mirror, the contrast in their coloring, he a shade lighter than her, his red hair to her dark brown, the flushed, breathless look on her face, the fierce expression on his.

His hands entwined with hers, pinning them down. He met her gaze in the mirror. "Would your friend do this?" he asked with a hard thrust.

"N-no," she gasped.

He kept going, pounding into her from behind. Despite the roughness of what felt more than anything like a claiming, she felt an intense spiraling building in her again. His hands released hers only to slip knowing fingers through her slick folds. She bucked backward at the touch, still raw from his earlier ministrations, and he slipped deeper inside. She gasped. His fingers became more demanding, increasing the pressure with every hard thrust. She whimpered incoherently, closing her eyes over the intensity.

He gave her a little shake. "Watch," he ground out.

She watched as he both took and gave to her. The climax hit her suddenly, shocking in its intensity, and she screamed.

He murmured sweet praise; then he pumped fast and hard. His teeth clamped on the side of her neck, and she panted, feeling positively animal as he held her in place for these last shuddering thrusts. He groaned, stilled, and they stayed like that for a minute, he covering her. His lips rested in a gentle kiss on the spot where his teeth had been.

He rose and carried her back to the bed, settling on his side next to her. He stroked her hair, her cheek, down her side, his hand coming to rest on her hip.

"We are not just friends," he told her. His blue eyes watched her intently, probably waiting for her to argue.

She couldn't.

She simply gazed at him in wonder, dazed by the contradictions in the man at once gentle and yet so...not forceful, she'd never felt like he'd used his superior strength against her, more like in charge. She flushed again, remembering.

He gave her a knowing smile, seeming pleased with her dazed state, and kissed her again, gently, lingeringly. Then he got up, got dressed, and left.

She spread her arms out on the bed and let out a deep, supremely satisfied breath. Her mind for once not racing from one thing to another on her long list of things to do. Wow. Just fucking wow.

19

Rachel opened Book It a little late that day, not even caring that it was late. It was a Tuesday, the first day of school, and she didn't anticipate many customers until the weekend. Luckily, Tanya had come through, opening Something's Brewing Café right on time.

She stopped by the café to get herself a latte and check in with Tanya. "How'd we do this morning?"

Tanya smiled. "Good. Not as good as four hundred cups sold, but we had a nice morning rush. Word got out, I guess."

"How much did we bring in?" Rachel asked.

"I don't know."

Rachel moved to the register to check for herself. She smiled. "Good. We're doing good."

"Shane's new delivery boy is cute," Tanya said.

At the mention of Shane, Rachel ran hot all over. Geez, he wasn't even here. Just the mention of his name had her near orgasm. She needed to calm herself.

"Oh, yeah?" she said casually. "He mentioned he hired someone to do the morning baking."

"His name's Ron," Tanya said. "I like that name. It's strong. He delivered it himself too."

"Cool." Rachel bought herself a maple blueberry scone. "I'll be next door. Let me know when you go on break."

"Will do."

She sat on the cushioned stool behind the counter, a little sore from last night and this morning's activities. The reminder sent another hot flash through her. She took a bite of the scone. It was effing delicious. Damn, Shane was talented. She had to stop thinking of him. Just because the man knew his way around a woman's erogenous zones didn't mean he got to take up so much headspace.

She got her laptop and worked on some accounting from yesterday's revenue from the bookstore and the café. She smiled. It was really gratifying to see Book It turn a profit like that. Too bad Janelle hadn't stuck around to see that happen. She missed her friend, but she knew she could only blame herself. She shouldn't have used Janelle to keep Shane at a distance.

Stop thinking about Shane!

She was turning into one of those pathetic, lovesick fools. Next thing you knew, she'd be picking out monogrammed towels and doodling their initials in hearts. She headed to the back storeroom. Keeping busy was key. She went through the shelves and made sure everything was organized and all inventory accounted for. An hour passed pleasantly with nary a thought of Shane. She breathed some relief. Okay, so they weren't just friends.

Shane's voice came back to her, *Would your friend do this?* She went damp at the memory. He'd driven his point home. Big time.

She needed fresh air.

The buzzer rang on the back door, and she saw red hair through the window. Her heart started pounding. She took a deep breath and opened the door.

"Delivery," a new delivery guy said. Not Shane.

Disappointment washed through her.

"Right over here, thanks," Rachel said, directing the delivery of six boxes of books.

By the end of the day, Rachel had worked up to a pretty good freak-out. She was feeling too much too fast for Shane, and it was scaring the crap out of her. She texted Liz to stop by after work. The Clover Park Elementary School was only a couple of blocks away from her store.

Thankfully, Liz showed up right on time before Rachel had a chance to call Shane and beg him to remind her how they weren't just friends.

"Hey, Rach!" Liz called as she breezed in. She carried a large purse and a second large bag full of papers.

"Hey. How was the first day of school?"

"Great! I love meeting the new crop of kids. This promises to be a great class."

"Awesome."

Liz wagged her finger at her. "Tell me. You look wound up as tight as I used to be."

Rachel tugged her friend to the small back office and sat down at her desk.

Liz perched on the edge of the desk. "So-oo?"

Rachel grimaced. "I slept with Shane."

Liz clapped. "Yay!"

Rachel scowled. "What are you so happy about?"

"I love you both, and I was hoping you'd get together. Everybody was."

Rachel's stomach did a few flips. "Everybody?"

"Well, you know. His family. And friends. We all knew he liked you."

She crossed her arms and hugged herself. "I, uh, don't know what to do now."

"What do you mean?"

"I mean, like, what now? He's my..." Shane's voice came back to her. *Would your friend do this?* She got another flutter low in her belly. "He's my business partner."

Liz waved that away. "And you work well together. So how was it?" She giggled. "No, don't tell me. He's my brother-in-law. I can't even think about him that way. Just tell me, did he blush when you got naked?"

Rachel flushed. Shane had been the furthest thing from blushing, much more sensual than she'd ever imagined. His obsession with good food, always rhapsodizing about the fragrant scents and flavors, should've given her a clue, in retrospect. She got another hot flash just thinking about the way he'd insisted on tasting every inch of her.

"He's fucking amazing," Rachel admitted.

Liz laughed. "Omigod, I'm so happy for you."

"So what do I do? Should I try to go back to strictly business? You know how important it is that we make the café work."

Liz smiled. "The café's already working. Just have fun, Rach. You're way overthinking this."

Rachel exhaled sharply. "I guess."

Liz beamed. "Wouldn't it be so cool if you were my sister-in-law?"

Rachel broke out in a cold sweat. "Liz!"

"Sorry. Forget I said that."

They chatted a few more minutes, and then Liz left to take Hagar for a walk. Problem was, Rachel couldn't help overthinking it. She'd never been so terrified it wouldn't work out. She didn't like Shane having that kind of power over her. Better to end things sooner before they both got in too deep. Someone would get hurt. Like her.

Shane stopped by the café before closing to check on everything. He hoped Rachel wasn't running scared after their night together. Last night and this morning had been everything he'd imagined and more. He'd thought of little else today, and giving her space had been just about the most difficult thing he'd ever done. But he knew her and knew she needed time to get used to this new side of their relationship.

"Hey, boss," Tanya called. "Can I get you something?"

His eyes went to the display case, where he took a quick inventory of what sold and what didn't. "I'm good, thanks. Busy today?"

"This morning we were."

He walked behind the counter and checked the two coffee machines, the espresso machine, the grinders, and the carafes. He poured himself a cup of light roast from a carafe and tasted a slight bitterness. "How long has this been sitting here?"

"Since noon?"

"After thirty minutes, you have to dump it and make a fresh pot. The coffee has to be freshly ground and freshly brewed, otherwise they might as well buy coffee at the gas station."

"Sorry." Tanya dumped it in the sink.

"It's okay. Just for the future." Shane wandered to the back and scanned the shelves of the storeroom. Looked okay. He checked the restroom. Paper towels were crumpled on the floor. Not good. He threw the paper towels in the trash can and washed his hands, making a mental note to hire a cleaning service for a nightly cleanup. They couldn't have any health code violations. It was the kiss of death for a food business.

He headed over to Book It. Rachel sat at the register, twirling the end of her braid while she read a thick book. He got closer. *Crime and Punishment*. Feeling guilty?

"Hey, Rach."

She startled. "Make some noise when you come in. Geez, you're like a cat."

"I know." He went behind the counter and kissed the tender spot below her ear, noticing the slight red mark on her neck from his love bite that morning. He liked that he'd marked her. She was his. He stroked a hand up and down her back.

She shook him off. "Don't do that here. It's weird. Main Street has a front-row view of my entire store."

He ignored her protest, turning her on the stool so her back was to Main Street and pulling her into his arms. He kissed her with all the pent-up passion he'd felt every time he thought of her today. Her book slipped from her hand and hit the floor with a loud *thwack*. He kissed her until she wrapped her arms around his neck and leaned into him, pliant and willing. He pulled back to look into her eyes.

She placed her fingers over her lips and stared at him wide-eyed. It was a good look for her. Shock and awe. Not to mention what it did for him. He wanted her again, and her apartment was right above the shop.

"Upstairs?" he asked.

She dropped her hand and scowled. "No, we're not going upstairs! I have to close out the register and make sure the café is ready for tomorrow. Tanya has to leave a little early today."

"I'll help you."

She gave him a squinty-eyed look that meant she was getting mad. This whole seduction thing wasn't going like he'd hoped.

"I thought we agreed," she said sharply, "you supply the food and drink, I run the café."

He raised his palms. "I just offered to help. It's my shop too."

"Ooh! I knew you were going to throw that in my face." She stomped off to the café.

He followed close behind. "I'm not throwing anything in your face."

"You can go, Tanya," Rachel said. "I've got it from here."

Tanya grabbed her purse. "Okay, I'll see you guys tomorrow."

Tanya left, and Rachel started checking the supplies under the counter.

Shane followed her. "I'm just saying I have a vested interest in the place, so I want to help out. And by the way, I'm calling a cleaning service to make sure the bathroom is cleaned every night. We don't want any health code violations."

She stood and headed to the storage room. "That's too expensive. I'll do it."

"You'll clean the bathroom every night?"

"Yeah, I do that at Book It." She grabbed a box of stirrers.

"Rach, I don't want you to have to do that. I'll get a service."

She whirled and pinned him with a flinty-eyed stare. "Last time I checked, I run the place. It's in the contract you signed. Therefore, I clean it if I want to."

It was classic Rachel. They'd gotten too close, and now she was all prickly defense.

He stepped closer. "You seem tense."

She backed up. "I'm not tense."

He took the box from her hands and set it on the shelf. "You were very relaxed last time I saw you, but now…" He ran a finger down her cheek, tipping her chin up, right where he wanted her. He ducked his head, easing in for a kiss.

She turned her head away. "Shane, I can't do this."

He kissed her jaw instead, kissing his way up to her ear. She pushed at him, and he stopped, biting back a breath of frustration.

Her eyes flashed. "Just because we…*you know* doesn't mean I'm going to marry you!"

Whoa. That had come out of nowhere. She was thinking about marriage? After one night? He must have made a mighty fine impression.

He bit back a smile. "I don't recall proposing."

She waved a hand in the air. "No, you didn't. Forget I said that. The point is…"

Her voice trailed off as he slid the band off her braid and unwound her hair. He slid his fingers through the silky strands. She shivered, and he took that as a good sign. He kissed the column of her throat, tasting as he went. Loving her taste and flowery scent. She let out a soft moan.

He pulled back and took her hand. "Let's go. We can come back to clean up."

She shook her head. "I've got to get things ready for the morning. You-you should go. Okay? Just go. Please. I can't work with you and-and…" She waved her hands. "Just go."

"Rach," he said gently. "Don't push me away. We're just beginning. Like starting a new chapter." He felt good he'd thought up a book metaphor, something she'd appreciate.

Her eyes were wide and panicky. "Then what? More chapters, the end?"

"Why are you thinking about the end when we're just beginning?"

"I'm not going to—" she gestured wildly "—talk this all out with you. Just *please* go."

She turned from him, grabbed the box of stirrers, and went behind the counter. She was spooked. And he knew the guys who clung to her were the first to get cut loose.

He went behind the counter opposite her, giving her some space. He focused on the prep area. A shiny aluminum canister caught his eye. He snagged it, finger on the trigger. He waited for her to stand.

"Rach?"

She turned. "What?"

He squirted her with whipped cream, aiming for her hair so he could wash it again.

"Ahh!" she hollered. She grabbed a shaker and threw cinnamon in his face.

He clapped one hand over his eyes while his other hand groped along the counter. "My eyes!"

She rushed forward, wiping his face with her fingers. "Omigod, Shane, I'm so sorry! I should've aimed lower."

"Like this?" He pulled her T-shirt forward and poured chocolate syrup exactly where he wanted to lap it up.

She gasped and staggered back. "My shirt!"

"I'll buy you a new one." He carefully peeled the formerly white T-shirt off her and dropped it on the floor. Then he slicked the whipped cream off the top of her head and dropped it on her shirt even though she looked cute like that —chocolate in front, whipped cream on top—his own personal sundae. "I'm going to lick you clean."

When she made no immediate protest, only stood there staring at him, he tugged her down to sit on the floor out of sight of the front windows and proceeded to do just that. He licked her chin where some had caught as the shirt lifted, then to her collarbone as he slid the straps of her bra down and unhooked the front clasp. He licked her cleavage clean, and she moved restlessly until he moved to her breasts, budding for him. She arched her back, offering herself to him, and he suckled the delicate morsel greedily. By the time he finished with the other breast, they were both panting. He wiped his mouth with his fingers to catch any stray chocolate. Rachel took his hand and sucked his fingers into her mouth, her tongue flicking over the tips. He groaned. He had to have her, like now.

"Rach," he said by way of warning.

"Give me your shirt."

He yanked off his T-shirt and handed it to her. She put it on, took his hand, and led him through Book It and up to her apartment.

He might not have her heart—not like she had his—but he'd work with what she willingly gave.

20

"I am such a slut," Rachel told Liz. She called her friend the minute Shane left to clean up the café. Most men would've conked out after sex. He let her rest and insisted on cleaning up since he was the one that made the most mess. What was she supposed to do with a man like that?

"You are not a slut," Liz said. Then she called, further off, "It's Rachel."

Rachel gritted her teeth. "Could you not tell Ryan every single thing?"

This was exactly why she'd turned to Shane as a confidant. Sweet, nonjudgmental, slut-inducing Shane.

"I'm not telling him every single thing," Liz said. "He just wanted to know who it was."

He wanted to know who was the slut. Ryan was no dummy. He'd put two and two together and have her and Shane paired off right away.

"Could you go somewhere a little more private to talk?" Rachel asked. "You're the only one I can talk to about this. And you have to swear you won't tell Ryan."

"Okay, I swear. Hold on." She heard a rustle, and then Liz was back. "Okay, I'm upstairs. Now why do you think you're a slut?"

"I told myself I wouldn't sleep with Shane anymore, and

one drop of chocolate and I'm riding him like a deranged rodeo star."

Liz giggled. "Did he bring you candy? That's so sweet. You know, Ryan got me Godiva chocolate truffles for my birthday even before we officially got together. It was so thoughtful."

Rachel rolled her eyes. *Yes, Ryan is dreamy, move on.* "No, he didn't...never mind. All I'm saying is he seems to have some kind of hold over me, and I just, I don't know, cave or something."

"You said he was *amazing* in bed." Another giggle. Obviously her friend couldn't picture it. Hell, Rachel wouldn't have guessed it either.

"I know!" Rachel cried. "I cave, and I like it!"

Liz giggled again. "I don't see the problem here, egg."

"Stop calling me egg! I don't call you chicken anymore!"

"Okay, sorry. I meant it affectionately."

There was a problem. It was too much, too fast, and she needed him to back the hell off, but he wouldn't. He couldn't. They worked together. They lived across the street from each other. This was why she didn't want to get involved in the first place.

"I screwed this up so bad, Liz. He's such a big part of my life with work and living so close." Her voice dropped to a pained whisper. "When this goes south, and you know it will, I'll have to close shop and leave town to get over it."

"Maybe you won't have to get over him. Maybe Shane is *the one* for you. Don't you remember when you told me to give Ryan a fair chance? When I was running scared, afraid to get my heart trampled on?"

Rachel went quiet. She remembered. But that was different. Liz had been into Ryan for as long as she could remember, Rachel had just given her the push she needed to go after what she wanted.

"This is different," Rachel insisted.

"You're scared, and I understand that, but now I'm telling you what you so wisely told me. Give Shane a fair chance."

Rachel murmured noncommittally. "I'm beat. I'd better go."

"Okay, call me anytime. Bye."

"Bye." Rachel hung up and went to bed, her hair still damp from Shane's gentle shampooing. She buried her face in the pillow and groaned.

∾

The next morning Rachel woke early after a long, good night's sleep and decided to help Tanya open the café. By eight a.m. there was a line out the door. Rachel was thrilled. She chatted up each customer and on the spot decided they would hand out reward cards—buy ten coffees, get one free. She wanted to keep people coming back. She told each person about the reward program and promised to bring the new reward cards soon. If they kept getting more people every morning, they might even need to hire another barista.

Things finally slowed down an hour later.

"Woo," Rachel said. "I'm glad I came down early to help you out."

"That was insane," Tanya said.

"If that keeps up, I'll have to hire another you. Know anyone looking for a barista job?"

"I'll keep my ears open."

"I'm heading next door. Call if you need backup."

"Will do."

Rachel headed to Book It with her latte, feeling really good about her new venture. At this rate, she'd be able to keep Book It and pay Shane back even earlier than they'd agreed. She really wanted to be a full partner, not just in name only with a huge loan hanging over her head. Not that Shane had ever once complained about the money, but she didn't like the imbalance in their relationship. Their business relationship. She wouldn't call a couple nights together a relationship. More like a long overdue...hookup. Yes, a casual hookup.

She opened her shop and helped a few customers. Some retired people came in, browsed, and bought nothing. A few young moms came in, looking for children's books. Rachel helped them and told them about the kiddie corner at the café. They headed over there, and she sent a silent thanks to Shane for thinking of it. There was a lull at noon, so she closed the shop for an hour and went to the small office supply shop in town to put in an order for some reward cards. They told her the cards would be ready by the end of the day. She made one more stop at a hobby shop in Eastman and bought a rubber stamp with a coffee mug on it to mark the cards.

The rest of the afternoon passed quickly as she dove back into *Crime and Punishment*, the man was so guilty from what he'd done. Rachel could relate. She felt guilty for breaking her promise to herself to keep things strictly business with her and Shane. Maybe Dostoyevsky would have some answers by the end of the story. She'd read it once in college, but the details were fuzzy in her mind. She greeted a few people who wandered over from the café to her store. Maybe she'd add a bargain-book section near the entryway to draw more people over. She got a small wheeled cart from her supply room and made an arrangement from a variety of genres meant to entice.

At the end of the day she closed her register and went to relieve Tanya from her long day. Tanya was already cleaning up the prep area.

Tanya handed her a slip of paper. "Shane left a note for you."

Shane must have stopped by when Rachel was out running errands.

Rach,

I noticed a line out the door this morning. You need to either open earlier or get another barista to move things along. We don't want to turn people away. Cleaning service starts tonight at seven. I gave them a key to get in, so make sure you've locked the register, though I'm sure it's fine, they've been cleaning my shop since the beginning.

Got a family thing tonight. See you tomorrow.
Shane

She read the note a second time, her irritation growing. He acted like he was the boss. They were *partners*. Maybe he did think he was the boss since he put up the money. She knew they might need another barista, but she wasn't going to rush into hiring someone only to have to let them go when business didn't keep up. Fine, she'd open earlier. That meant she'd have to do it, she already had Tanya putting in eight hours a day. And how dare he hire that cleaning service! She said she'd take care of it. And he copied the key and gave it out? How many keys would the cleaning service make? Anyone could get in here now! Was this how he ran his shop? Well, it wasn't how *she* ran a business.

She crumpled the note. She couldn't wait to pay him back her share. In fact, she'd love to buy him out entirely and take complete control. She'd wanted it to be her business from the beginning. She knew she couldn't have gotten it off the ground without him, but now she wanted it back. She couldn't take this micromanaging. She'd had enough of that from her demon boss. It was why she owned her own business. She answered to no one but herself. She threw the note in the garbage; then she called the cleaning service, asked for the key back, and cancelled the job.

She poured her aggravation into cleaning the café. Then she restocked everything for the morning and headed out to the supply shop to pick up her reward cards. She knew how to run a business very well, thank you very much.

The next morning Rachel was gratified to see another line out the door of the café. She changed the store's hours on the sign to an hour earlier and told each customer as she handed them their order. Tanya gave out the reward cards already stamped with one mug. Everyone seemed happy with the reward program, and several people said they'd come by at the earlier time to avoid the rush.

She smiled to herself as she headed over to open Book It. Hopefully some of the people who stopped by the café during the day would notice her new bargain-book display and stroll on over. Maybe she'd even have some readings at Book It after hours and leave the café open. Her mind was humming happily along with ideas for boosting the bookstore and café together, until Shane walked in holding a reward card.

"What is this?" he asked, holding up the card accusingly.

She smiled and said calmly, "It's a reward card. I just started giving them out this morning. Everyone loved them."

He slapped the card down on the counter. "We never talked about this."

The inklings of anger crept into her voice. "We never talked about the cleaning service, but you went ahead and did that. I'm running the shop how I see fit. That's my job."

"You cancelled the cleaning service. Why?"

"I told you I'd handle it. We're just starting to make a profit. I don't want the expense right now."

He blew out a breath. "Rach, I don't do coupons. People come back for a quality product, not coupons. This is the kind of cheap sales crap that Barry has to pull with his fro-yo. Our coffee is superior, so are the baked goods. We don't need it, and it makes us look bad."

She lifted her chin. "We might not need it, but people love it. It inspires loyalty."

His mouth formed a flat line. "We should talk about stuff before you do it."

His attitude was really getting under her skin. She managed to hold onto her temper. Barely.

"You supply the food," she said in what she hoped was a cool, professional voice. "I run the shop. That was the deal."

His jaw tightened. "We're partners."

She really should just ignore him and go about her business, but she couldn't let him act like the boss.

"You're the silent partner," she said. "I'm the one who runs things."

He fixed her with a calculating look that made tingles run down her spine in anticipation. He moved fast. One minute he was across the counter from her, the next he was behind it, his hands boxing her in. Her pulse quickened. He spoke in a low tone, not touching her, just hovering close. "I am *not* a silent partner."

Her body heated, and she felt weak in the knees. She couldn't just cave because she wanted him. This was all mixed up and messed up, and she was torn between stomping on his foot so he'd back the hell off and stripping naked right there in full view of Main Street.

Show me, Shane. Show me how you're not a silent partner.

Yup, I'm a slut.

"Rachel, great idea with these reward cards!" a cheerful voice called.

Rachel turned as Barry walked into Book It. Shane released her and narrowed his eyes at his nemesis.

Rachel took a deep breath and smiled at Barry, who appeared completely oblivious to the tension between her and Shane. He strolled over with two to-go cups in hand and handed her one.

"Thanks, Barry, you didn't have to do that."

He waved his card. "Got two mugs, only eight more until my free one! And I love the mug stamp too."

Shane tensed by her side.

Rachel beamed. "Thanks, it's been going over really well."

"Where'd you get them?" Barry asked. "I'd love to do the same for my shop. Maybe with a cow stamp. Hey, Shane, you could do one with an ice-cream cone."

Shane stiffened even more, if that was possible. "I have to get back to work."

He left, stalking out of the shop, tension in every step.

Barry sipped his coffee. "This is the best café mocha I've ever had. And I've tried them all."

"Thanks," Rachel said, her eyes following the man who knew how to make divine food and drink happen, but didn't have a clue how to deal with a business partner.

21

The next two weeks left Rachel frazzled and working harder than she ever had in her life. Word of mouth made both the café and her bookstore suddenly popular, attracting people not just from Clover Park but from nearby towns too. It was everything Rachel had ever dreamed of for Book It. Every night at closing Shane stopped by the café to help her get things ready for the next day. And every night they fought. Every damn night. It wore on her. The long days, the fights.

She would close out the register, which tied into their inventory system, then get the bank deposit ready to go and put in the order for the next day's supplies. Shane cleaned the prep area. As they worked around each other, Shane would say, "Another employee and we could get this done a lot faster."

To which she'd reply, "I'm managing just fine. Besides, we haven't made enough money to justify one."

"We have money," Shane always said. "Besides, you have to spend money to make money."

"I have to pay my debt. I don't have to do anything else. I know how to run the shop."

"You don't. You're still learning."

"You can stop *teaching* me. I've got this."

"We're *partners*."

"The deal was I run it. I'm the boss."

"Dammit, Rachel!"

She knew he'd take over if she let him. So she never gave him even one inch.

Then before she moved to clean the bathroom, he'd say, "If we had a cleaning service, we'd be outta here."

To which she'd sing, "Money, money, money."

"You're just being stubborn."

"You're just being a nag."

Sometimes it varied. Sometimes Shane got irritated enough to huff and puff and threaten to call the cleaning service anyway. She ignored this because even if he did, she'd just cancel it again. Sometimes her temper flared over his constant micromanaging over pricing and inventory, and she ended up hollering at him. He always hollered back.

Maggie had said Shane didn't like fighting, but he didn't seem to mind with her. They went toe to toe, round and round, every night about the way the café should be run. Every freaking night. Honestly, she didn't know why he kept coming back. He didn't have to help her close the shop.

Then again...

Every night when the café was clean and ready for the next day, Shane would take her hand and walk her out the back door and up to her apartment. And every night she let him. They had an unspoken agreement to leave work and their fights over the café downstairs. Upstairs was just for them.

They always took a long shower that left her squeaky clean and boneless, made love, and then she'd kick him out. She needed her space and told him so. He accepted this without argument.

But his scent, his remembered touch, lingered with her as she dropped into a deep, exhausted sleep.

∾

Shane spent Friday at a workshop for coffee roasters, hoping to glean some new contacts for high-quality beans. He was

thinking about targeting health-conscious, socially respon-
sible customers with fair-trade coffee. The beans were superior in many ways, as he'd discovered from the cupping he'd
done today at the workshop. When he'd left Clover Park this
morning, he'd seen another line out the door at the café. And
while it was great to see all the business, it was grating on
him the way Rachel was fighting him on hiring more people.
If they couldn't keep up with demand, those customers
would go elsewhere.

Rachel was fighting with him over the running of the café
just to keep him at a distance, he was sure. She insisted on not
spending any money and doing everything herself. It was
ridiculous. And yet she let him in every night. Her brain and
her body were saying two different things where he was
concerned, and while he didn't want to let go of her body, he
wanted her brain on board too. She was making him crazy.
This wasn't how he ran a business.

The fact that he'd been running a successful ice-cream
shop for six years seemed to mean nothing to her. He
knew food. He knew how to keep customers coming
back. He knew how to keep things running smoothly. He
let out a frustrated breath as he drove home. He parked
and walked over to the café as he did every night. He
could see Rachel in there closing up shop. Tanya was
already gone. Rachel was working too hard—opening the
café early, helping with the morning rush, running both
the café and the bookstore, staying late to close. He had
a good team behind him at Shane's Scoops, guys that did
the morning baking and ice-cream base making, people to
run the registers, serve customers, and close up shop,
and a cleaning crew. He jumped in now and then at his
shop when there was a rush or when he felt like it, but
he was more a manager than someone forced to work
shifts.

He knocked on the front door of the café so he wouldn't
startle Rachel. She unlocked it and let him in.

"Hey, how'd it go today?" He took a quick look around,
making sure everything looked in order, clean and inviting.

"Busy," she said, turning away and wiping down some tables.

He went behind the counter to see what needed doing, but she'd already cleaned up and restocked. She was getting the hang of the food business. Now they just needed to hire some staff so she didn't have to do everything. He didn't want to have that same old fight again. He had to work around her stubborn resistance.

"I got a lead on some fair-trade coffee that's really good," he said. "Almost a hint of pepper to it. It's something really different that would attract real coffee lovers. We could even sell the beans. I was thinking we could sell stuff for the home too. Like personal coffee grinders, high-end espresso machines. What do you think?"

She kept scrubbing.

"Rach?"

She stopped scrubbing and slowly turned to face him. "I have to tell you something."

Her tone sent alarm bells off in his head. This sounded bad. Was it the café? Another man? Was she in love with Barry? *Get a hold of yourself, man. Let the woman speak.*

He crossed to her and sat down at the table. She sat across from him, took off her glasses, and cleaned them.

"Stop stalling," he said.

"Only if you promise not to get mad."

He crossed his arms. "How can I promise when I don't know what it is?"

"Promise."

"No."

She shoved her glasses back on. "Fine."

She stood and turned away, actually turned away from him and went back to scrubbing tables. Her arms were rigid as she took whatever was bugging her out on the table.

He knew how to soften her up. He slipped behind her, half bending with her, pressing his lips to the side of her neck where he liked to give her love bites when he was deep inside her. The position at once turning him on and loosening her up. She dropped her hold on the rag.

"Shane," she whispered, straightening and turning in his arms.

He couldn't resist kissing her. He cradled her face, momentarily forgetting his original purpose at the touch of her soft lips, her taste like the most delicious sweet honey, his personal nectar. He slowly pulled back, already thinking about taking this upstairs.

Then she said all in a rush, "The health inspector stopped by this morning, and we failed, but we get a second chance in two weeks."

He jolted and stepped back, feeling a little dizzy. This was almost worse than Barry. His reputation was on the line with the café. He'd gone through all his usual suppliers, spread the word that it was his product at the café, and now a failed health inspection. The absolute kiss of death.

"Why?" he asked. "What was the score?"

She grimaced. "F."

"F?" he roared. "How did we get an F?"

"Don't yell!" she hollered.

"I'm upset. People don't give you a second chance if they think it's not hygienic to eat at your place. What did they say?"

"There wasn't any soap in the bathroom dispenser. I forgot to refill it last night, and the morning rush was so busy I had no idea we'd run out."

He hadn't checked it last night either since Rachel insisted on handling the bathroom herself just to show him they didn't need to pay a cleaning service. That damn bathroom. It was worse because it was the same bathroom the employees used, which made it look like no one had washed their hands before preparing the food. Even if it wasn't true. Rachel and Tanya had probably been too busy to even think about taking a bathroom break.

He scrubbed a hand over his face. "This wouldn't have happened if you had let me hire the cleaning service."

Her eyes flashed. "I knew you would say that! Look, I'm handling it. We'll be ready next time. It'll never happen again. I'll double-check everything every morning before we open."

"Rach, this is not how I run a business."

"Good, because this is how *I* run a business, and it's fine."

He narrowed his eyes.

"Nobody will know," she said. "They're giving us a second chance."

He shook his head. "I've tried to let things go. Let you have your way, but this I can't stand for. This doesn't just affect you. My rep is on the line. Everyone knows I supply all the food and drink here. I've got loyal customers from my shop and local restaurants I supply. I can't have the threat of health code violations tied to my name."

"They won't be. Next time we'll pass!"

"You're the stubborn one who insists on making all the decisions when there's two of us affected by it. I'm not going to stand here and let you ruin everything I've worked so hard for."

She crossed her arms. "Then leave!"

Wouldn't she just love that? Pushing him out and away like she did every other man in her life. He wasn't going anywhere.

He crossed his arms too. "Make me. I'm a partner here. More than an equal partner."

He knew he was pushing it with that last remark, but she was way out of her league with this café, and it was high time he took control.

She sputtered, her hands in fists, and he waited for some sharp retort.

Instead she shocked the hell out of him when she let out a primal scream and launched herself at him. They went crashing to the ground.

22

Rachel's fists were flying as she pummeled Shane's chest, feeling like a crazed banshee. "You are not the boss! You will never be the boss! I hate bosses!"

Then he had her wrists manacled in each hand, restraining her.

"Rachel! Get a hold of yourself. Are you crazy?"

She struggled against him, breathing hard. "This is all your fault!"

He looked up at her from the ground where she'd flattened him. "How is this my fault? I'm flat on my back with a crazed woman trying to kick my ass."

She stood and wiped at some dirt on her shorts. "I don't care if you put up the money. I'm going to pay you back as soon as I can." She glared down at him. "You knew that going into it."

He stood and glared back. "I didn't know you were going to fail health inspections or be so stubborn you couldn't handle basic business decisions."

"Basic business decisions! I know how to run a business!"

"So do I!"

Rachel was having trouble calming down. She eyed his hair, itching to give it a good pull. But violence wouldn't solve anything. She shoved her hands in her pockets.

"Can we please talk about this rationally?" Shane asked in a typical superior male voice.

Her palm came up by pure instinct, and Shane backed up a step and pointed at her. "You stay there. I'm going over here so we can talk without anyone getting smacked." He walked to the other side of the table.

"You are not the boss," Rachel ground out.

"Neither are you," he shot back.

"I am the boss of this shop. I say who gets hired, how it's run…" Her voice rose in volume as she jabbed a hand in the air. "I say we get freaking reward cards with little mugs stamped on them!"

He shook his head. "I hate those fucking reward cards."

She knew he did. Tough, it was her idea, and it worked. "Well, the customers love them."

He ran a hand through his hair. "Look, I don't want to fight. I just want to be sure this kind of thing never happens again. You don't understand how important it is. One bad mark and people avoid your place like the plague. The reputation for my name and my food is everything. Nothing else matters as much as that."

It was her reputation too. Did he really think that she would do anything to harm it? She had just as much riding on the success of this business as he did. Maybe more since her bookstore had nearly gone under only weeks ago. She couldn't do this anymore. She hated having to answer to Shane, constantly having to defend her decisions.

"I can't work this way," she said. "If you can't go back to just being my supplier, then I can't do this."

"I was never just a supplier," he said evenly. "I'm an equal partner."

"I'll find a new partner. Maybe the bank will reconsider now that the shop is doing better."

He regarded her with irritation. "Fine, go to the bank. Good luck with that. Maybe you should find another supplier too."

She raised her chin. "Maybe I will."

They stared at each other, each refusing to budge one inch.

Shane shook his head. "Suit yourself."

He stalked out. Rachel sagged to a chair, suddenly exhausted. It was nothing less than she'd expected all along. The end of their partnership. The end of their friendship.

Being right had never felt so wretchedly wrong.

~

Shane was in a foul mood when he woke on Sunday morning after two long weeks of not being with Rachel. Without any prompting from his uber-fit brother, he went for a run, hoping that physical exhaustion would help him stop thinking about her. He'd stayed away from the café. He couldn't bear to go in these last weeks, knowing it had failed the health inspection.

He couldn't stand watching Rachel run the café like she ran the bookstore, oblivious to the fact that selling books was very different from selling food and drink. Not to mention the fact that she'd tried to beat him up. Clearly she didn't trust him. She'd rather flatten him than let him help run the café, even with the great success he'd had with his own shop.

He was starting to wonder why he'd ever thought he could get past her defenses and into her heart. He beat feet up the hill to the high school, the journey not difficult anymore after all the morning runs he'd done with Ryan. Now that it was October, the cooler temperatures made it much more comfortable. He bit back a groan at the sight of Ryan and Liz standing at the top of the hill in their running shorts, Hagar at their side. He knew they'd bug him about Rachel, and he didn't want to go there.

"Shane, look at you!" Ry hollered. "Running on your own. And not even winded."

Shane stopped, hands on his hips. "Yeah, you got me in the bad habit."

Liz stood on tiptoe and kissed his cheek. "Morning, Shane. You want to join us for breakfast? It's no problem making extra toast." She grinned and looked sideways at Ry. "We've got a four-slice toaster."

Ry grinned and shook his head. *Inside joke*, Shane figured.

But he wasn't doing himself any favors brooding in his apartment, so he accepted the invitation.

They jogged back to Ry's place. Hagar tried hard to pull on the leash with Liz, so Ry took him, keeping up a brisk pace so the dog could naturally run at his side. Liz and Shane trailed behind.

"The café's doing well," Liz said. "They just had their new health inspection. There's a big ol' A on it in the front window."

She watched him for his reaction. Rachel must have told her about their fight. He wasn't going to tell Liz anything. If Rachel wanted to talk to him and actually admit that they had something special together, then she'd have to do it herself. He missed her a lot, but he was giving her space to decide what she really wanted. If she wanted him fully on board as a partner and as a lover, then she had to let him in. Their lives were all wrapped up together. He was unwinding them because she wasn't thinking clearly.

"Yup, I heard that too," Shane said. "It's great."

He'd called a guy he knew over at the inspection department to be sure they'd passed last Friday. Now he was back to sending a delivery guy over with the supplies. He was the supplier, period. He figured Rachel hadn't gotten a bank loan either because she hadn't tried to pay him back.

He blew out a frustrated breath. Rachel just didn't get it. He didn't give a shit about the money, as he'd told her more than once. It was his reputation. His name was everything when it came to good food.

They were getting close to Book It. Shane purposely didn't look in that direction. Rachel wouldn't be there at this time of morning, but lately even looking at her shop was difficult.

"Rachel says you haven't been at the café for more than two weeks," Liz said.

Shane stopped short. "She doesn't need me there."

Liz stopped next to him. Ry kept going with Hagar. She put a gentle hand on his arm. "I'm sure that's not true."

"If she wants to see me, then she can talk to me herself," he gritted out.

Ry turned. "Come on, slowpokes!"

Shane began a slow jog with Liz at his side.

"Be patient with her," Liz said. "Rachel's never had a real relationship. Only a long history of disasters. She probably doesn't know what to do with a great guy like you."

Shane grunted in response. He had been patient. Hadn't he patiently waited for *two years*, ever since Rachel moved back to town, and bided his time while she went through a string of losers? Hadn't he patiently waited for seven months of hanging out as friends until he was sure she was ready for more? He liked spending time with her, true, but he'd always wanted more than friendship. He loved her, but he was out of patience. Their relationship couldn't be so one-sided.

He said none of that, knowing it would get back to Rachel. He didn't want other people negotiating between them. He wanted Rachel all-in. He wanted her heart.

"Thanks, Liz," he muttered.

She smiled and patted his arm. Shane continued his run as something very close to despair seeped into his bones.

∾

Rachel had her usual chaotic Monday morning as the commuter rush hit the café. She probably should hire another barista, but it was so gratifying to see the profits rolling in, she just couldn't do it. She wanted to pay for her part of the partnership and buy out Shane. Now more than ever she needed to be the boss—complete control, full ownership, reporting to no one. Being in business with Shane had ruined everything.

She crossed back to Book It with her latte and sighed. Not that the café, or her, seemed to matter to him anymore. He hadn't returned to the café ever since the failed health inspection. He sent over his supplies through Ron. He didn't help her close up shop either. Every night when she did the task alone, she thought of him. Of the way they used to work side by side, cleaning and prepping for the next day, both knowing what came next. Their time together upstairs in her apartment. She pushed that thought away. Amazing sex does not a happy-ever-after make.

She missed talking to him. She loved their daily chats, the casual sharing of confidences. As soon as she could, she'd pay him back; then maybe they could at least be friends again. Her dad was right. She never should've borrowed money from a friend.

The day dragged on, with only a few people stopping into Book It, and Rachel's mood sank to an all-time low. She wanted so badly to fix things with Shane, but without the money to pay him back, she was stuck. The bank had turned down her second attempt to get a loan. Not enough time had passed with profits to make her a good risk.

A car horn honked insistently in front of her shop. She ignored it.

Beep-beep-beep-beep!

She stood and went out front to tell them to knock it off. It was a shiny red Mustang convertible. *All right, hot shot, this is a quiet town.* But then she saw who it was—Maggie. The woman was nuts in the best kind of way.

Rachel stopped at the car. "Hey, Maggie, what's up?"

Maggie pushed huge round sunglasses to the top of her head. Her leopard-print bodysuit left nothing to the imagination. *Oy!* "I'll tell you what's up, girlie, we're going for a ride."

Rachel looked back to her shop. "I don't close for two more hours."

Maggie craned her neck to peer around Rachel. "Nobody's in there. Put up that closed sign and hop in."

It would be a relief from the constant rehashing over where things had gone wrong with Shane and how she was going to come up with the money to make things right again.

"Okay," she said. She ran inside, grabbed her purse, flipped the sign to Closed, and locked up. She slid into the passenger seat. "Where to?"

Maggie pulled out onto Main Street and headed out of town. "It's a surprise. You like surprises?"

"Sure, surprise me."

"So how's the café?" Maggie asked.

"It's great. We're clearing a profit, and more people are coming in every day. Plus we have lots of repeat customers."

"I heard about your coffee reward card. Very smart."

Rachel smiled. "Thanks."

At least Shane's grandmother appreciated her marketing efforts, unlike her big lunkhead of a grandson.

Maggie hit the highway and floored it. The wind whipped around them, and Rachel could barely hear Maggie over the radio and the wind whipping past. She pushed some hair behind her ear that had escaped her braid. The older woman was saying something about tea or coffee or maybe she said toffee? Rachel just smiled and nodded.

Finally, they pulled into a parking lot with a lot of old and classic cars. The sign on the large garage read Exotic and Classic Restorations. Maggie got out, and Rachel looked around in confusion.

"Are you buying a new car?" she asked, surprised because the convertible looked brand new.

"Come with me," Maggie sang, heading to the side of the garage where a door led into a small office. "Hello-oo-oo, I'm looking for Kevin."

"Just a minute," a receptionist said. She hit the intercom. "Kevin, someone to see you."

Kevin, a middle-aged man with a full head of white hair, came out of the work area in coveralls. "I'm Kevin."

"Hi, Kevin, I'm Maggie O'Hare. We spoke on the phone. This is my friend Rachel. Can you show us that surprise?"

Kevin grinned. "Sure. I keep her under lock and key in my private garage. Right this way."

Rachel followed with a sinking feeling. They walked to the back of the property. Kevin punched in a code, and the garage door opened. An older model shiny red Mustang. This had to be the Shelby. The car was gorgeous. Shane giving it up was even worse than she'd thought. Guilt swamped her.

Kevin gestured to the car. "Check her out."

"Can I get in?" Maggie asked. "I've missed it."

"Of course."

Maggie waved Rachel over to the passenger side while she got in to the driver's side.

"This was my departed husband Patrick's car," Maggie said. "It's a Shelby Mustang. See the signature." She pointed to the glove box in front of Rachel. "He took such good care of it. Only took it out on sunny days. We'd take these adventures, driving to beautiful parks for picnics, cruising the highway. It's a powerful car." She turned and looked Rachel in the eye. "It makes you feel *alive* to ride in one of these."

"Spoken like a true Shelby lover," Kevin said from outside the garage, where he was smoking.

"Maggie, I'm sorry," Rachel said. "I wish I could buy it back."

Maggie shook her head, fondling the wood steering wheel. "After Patrick died, it sat in the garage for years, untouched. Then when my son, Jack, moved nearby, sober again, I gave it to him so he'd have a project. My boy always did love cars. And after many, many weekends of working with Shane to fully restore it, he gave it to him."

"I tried to pay Shane so he could get the car back," Rachel said over the tightness in her throat. "I gave him a check from another investor, and he ripped it to bits."

Maggie raised her brows. "That sounds like my Shane. It's not about the money. This is your café. He did it to make your dream come true."

Her voice came out small. "Why did you bring me here?"

"I wanted you to see with your own eyes what you mean to Shane."

She turned despairing eyes to Maggie. "How can I ever repay him?"

Maggie patted her hand. "I'm sure you'll figure something out. Just remember it's not about the money."

Rachel's stomach churned. She had no clue what to do. She just had this awful, awful feeling that she'd been in the wrong all this time, not Shane.

They drove back to Clover Park with the wind whipping through their hair. Rachel was too depressed to even attempt conversation.

Maggie dropped her off at the front door of her shop. "See you soon!"

Rachel waved weakly, completely bypassing Book It and slipping into the café. She sat down in the shop, only a few people were hanging out in it, writer-types with laptops. She barely heard Tanya's cheerful greeting. She just stared at the table. She owed Shane so much. And how had she repaid him? By kicking his ass. She could at least apologize for that. The rest she hoped she'd figure out when she saw him.

23

Shane was behind the counter of his shop, feeling tense and restless. Things were slow at his shop now that the weather had cooled. He went to the back to the kitchen, thinking of baking something with pumpkin for the café. Maybe he'd make pumpkin cupcakes with cream cheese frosting. He'd just started gathering ingredients when he heard the bell from the shop indicating he had a customer. He went back behind the counter. Rachel.

He blew out a breath. He wouldn't bring up the café or the health inspection or the need for more staff. He missed her way too much to get into all that.

"Hey," he said.

"Hey," she said softly.

When she said nothing else, he looked around to see what he might have on hand that she'd like. "Want some ice cream? I've got a new flavor. Honey swirl."

He'd created the flavor with her in mind. He always said she tasted like honey. It had been a hit in the shop too.

Her gaze jerked to his. He smiled. She remembered all right.

"Can we talk?" she asked.

Dammit. When a woman wanted to talk, it was usually

about the relationship. And the way things had ended the last time he'd seen her, this couldn't be good.

He took off his apron and joined her at a table. "What did you want to talk about?"

Her chocolate brown eyes met his, full of remorse. "I want to apologize for kicking your ass the other day. It was wrong. Vio—"

He held up a hand. "You *tried* to kick my ass. You didn't actually kick my ass."

She waved that away. "I knocked you down, and I was punching—"

"You didn't kick my ass," he barked.

"Um, okay." Her eyes darted to the side. "Anyway—"

"You could never kick my ass. No lightweight has ever kicked my ass."

She nodded. "Okay. I, uh, know I can never repay you for all you've done, but—"

"I thought we covered this. You don't owe me anything."

"Are you ever coming back to the café?"

"Do you want me to?"

She stared at him, her expression serious. "I want to be in charge."

"Then there's your answer."

Her shoulders drooped. "I have to get back. I'll see ya." Her voice came out sounding choked at the end.

He didn't mean to upset her. "Rach, wait."

She waved a hand behind her back and kept going.

"I love you!"

She froze, and he held his breath, waiting for her to come back to him, hoping she'd say the same.

But to his utter alarm, Rachel, his strong, sarcastic, tough Rachel, turned around and broke down in tears.

Rachel was so embarrassed about crying in front of Shane, but she couldn't seem to stop the tears now that they were flowing. She never cried. It was just that Shane was so loving and so sweet, and she'd almost thrown it all away. She felt strong arms around her, and then she was in his lap, sobbing into his shirt. She could hear the steady thump of his heart beating strong and true.

She grabbed a napkin off the table and wiped her tears. Then she blew her nose in it and crumpled it in her hand.

He stroked her hair. "Tell me why you're crying."

"Because I finally realized that the problem I needed to fix, the thing that was wrong with this relationship was me!" She sobbed again, feeling absolutely ridiculous, but unable to stop. "I'm Mr. Darcy!"

"You're who?"

She sniffled. "I'm the arrogant cad brought low by love!" Fresh tears poured down her cheeks.

He wiped some tears away with his thumbs. "Oh, Mr. Darcy. Am I Elizabeth Bennet? Cuz I gotta say—"

"No, you're just Shane," she choked out. "Perfect Shane."

"Honey, I'm not perfect."

"You're a lot closer to perfect than me." Her shoulders sagged. "You've done everything you could to show me you loved me, you confronted my stalker, you sold your inheritance—" she threw her hands up, and the napkin went flying "—you bought all those cookbooks! Who knows what other wonderful things you did! And what did I do? I pushed you away."

"No—"

"Yes! You know I did!"

One corner of his mouth curled up. "Maybe a little."

She nodded vigorously. "A lot! First I told myself we were just friends and no more when I always knew…"

"Knew what, sweetheart?"

"I always knew I had strong feelings for you," she admitted.

He kissed her hair.

She wasn't done. "And then once we hooked up, I told myself we could only be business partners, but then I kept sleeping with you. And every day I fought with you again, trying to keep things all business and failing miserably." His warm hand rubbed her back. "And then when you got mad about the business side of things, I tried to end that too."

"But I didn't go for it."

She looked at him. "No, you didn't. And then...I saw the Shelby, Shane! It's gorgeous! I can't believe you gave up that car!"

He shook his head. "Gran," he muttered.

She took off her glasses and wiped them clean from the tears. "I owe you too much. Too much money, too much making up for how I treated you." She slid her glasses back on. "I mean, I kicked your ass when—"

"I think we've already established that you did *not* kick my ass."

She smiled through her tears, and he kissed her. She kissed him back, taking every bit of comfort she could, missing this part of him, of feeling connected so fully to someone who knew her so very well.

She pulled back and stroked his strong jaw. "I love you. It scares me, but I do." She shook her head in amazement. "It finally happened for me."

"I love you too," he said huskily. "*Amor vincit omnia.*"

She bit her lip. "Love conquers all."

He smiled. "I was saving that one. Let's get out of here."

Shane locked up, and they walked outside. Rachel stopped on the sidewalk and took a deep breath for courage. Now that they were together, really together, she didn't ever want to be apart. She pulled her keychain from her purse. She slid off the key to her apartment and gave it to him. "I want us to have a place together. I don't want to be away from you anymore. I want to be with you every day and every night."

He closed his hand around the key. "Are you sure? Be sure. Because once I move in, I'm never gonna leave."

She nodded, her eyes stinging with tears. "I'm sure."

He gathered her in a warm embrace and kissed her tenderly. "Let's go home."

They walked to her place, and Shane stopped at the door to kiss her. She threw herself into the kiss, her hands running all over him, needing to feel that closeness with him again.

Her entire world narrowed down to simple burning need. He broke the kiss and gazed into her eyes with a hungry look. She knew they were both thinking the same thing —bed. Now.

He tucked a lock of hair behind her ear. "Of course, there won't be any funny business between us until you agree to marry me. I've been there, done that, got the keychain."

She stared at him. She was just coming to terms with the fact that she loved him so deep and true. She'd never been in love before. Marriage was like a whole new terrifying level.

She socked him in the arm. "Very funny, mister, now get that firm ass of yours upstairs!"

A corner of his mouth kicked up. "Okay, but you're still not getting any until we're married."

"What!"

The look on Rachel's face was priceless, and Shane bit back a laugh. There was one thing he was beginning to understand about Rachel, and that was sometimes she needed a little push to bring out what was really going on in that heart of hers before her big brain had a chance to rationalize it into something else.

She sputtered, and he kissed her again. He stroked a hand up and down her side, purposely slipping close to her breast. Her breath was coming faster now. He pushed her a little further, placing a kiss on the side of her neck in the spot that always made her soft and pliant. This time was no exception. She sank against him.

"Okay, I'll marry you!" she exclaimed.

He grinned. "You're so easy."

"Only you would say that."

He swept her off her feet, carrying her upstairs to her apartment, remembering the first time he'd carried her up the stairs when she'd sprained her ankle. And now look at them, getting married. He set her down in the apartment. There was just one more thing he had to make clear to her.

Before he could get out a word, she launched herself at him. He caught her, walking back to the bedroom with Rachel's arms and legs wrapped tight around him. She kissed him frantically, and he laid her down on the bed, returning her passion with everything he felt inside. Finally, he nuzzled her neck and moved up to her ear so he could tell her what was on his mind.

"I want a big family," he whispered, his hand slipping under her shirt, caressing her breast. "A house full of love."

"Are you nuts?" she asked, shoving his hands away. "I just agreed to marry you and now you want to knock me up?"

He laughed. "Yes."

She thought about that. He leaned against the headboard and pulled her close, cradled in his lap, savoring the honey lavender of her skin as he kissed along her cheek, her jawline, her throat, waiting for her to decide. Now that he had her love, he wanted her to know just how serious he was, how much he dreamed for them.

"How many kids?" she asked, breathless as he sucked one erect nipple through her shirt.

She tangled her hand in his hair. He peeled off her shirt and bra and suckled at her other breast, teasing with his tongue and teeth. She moaned again, and he looked up. Her eyes were closed; head thrown back.

"Six," he said.

Her eyes flew open. "Four."

He slid a hand across her inner thigh, nudging her legs apart. His knuckles brushed her center, and she jolted.

"Really? Four?" he asked.

Her eyes flashed fire. "You are the biggest tease. You really want to talk about this now?"

He kissed her until she settled down again; then he laid her out on the bed, sliding off her jeans and panties, arranging her so her legs were spread wide. He left her glasses on so she could watch. He kissed his way down her body and stopped at her belly. "Four kids sounds good."

Their eyes met. He grinned up at her. She looked disgruntled. He kissed her center and looked up at her lovingly.

She groaned and closed her eyes. "Why did you say six?"

He smiled devilishly. "Because I wanted you to say four."

"Ergh! You wanted—"

He silenced her protest by clamping his lips around her hard nub. She arched up into him, and he savored his personal nectar. Within minutes he had her on the brink. He teased her with soft kisses and flicks of his tongue until she was writhing under him, murmuring, "Please, please."

Then he sent her over, loving watching her in full ecstasy. When she came back to earth, she reached for him.

"I love you so much," he said, sliding into her.

She wrapped her arms around him. "I love you too. So very, very much."

He had her heart now, just like she'd always had his.

EPILOGUE

Rachel brewed another carafe of coffee to go with the pancakes Shane was making by the dozen at the annual Clover Park Breakfast with Santa. Shane always volunteered to cook at the breakfast, but it was Rachel's first time working the event. Her shiny diamond engagement ring flashed as she worked expertly to fill the machine with freshly ground beans. She still couldn't believe she was getting married in just a few weeks. They planned to marry on New Year's Eve, both wanting to get started on a family right away. They'd agreed to raise their children both Jewish and Christian, double the holidays. Her parents were thrilled. Maggie was happy she'd get her great-grandkids to visit every Christmas Eve.

Daisy and Trav brought Bryce to sit on Santa's lap. Bryce pulled on Santa's beard and patted his face. This year Trav's friend Rico had stepped in to play Santa at the last minute and was extremely uncomfortable with the gig. They'd been laughing at Rico all morning. Clearly Bryce recognized him, but since he couldn't talk yet, he didn't give Rico away.

"Hey, Rach, check it out," Shane said, pointing as Maggie sat on Rico's lap.

Apparently Maggie had a long list for Santa.

Rachel giggled. "You think she's naughty or nice?"

He held up the pancake flipper and pointed it at his grandmother. "She's naughty, but makes you think she's nice."

"I'm on the nice list," Rachel said.

"You are most definitely gonna be naughty tonight."

A hot flash went through her at the hungry look in his eyes. Thankfully he was a distance away. She turned back to the coffee brewer. Two large hands wrapped around her from behind. Shane kissed the side of her neck. He still snuck up on her, but her body knew his scent, his touch immediately. He bit gently on the side of her neck, and she felt an answering throbbing between her legs.

"Shane, stop," she said breathlessly. "Not here, there's kids."

He chuckled, turned her for a quick kiss, then went back to pancakes. She found herself staring at the rear view. It amazed her how a man in an apron could look so sexy.

He turned. "Like what you see?"

"Mmm-hmmm."

He laughed. Ryan and Liz stopped by to grab more pancakes and coffee to deliver to the families.

"You guys need any help back there?" Liz asked.

"We're good," Rachel and Shane said in unison.

They were better than good. They were a team both at work and at home. Their café was doing so well they'd hired a second barista and a cleaning service. Together, they'd created an employee handbook that spelled out the café's policies and procedures for all the employees' benefit. And nothing ever slipped through the cracks with his training. Book It was in the black, doing even better now with her new rewards program: buy ten books, get one half price. And she'd started a romance section now that she understood what it meant to be in love. It was the best-selling section of the store.

Rachel had even opened a savings account where she stashed away some of the profits from the café for a down payment on a home. She rubbed a hand over her belly. They'd be needing that house soon. She hadn't told Shane yet.

It would be his Christmas present.

Don't miss the next book in the series, *Kissing Santa*, where Rico hears a secret Christmas love wish from the woman who might just reform his player ways! And there's big news from the O'Hare family!

Kissing Santa

Samantha Dixon is about to confess her most secret, romantic Christmas wish to Santa. Heck, what's she got to lose with her disastrous romantic history? Like that player from her horrible blind date last week arranged by her mother. Only guess who's Santa?

Rico del Toro loves women. So one bad date with the beautiful Samantha in a string of many, ahem, successful evenings is no big deal. But when a friendly favor playing Santa unexpectedly lands Samantha on his lap for a romantic confessional, he's intrigued. He's never heard a woman open her heart like that before.

But if this Santa wants a second chance, he'll have to rethink his womanizing ways and convince her that he is the perfect package.

Sign up for my newsletter and never miss a new release! https://www.kyliegilmore.com/newsletter

ALSO BY KYLIE GILMORE

Unleashed Romance <<steamy romcoms with dogs!

The Clover Park Series <<brothers who put family first!

The Clover Park Charmers series <<sweet and sexy charmers!

Almost Over It (Book 1)

Almost Married (Book 2)

Almost Fate (Book 3)

Almost in Love (Book 4)

Almost Romance (Book 5)

Almost Hitched (Book 6)

Happy Endings Book Club Series <<the Campbell family and a romance book club collide!

Hidden Hollywood (Book 1)

Inviting Trouble (Book 2)

So Revealing (Book 3)

Formal Arrangement (Book 4)

Bad Boy Done Wrong (Book 5)

Mess With Me (Book 6)

Resisting Fate (Book 7)

Chance of Romance (Book 8)

Wicked Flirt (Book 9)

An Inconvenient Plan (Book 10)

A Happy Endings Wedding (Book 11)

The Rourkes Series <<swoonworthy princes and kickass princesses!

Royal Catch (Book 1)

Royal Hottie (Book 2)

Royal Darling (Book 3)

Royal Charmer (Book 4)

Royal Player (Book 5)

Royal Shark (Book 6)

Rogue Prince (Book 7)

Rogue Gentleman (Book 8)

Rogue Rascal (Book 9)

Rogue Angel (Book 10)

Rogue Devil (Book 11)

Rogue Beast (Book 12)

**Check out my website for the most up-to-date list of my books:
kyliegilmore.com/books**

ABOUT THE AUTHOR

Kylie Gilmore is the *USA Today* bestselling author of over fifty humorous contemporary romances. Her series include Unleashed Romance, the Rourkes, the Happy Endings Book Club, Clover Park, and Clover Park Charmers. With more than three million downloads of her books, readers all over the world love escaping into her hilarious feel-good romances featuring strong bonds with family, friends, and community.

Kylie lives in New York with her family, a demanding cat, and a nutso dog. When she's not writing, reading hot romance, or dutifully taking notes at writing conferences, you can find her flexing her muscles all the way to the high cabinet for her secret chocolate stash.

Sign up for Kylie's Newsletter and get a FREE book! kyliegilmore.com/newsletter

For text alerts on Kylie's new releases, text KYLIE to the number (888) 707-3025. (US only)

For more fun stuff check out Kylie's website https://www.kyliegilmore.com.

Thanks for reading *Bad Taste in Men*. I hope you enjoyed it. Would you like to know about new releases? You can sign up for my new release email list at https://www.kyliegilmore. com/newsletter. I promise not to clog your inbox! Only new release info, sales, and some fun giveaways.

I love to hear from readers! You can find me at:
kyliegilmore.com
Instagram.com/kyliegilmore
Facebook.com/KylieGilmoreToo
Twitter @KylieGilmoreToo

If you liked Shane and Rachel's story, please leave a review on your favorite retailer's website or Goodreads. Thank you.

www.ingramcontent.com/pod-product-compliance
Lightning Source LLC
Chambersburg PA
CBHW070639100726
47907CB00007B/2034